CRESCENT COVE series
Christian Romance

Testing the Waters
Book 1

Oceans Apart
Book 2

Sink or Swim
Book 3

MADISON FALLS series
Christian Romantic Suspense

Saving Grace
Book 1

Jill Came Tumbling After
Book 2

Find out more at **lesleyannmcdaniel.com**

Jill loved Madison Falls. It was the only place she had ever lived or had ever wanted to live. She had to figure out a way to keep her life there.

And life *for everyone here…*

The unsettling feeling that the last thought had come from somewhere outside of her own head sent a shiver through her. The thought that she hadn't stumbled on this issue at the factory by accident but had in fact been given an assignment started to take root. Could that be true?

She gazed at the snow, which was coming down heavier now. In spite of everything, the soft blanket of white on the ground felt like a reassurance from God that they were covered.

Realizing that she'd probably stayed up way past her intended bedtime, Jill bent to turn off the battery-operated candles inside each of the jack-o-lanterns. As she stood, a flash caught her eye and she noticed for the first time that there was a dark-colored sedan parked almost directly across the street. She wouldn't have noticed it at all, but the light from what had probably been a phone had momentarily illuminated the silhouette of a person sitting in the driver's seat.

A chill passed through her. This was a small town, and it was pretty unusual to see cars in her neighborhood that she didn't recognize. And for someone to just be sitting there, at this time of the night…er body began trembling. Whoever it was had been sitting there this whole time.

Other books by Lesley Ann McDaniel

HOLIDAY HEARTS series
Christian Romance

Christmas Bells are Ringing
Book 1

Heavenly Peace
Book 2

Home for the Holidays
Book 3

Comfort and Joy
Book 4

To Hear the Angels Sing
Book 5

Laughing All the Way
Book 6

My True Love Gave to Me
Book 7

Newsletter Invitation
My Thank You Gift to You...

High and Dry

CRESCENT COVE series Prequel
Available only to my newsletter
subscribers. Get your copy for FREE!

Do you love Inspirational Fiction? Join my
Newsletter family and receive all the latest
news about my books, plus contests,
giveaways, and insider info.
**www.lesleyannmcdaniel.com/newslett
er**

Jill Came Tumbling After
Madison Falls, Book 2
Copyright © 2018 Ark Ink
All rights reserved.
ISBN-13: 978-1723479694
ISBN-10: 1723479691
Cover design by Lynnette Bonner of
Indiecoverdesign.com
images ©

www.dreamstime.com, ID 5596382
www.peopleimages.com, ID 384052
Photoshop Swirls by Obsidian Dawn,
www.obsidiandawn.com

Jill Came Tumbling After is a work of fiction.
References to real people, events, establishments,
organizations, or locales are intended only to
provide a sense of authenticity and are used
fictitiously. All other characters, incidents, and
dialogue are drawn from the author's imagination.
Printed in the U.S.A.

MADISON FALLS - BOOK 2

Jill

CAME TUMBLING AFTER

By Lesley Ann McDaniel

Chapter 1

Jill Martin flung open her front door with a burst of uncharacteristic boldness, then whirled around to face her husband. "Get out."

Caleb's bloodshot eyes widened with either surprise or amusement. "Ge'out?" The two words slurred together into one. "Where am I supposta go?"

"You seem to be an expert at finding places to be other than home." She dug her nails into her palms, determined to hold her ground. It was about time she did this. In fact, she should have done it ages ago.

"Bu' honey." Taking a step toward her, he reached for her cheek but staggered, giving her nose a decidedly unromantic flick.

She slapped his hand away. "Don't call me that. I'm not your 'honey' anymore. I'm not your *anything* anymore."

"Hey." He held both palms out from his sides like a statue of the Virgin Mary. "Wha'd I do?"

Disbelief puffed out between gritted teeth. How could he be so incredibly manipulative? And why had she put up with it for so long?

"What did you *do?*" Planting her hands on her hips, she braced herself against the cold October night air now gusting into their entryway. "For starters, we don't have any food in the house, and you just blew my grocery money on beer."

"Jilly…" His attempt at the boyish grin that had won her heart all those years ago in high school faltered under the influence of the two six-packs he'd just polished off in front of the TV. "I tol' you I'd pay it back."

"Oh really? Well, that's going to be a neat trick, considering you don't have a job."

He dropped the grin along with what looked like his hope of sweet-talking her. "You can't kick me outta my own house."

"Maybe not." She reached for the cordless phone, perched in its stand on the hall table next to the stairs. "But I'm sure Sheriff Drew would be happy to do it for me."

Fear flashed across his face like a brushfire. He'd had enough encounters with the sheriff of Madison Falls to know that if he found him in this condition, he'd haul him away to cool his heels overnight in a jail cell. Jill grimaced. It wouldn't be the first time.

Giving her a glare that was no doubt intended to intimidate, Caleb stumbled past her and on out the door, then nearly tripped down the porch steps.

Firming her jaw, she glanced up and down the street. A couple of curtains parted and faces peered out. If this had been his first public display of drunkenness, she would have been mortified. As it was, the neighbors were probably wondering why she hadn't kicked him to the curb years ago. She shivered. At least she wouldn't have to announce the news of her situation. Between the gossips and the prayer warriors, news traveled fast in this small Montana town.

Caleb hit the bottom step and whipped around to look up at her, waving an arm and probably thinking he looked threatening.

"I'll be back, Jill," he growled. "You can't keep me from seein' my kids."

A pain shot through her heart at the reminder of the two innocent little ones sleeping upstairs. At least she *hoped* they were still sleeping, with all the yelling that had gone on for the past fifteen minutes.

As he turned and stumbled toward their car in the driveway, her stomach buckled. She quickly glanced at the hooks that edged the bottom of the vintage white mirror hanging next to the door. Her keys were there as usual, but where were Caleb's? He was always losing them.

She looked back out to see him pat the pockets of his jeans then roll his gaze toward the house. Their eyes met in a strained mutual acknowledgment of the situation. He was keyless, and he shouldn't drive in his condition anyway. Not that that ever stopped him.

He sneered, then started down the sidewalk on foot.

Releasing a prayer of thanks along with the breath she'd been holding, Jill rested the phone on the table next to the door. She would need the car more than he would, what with the kids and all.

The kids. Keeping an eye on Caleb as he swaggered into the night—probably to hit the Spur before last call—she strained her ears for any sign of wakefulness upstairs. She let out a long breath. Nothing but blessed silence.

Shaking from the dissipation of adrenaline, she shut the door and twisted the deadbolt, hopeful that Caleb wouldn't find his keys somewhere and be able to get back in. She made a mental note to track down Sam tomorrow and tell him not to give Caleb the spare set of keys for their house, no matter how much he begged him. Sam would do that for her, she was certain of it.

She sighed. Even though Sam had been Caleb's best friend since they were kids, he saw through him. He wanted to help Caleb, but he was more concerned with keeping Jill and the kids safe. It was good to know she could trust him.

She sighed again, leaning her back against the door. Too bad she couldn't trust her husband the same way.

Running her hands through her unkempt hair, she let the silence soothe her ears. She'd done it. After years of thinking about it and making halfhearted threats, she'd finally made her husband leave. Closing her eyes, she sent up a quick prayer, thanking God for the surge of strength that had apparently lasted just long enough this time to get him out the door. Even as she said a silent *amen*, her knees turned to mush and she sank to the cold hardwood floor.

Relief gave way to a wave of anger. She picked up a mountain ash leaf that had blown in while the door had been open and crunched it in her fist. She'd been such an idiot for marrying him. And then for having children with him.

No. She wiped her palms across her thighs, flicking away the bits of dried leaf. She couldn't go there. Couldn't regret having her precious children.

Her hands dropped to her lap and she expelled a breath, then twisted the band around her left ring finger. He had promised— no, *vowed*—to take care of the family. *Right.*

Did he really think that "taking care" of them meant spending half his time drunk, losing his job…then getting into trouble with the law for associating with a drug dealer?

Her jaw clenched at the memory. It made her sick to her stomach to know that her husband had put food on the table for weeks using the money he'd earned making deliveries for Carson. Claimed he didn't know what he was delivering and had gotten out of doing jail time because there was no concrete proof that he'd been directly involved with either using or dealing. Not even Jill had anything to go on but her suspicions. She would have pressed the sheriff to put Caleb behind bars if she'd known he wasn't going to make good on his promise to look for honest work. What a waste.

And now that he was out of the house, how low would he sink to ensure his own survival?

Oh, come on, Jill. She shot a glance into the darkened living room, at the family portrait hanging above the fireplace. A reminder of happier times.

She rubbed at a dull pain in her chest. *He's got a drinking problem, but he's not a monster.* It was just that it had been so long since she'd been able to trust him. Perpetual suspicion had come to feel like a normal condition.

With her head throbbing like it might explode, she pushed to her feet. She took a step, realizing too late that Riley's mini soccer ball had rolled underfoot. She stumbled, catching herself as exhausted frustration surged afresh.

Unable to control the new groundswell of rage, she hauled off and kicked the ball, aiming for the hall table as if it were a pintsize goal. The ball ricocheted off the table leg, amputating it from its top and sending an accumulation of mail—along with the phone stand—plummeting. Jill lunged, catching as much of the load as she could before it thundered to the floor.

With her arms full, she held completely still. No sound came from upstairs, and she eased out a breath.

An uncharacteristic curse word rolled around in her head and landed on her tongue, which she bit down on to silence. She'd been asking Caleb for weeks to fix this table leg, but of course he hadn't gotten to it. Another empty promise. Life with him had been full of them.

Leaning forward, she propped the table on its three good legs and held it there with her hip while easing her load down onto it. Then she braced it with one hand and retrieved the wayward leg with the other, then slid it under the fourth corner. It seemed okay, but the slightest provocation would jar it out of place again. Just like her life. It looked fine, but it had no security.

Who was she kidding? Her life didn't even *look* fine anymore.

As she started to tidy up the papers, something colorful snagged her attention. She pulled a bright-yellow sheet from the pile and just about choked.

A shut-off notice? She gaped at the red print screaming from the page. Their power was going to be shut off? *When?*

Her eyes darted around the paper. *Ten days from this notice.* She tried to read the details, but her mind boggled and her vision blurred. Where was the date? Why couldn't they at least make it clear?

There it was…ten days from…*October thirteenth.* And what was today?

Clutching the rest of the papers, she hurried to the kitchen and the calendar on the wall next to the back door. *October twentieth.*

Her lungs pushed out air like a spent bellows. By the look of things, she had two days to come up with…how much? She surveyed the paper in her hands.

"Three hundred and eighty-seven dollars?" She could barely breathe out the words. It might as well be a million.

Her teeth gritted. Caleb had to have known about this. Of course he had—he'd opened the notice. When had he intended to tell her about it? Was he going to let the man from the power company break the news when he came to shut off their service?

She fumed. No wonder Caleb had gotten smashed tonight to escape reality. Their reality stank.

Focusing now on the rows of numbers on the page, she tried to decipher how long it had been since a payment had been made. Caleb had been out of work for so many months, she could barely even remember what it felt like to know that money would be coming into their account on a regular basis.

Giving up, she tossed the papers onto the kitchen table like they were on fire, afraid to check if anything else was going to be shut off or taken away. Her stomach clenched. Exactly how bad had he let things get while she'd kept her head buried safely in the sand?

A wave of panic rolled over her. What had she done? Here she was with a three-year-old and a baby to feed, a stack of unpaid bills, no money, no job, and no husband to help her. Where was the hope she had expected to feel when she finally took control of her life?

Swallowing a sob, she sank into a kitchen chair. Telling Caleb to leave had taken all her reserves. What was she supposed to do now?

Jill Came Tumbling After

Chapter 2

Shaking off the disorienting feeling that she'd stepped out of her own life and into someone else's, Jill poured Cheerios from a baggie onto Emma's highchair tray at the Country Kitchen. She looked down at Riley, who made motor sounds and raced his cars around on the seat of their booth. If only she could be so carefree.

Across the table, her best friend, Colleen, tapped away at her laptop.

"I'm glad you could meet us, Cole." Jill wrapped both hands around her coffee mug, grateful for its comforting warmth. Over the years, she and Colleen had bolstered each other through every little thing from homework to heartbreak, and she needed her now more than ever. After all, Colleen had always been supportive of Jill's marriage. It was Caleb she disapproved of.

"Are you kidding?" Without looking up, Colleen flipped a strand of honey-blonde hair into submission and continued to type. She always managed to look completely pulled-together—a feat that in Jill's estimation could only be achieved by women who were still single and childless. "What are best friends for if not to do a little emergency brainstorming and résumé writing?"

Jill managed a tight smile. Caleb hadn't had steady work in months, but at least he had brought in sporadic income from odd jobs. Now with no guarantee of any further funding from him, getting a job herself seemed like the obvious plan of attack. Trouble was—she glanced down at Riley's rumpled mop of blond hair—she already had a full-time job.

"I appreciate it." Jill felt her sleep-deprived body tense. "But, I don't know what I want to do. I've never even had a job."

"You've had a job." Colleen arched a brow in a show of mild offense. "That summer before our senior year."

"When you and I worked at the Tastee Freez?" Jill's mood lifted slightly at the memory. "If I recall, we spent more time gabbing with our friends and talking about boys than actually working."

"Hey, it still counts." Colleen flicked a dismissive wave. "Everybody has to start somewhere."

Jill gave her a feeble nod. "I've never thought about what I wanted to do besides being a mom."

"Don't worry. There are lots of things you could do." Colleen turned the laptop so the screen faced Jill. "And this is your first step."

Still uncertain, Jill quickly scanned the surprisingly detailed outline of her skills. "'Demonstrated competency in management'?" She frowned over the top of the screen. "When exactly have I done that?"

"*Hello.*" Holding up a hand, Colleen counted on her fingers. "You've managed a household. You've managed a team of volunteers making costumes at church." She leaned closer, her eyes narrowing as her voice lowered. "And you've *managed* to stay married to that bum for five years."

Jill made a shushing motion as she looked down at Riley, who seemed blessedly immersed in his own play world.

"Just trust me, Jill." Colleen turned the computer around again, looking pleased with her creation. "This résumé is going to sell you like ice water on a hot Montana day." She directed a neatly manicured finger in Jill's direction. "It'll get you the interviews and your skills and personality will do the rest."

"Skills and personality, huh?" Jill plunked

the baggie of Cheerios back into her diaper bag. "Then I'm in big trouble."

"Jill." Colleen's warm, loving expression communicated an unwavering confidence draped in unconditional love. "You're going to come out of this just fine."

Jill bit her upper lip. Why couldn't *she* be so confident about that?

Just then, Emma let out a little chortle and hurled a fistful of Cheerios at Riley's head.

"Emma!" He shot his sister a disapproving glare, then looked to Jill with a clear expectation of instant justice.

"Emma, don't throw your food." Carefully, Jill picked a soggy cereal loop off one of Riley's ringlets as she inched the conversation down an alternate path. "Maybe there's a way for me to make money but not be away from my kids all day."

Colleen pursed her precisely lined lips. "You mean like some kind of home-based business? Well, maybe…" Her eyes rounded in that I-hate-to-break-it-to-you way that never preceded good news. "But those usually take time and money you don't have right now."

"Oh." Tears pressed behind Jill's eyes. She shoved her hand into the diaper bag and rooted around for Emma's teething ring.

Colleen reached across the table and gave Jill's arm a squeeze. "I know you don't want to leave the kids with a sitter, but…" The end of the sentence drifted off along with her gaze, as if her train of thought had just been derailed. She pulled her hand back and started tapping at her computer again. "I should have thought of this ages ago."

Handing a binky to Emma, Jill twisted her upper body in a futile attempt to see the screen. "What?"

"Welfare." Colleen blurted out the word with such vigor that a couple of women in the next booth stopped talking and turned their heads.

Welfare? Jill opened her mouth to protest but stopped when she saw Glo, the diner's head waitress, approaching with a tray balanced at shoulder level. From the look of unease on her face, it was clear that she'd heard Colleen too. Jill tried to silence Colleen with her eyes, but her best-friend-telepathy powers failed her.

"There's no shame in it, Jill." Clearly oblivious to Jill's discomfort, Colleen increased her volume along with her enthusiasm. "You and your kiddos have to eat."

Jill sighed as she manufactured a smile for Glo. A warm rush of humiliation trekked through her. How had her life come to this?

"Here you go." Glo set a small plate of chocolate chip pancakes in front of Riley.

"Pa'cakes!" Snapping his attention from his cars, Riley sat up and seized his fork.

Glo gave Jill a kind smile as she placed a bowl of yogurt in front of her. "Nice to see you sometime besides on Sunday mornings, honey."

"Yes." She returned the smile, now a little

less forced. "Some weeks it seems like church is the only time I get out of the house."

"Well, you and these precious little ones are always welcome here." She gave her a wink that communicated more than her words.

Jill blinked back the persistent pressure behind her eyes. It felt good to live in a place where the majority of people stood behind you not to stab you in the back, but to catch you when you fell. She nodded her appreciation.

"Thanks." Colleen moved her laptop aside as Glo set a dish of mixed fruit next to it. "Hey Glo, can we print something here?"

"Why sure, honey." As Glo tucked the tray under her arm and cast an assessing look at the roomful of customers, she managed to look amenable to the request. "You just send it to me in an email and I'll open it up on the office computer. Won't take but a minute."

"Thanks. I'll do that right now." Colleen tapped the contents of a sweetener packet into her coffee. "We could use maybe ten copies to get us started. I'll pay you for the paper."

"I'm happy to do it." Starting toward the office, Glo spoke over her shoulder. "You ladies need anything else, you just let me know."

After saying a quick prayer of thanks for the food—more to set a good example for Riley than for her own spiritual fulfillment— Jill forced down a tiny bite. She cringed. Even yogurt hit her stomach like a rock this morning. "So, about your welfare idea. That would just feel like giving up."

"Think of it as a stepping stone, not a landing place. It's a way of keeping the boat afloat until the kids are in school."

"It just seems like...*cheating*, somehow."

"Jill." She gave her a firm look. "Just because some people take advantage of the system doesn't mean that the system itself is bad. Sure, people generally follow the path of least resistance, but I don't think that's what you'd be doing."

"I don't know..."

"Let's at least keep it on the back burner

for now." Colleen speared a chunk of cantaloupe. "I'm sure there are plenty of other alternatives."

Forcing herself to look hopeful, Jill reached for a triangle of thick, buttery toast. "So now that I have a résumé, what's next? Want ads?"

Colleen shook her head. "Unless you want to haul hay bales for old man Willis or pump gas over at the filling station on Route Six, Madison Falls isn't exactly the land of opportunity."

Jill twisted her mouth. "So if nobody in town is hiring, what am I going to do?"

"It's okay." Colleen lifted a cube of pear to her lips. "Everyone knows you don't find the real jobs advertised in the newspaper anymore."

"No? Then how do you find them?"

"Well…primarily from word of mouth, I suppose." Swallowing, she crinkled her nose. "I wish my office was hiring. But the attorneys can barely afford their receptionist and me right now. I'll start asking around, and in the meantime—"

"In the meantime, I'll go see if the Tastee Freez has any openings. Minimum wage, here I come."

Colleen huffed out a breath. "Now, don't give up before you've even started. There has to be something." She tilted her head toward the window as if someone might be waving a *Now Hiring* sign in a fortuitous parade of perfect timing. Something she saw jostled a thought. "Hey, maybe Grace would hire you at the bistro."

Jill flinched. What was it about that name that always tied her stomach in a knot?

"I don't know." She shrugged. "She's got mostly high schoolers working part time right now."

"Oh." Colleen took another bite and continued to think.

Letting out a breath, Jill surveyed Main Street. There were two full blocks of businesses just on this street alone. One of them had to have an opening for something she could do. Anything would be better than going on welfare.

Starting at the corner across from the park, she scanned the far side of the street. She could talk to Spritz at the real estate office, or maybe Dr. Fleming was in need of a new receptionist.

Ew. The thought of working in a dental office set her teeth on edge.

Her gaze moved down the block. Past Roberts and Son Hardware—the store Sam owned with his dad—and Colleen's apartment above it.

Then her perusal stopped cold, along with her optimism. *The Spur Tavern.* How many times had Caleb gone in there when he should have been doing something else? Like looking for a job or going home to her and the kids. How many times had he confided to his cronies there how unhappy his homelife was or what a shrew he had married? The injustice of it dredged up a sour taste from her throat as the yogurt she'd managed to choke down turned her stomach into a butter churn.

Swallowing hard, she tried to ignore the bitter reminder that she was married to an alcoholic. Her face pinched with an effort to stave off tears. She had done her best against impossible odds. Hadn't she?

"Well, it's about time they got that thing finished."

Colleen's light tone heaved Jill out of her grim contemplation, leaving her with a vaguely unsettled feeling. She shifted her focus back to the hardware store, where Mr. Roberts—Colleen and Sam's dad—wrestled a scarecrow into position near the door. A measure of burden lifted from her heart. The town council's annual scarecrow competition was one of her favorite local traditions.

"Wait…" Jill squinted. "Is that one of Sam's shirts?"

Colleen giggled. "Dad's idea for their entry this year was to make it look like Sam performing in that big songwriting competition. Dad says it's his way of showing the town how proud he is of him for making the finals. They've been arguing over it all week."

The women watched in amused silence as Mr. Roberts went back into the store, then came out again carrying a guitar, which he positioned in the effigy's gloved hands.

"You looking for a job, honey?" The women looked up to see that Glo had returned, carefully carrying a small stack of papers in one hand and a coffee pot in the other.

Jill felt a blush crawl up her cheeks. "I'm thinking about it."

Glo handed Jill the résumés as she replenished her caffeine supply. "You know the old sapphire mine just past the falls?"

"Yes…" Jill crinkled her brow, trying to determine if Glo had something to offer apart from a quiz on local history. "What about it?"

"I hear they're hiring."

"The sapphire mine?" Jill studied Glo. Sure, the woman had her finger on the pulse of all the local goings-on, but the old mine had been shut down for at least sixteen years. "But, how—"

"It's being turned into a factory. Bob Branigan—you know, Lucy's husband—his company is doing the renovation."

"Seriously?" Jill perked up. That old mine had always fascinated her. She'd been inside once, on a third-grade field trip, and she still had the tiny sapphire she'd been given as a memento. "What kind of factory?"

"Manufacturing something to do with clean energy." Glo seemed to study the ceiling for a moment. "I don't know what it is exactly, but it's supposed to be a real good thing for the environment."

"Oh right. Geothermal energy. Turning underground heat into electricity." Colleen sat forward. "Why didn't I think of that? My bosses have been talking about what a great guy the new owner is. They say he's really concerned about the community and all."

"A couple of my regulars were talking this morning." Glo continued. "Apparently, today's the day for the open interviews. You don't have to make an appointment, just go up there and wait in line. And with times being what they are, everyone around here who needs work is applying."

Jill's stomach clenched. If everyone who needed work would be there, why would they even look at her?

"Perfect!" Colleen beamed. "See, Jill. God is smiling on us."

"He is, indeed." With a quick mascara-encased wink, Glo went on about her business.

Colleen glanced at her watch. "I have to get to the office, and you had better hit the road."

"But..." Jill looked down at herself. Knowing she'd be out job hunting today, she'd put on her favorite pale-pink cotton dress topped with a white cardigan. Now she realized she had dressed more for a picnic than to impress a serious business owner.

Colleen seemed to read her mind. "Here." She grabbed the beige linen blazer she'd draped across the back of the booth bench and handed it across the table, then kicked off her matching open-toe pumps. "Good thing we wear the same size."

Jill smiled as she swapped her ballet flats for the pumps, praying she wouldn't break her ankle. She couldn't exactly borrow Colleen's health insurance. She removed the sweater and handed it to Colleen.

"One last thing." Colleen grabbed her ecru leather bag that looked more like a purse than a briefcase. She removed a yellow legal pad and an energy bar and replaced them with the stack of résumés. "On second thought…" She slipped the energy bar into an outer pocket. "You might need this more than I do."

"But, what about the interview? How will I know what to say?"

Colleen chewed on her lower lip for a moment. "Just be yourself and answer all the questions they ask in a positive way."

"Okay. I'll try."

"And remember, your goal is to convince

them that hiring you will benefit them. Pretend you're trying to get a kid to do something you want him to do. It's kind of the same thing."

"Great. And if all else fails, can I bribe him with gummy worms?" Tugging on the blazer, Jill regarded herself with an air of confidence. Maybe things were going to be okay. She could get a factory job and support her kids. Do something with her life besides washing dishes and changing diapers.

Glancing down at Riley's chocolate-smeared face, her burst of *I-am-woman-hear-me-roar* enthusiasm was quickly squelched by a rush of *what-do-you-think-you're-doing* terror.

"Cole…" She let her voice trail off as her head inclined toward the kids.

"Oh. Right." Colleen lowered her voice. "If we weren't so swamped at the office, I'd offer to take them with me. It's just that we're getting ready for a big trial, and—"

"No." Jill held up a hand. "I wouldn't even ask. But it does bring up the question of what

I'm going to do if I get a job. I can't afford daycare."

"Well..." Colleen angled a coy smile. "You do have one option. I mean, there's always your m—"

"Don't even say it." Jill held up her hand. Noticing how ragged her nails looked, she quickly clenched it. "I would have to be really and truly desperate to ask for that kind of help."

"Oh, and just how serious do things have to get in order for desperation to set in?"

"Colleen..." She flashed a warning look.

"I know, I know. So, what are you going to do?"

Jill looked out the window just as Sam exited the hardware store and started across the street, obviously headed for the bistro. Her heart lifted.

"Well, I'm pretty sure I have a solution for today, anyway." She glanced down at Riley. "Hurry and finish your pancakes, buddy. We're going to see Uncle Sam."

Jill Came Tumbling After

Chapter 3

As Jill braced the diner door open with one hip and hoisted Emma higher on the other, something whizzed past her legs. She looked down to see that Riley had just propelled himself out the door and toward the street.

"Riley!" Darting after him, she felt the diaper bag, purse, and briefcase she had strapped across her shoulder all threaten to obey the law of gravity and take her down with them. One of her borrowed shoes skidded on the pavement, giving her a painful reminder of why her own high heels never left the closet these days. They were totally impractical for keeping up with a three-year-old.

"Sweetie!" She somehow managed to stay balanced while dipping down to redirect him. "We're heading this way."

"But…" Lifting his arm in the direction of the hardware store, he looked like a tiny, distraught Indian scout. "You said we go'a see Unca' Sam."

"Yes, baby. But he's not at his store. He's at Miss Grace's bistro."

"Oh boy." His tantrum-tinged whine instantly dissipated as he pivoted toward the rustic brick building on the corner of the next block. "I like'a Miss Gwace."

Of course. Snorting out a breath, Jill shifted her momentum and quickstepped to keep up. *Everyone loves Grace.*

Grace had pretty much become a local heroine when she'd saved both the community theatre and the old storefront next to it from the wrecking ball the previous summer. She'd been the new girl in town, intriguing to everyone, especially Sam. When it turned out she was actually an opera singer named Tracy Fontaine, and that she was hiding out in Madison Falls to escape an obsessed fan, the intrigue factor had shot through the roof.

Now she ran both the Madison Falls Playhouse and the Backstage Bistro, in addition to maintaining her career as a professional opera singer. *Oh yeah.* And she was gorgeous too.

Jill sighed. What wasn't there to love?

"We get'a see Angel?"

Jill swallowed hard as they stopped at the corner just past the flower shop. Riley, who had a typical little-boy-adoration of dogs, had fallen for Grace's border collie, adding to her superhero persona and Jill's resultant frustration. Of course Grace had an angelic dog when Jill couldn't even afford to keep a goldfish.

After making sure Riley took her hand and

looked both ways, Jill stepped into the street. "I don't know if she'll have Angel at work with her today, buddy. Sometimes he stays home with Mrs. Fontaine in the mornings, remember?"

A hopeful light flickered in his little eyes. "Then we go'a see Ms. Fon'ane too, 'k?"

Jill couldn't help but smile at Riley's tenacity. Too bad she couldn't duplicate that attitude for herself today.

As they neared the old-west-style bistro, with its square front and towering windows, Jill let her gaze wander to the inviting brick structure next to it. A surge of muddled feelings washed through her. As a kid, she had loved having free rein of the theatre with Sam and Colleen. It had been devastating last summer when their dad had nearly sold it, along with the building next door, to a developer who'd wanted to tear it down and replace it with a casino. Now, thanks to Grace, it glistened like new, its brick front freshly power-washed, and its marquee proudly announcing the upcoming fall production.

Jill let out a long breath. True, Grace could have done plenty of things with her money other than rescue their little town from losing a piece of its history. Why did a residual coating of resentment have to cling to Jill's sense of gratitude?

"C'mon'a, Mama."

Riley yanked her onto the curb and out of her rumination. *Right.* She had important things to do here.

When they got to the area where café tables had adorned the sidewalk until the fall weather had set in, Riley let go of her hand and took off at a trot. He slapped his palms flat against the distressed wooden door of the bistro as Jill peered through the window just above his head. The place bustled as usual. *Good.* That meant that Grace would be busy, and Jill could speak to Sam in private.

As she reached for the door handle, the sight of Sam leaning against the espresso counter quelled her anxiety. Besides Colleen,

Sam had always been the one person she could count on, and she needed him now more than ever.

Twisting Emma further to the side, she pressed her left shoulder against the obstinate old door. Just as it shuddered open, a lithe blonde glided through the batwing doors which led from the kitchen to the area behind the counter. Sam stood straighter, and Jill stopped cold in the doorway. *Grace.*

Sam and Grace shared a look—the kind that made it clear that, for the moment, the rest of the world might as well not even exist.

Suddenly, a gaping cavern of neediness opened in Jill's chest. She had grown so accustomed over the years to having Sam fix everything—her dryer, the plumbing, Caleb— that she hadn't even thought about how different things were now. She couldn't expect him to just drop everything to help her. Not anymore.

That realization pummeled her into pure panic. What was she doing? She couldn't make it on her own. She had to go find Caleb and beg for his forgiveness.

The urge to slink away unnoticed grew, in spite of her being hobbled by three bags, a baby, a pair of two-inch heels and an unfettered preschooler. Hoisting Emma higher on her hip, she carefully reached for Riley, but as her fingers brushed against his tiny shoulder, he lurched forward.

"Unca' Sam!" His high-pitched squeal turned several heads, including Sam's and Grace's.

Jill bit her lip and sent Grace an apologetic look. Touching Sam's arm, Grace seemed to encourage him to go to Jill. Resigned, Jill took a few steps into the room and hip-bumped the door shut.

"Morning, partner." Sam met Riley halfway and scooped him up in his arms before focusing on Jill. "I just called your house, but I guess I missed you."

"If only I had a cell phone." Jill imitated the sing-songy admonition she generally received whenever anyone informed her of an unsuccessful attempt to reach her on her landline.

"We went'a the dine'a." Riley made the announcement as if breakfast out were as special as a trip to Disneyland. In his world, that was pretty much the case.

Seeing Grace come around the end of the long, antique counter, Jill stiffened.

"Morning, Jill." Flashing an easy smile, Grace brushed a lock of her almost-shoulder-length blonde hair off her face and onto the side of her head, where it remained as if obeying a command. "Can I get you some coffee?"

Jill blew a strand of her own hair out of her eyes. She had attempted that morning to catch it all up into a tidy bun at the nape of her neck, but no matter how much product she used, a bit of hair always escaped, usually to block her vision.

"No, I don't need anything." Feeling ridiculous now, she flipped through a litany of explanations for their presence there, wanting the reason to be anything but what it really was.

"Well, it's chilly out this morning." Leaning in, Grace lowered her voice. "How about if I make the kiddo some c-o-c-o-a while you talk to Sam?"

"Oh, sure. That would be great." Relief mingled with appreciation, lessening Jill's feeling of humiliation. The gesture was genuinely sweet, and the contribution to Riley's sugar high would be the least of Jill's worries this morning.

She looked at Riley, who played with a pack of gum he'd just lifted from the pocket of Sam's work shirt. "Riley, you want some hot cocoa?"

"Yeah!"

As Sam lowered the wriggling Riley to the floor, Grace took his little hand. Sam let his gaze linger for just a moment on her as she led the tyke toward the espresso area.

"Let's grab a table." Taking the bags from

Jill's shoulder, Sam started toward some vacant seats near the front window.

As he veered to grab one of the old-fashioned wooden highchairs from its place next to the wall, Jill assured herself that the closest customers weren't paying them any attention. He set the chair next to a table and helped her lower Emma into it.

Feeling secure that she did still have a place in Sam's life, she blurted out an all-too-common phrase. "I have a favor to ask."

"Uh-huh." He pulled out a chair so she could sit. "And does it have anything to do with Caleb showing up at my place last night?"

"He did?" Sinking into the chair, she let out a long breath. It hadn't occurred to her that Caleb might be with Sam today. She'd assumed he'd go where he could expect some sympathy. Suddenly, her idea of having Sam watch her kids seemed impossible.

A sense of defeat set in. Everyone she trusted already had something that kept them busy during the day. What was wrong with her life that she didn't have a support system?

Defeat mutated into resentment. Why was she always the one who had to shuffle everything around while Caleb slept late and felt sorry for himself?

She firmed her resolve. "So where is he now, on your couch?"

"Nope." Sam sat across from her. "I put him to work."

"Work?" She took Emma's rubber giraffe out of the diaper bag and handed it to her.

"He's unloading some pallets in the back of the hardware store. But don't worry." He lifted a palm like a traffic cop. "He's not going to show up over here. I told him to stay in the back of my store so he wouldn't scare the customers."

"Scare them?" Her anger suddenly melted into a more familiar protective concern. "He looks that bad?"

"A hangover doesn't look good on anybody. He didn't have time for a shower this morning, but at least I loaned him some clean clothes." He rested his arms on the table, like he had all the time in the world to listen. "So, tell me what happened."

She leaned forward, keeping her voice down. "Well, it all started when he rolled out of bed yesterday afternoon at around three."

"Three?" Sam worked his jaw, wisely stifling what he was no doubt thinking.

"That's typical." Jill continued. "I was looking through my practically empty cupboard when he came into the kitchen. I asked if he was going to be home to eat with us, because I never know. Before I knew it, we were fighting again. About our empty cupboard and the reasons why I have to plan our meals down to the penny. Meals and everything else." Her stomach twisted. Why did it always have to feel like they were on opposite sides in a war?

Sam's voice sliced into her self-pitying silence. "So, what happened next?"

She swallowed back tears. "Well, I heard

Emma waking up from her nap, so I went to her. I could hear him banging around downstairs, then the back door slammed. He had stormed out, like he usually does. All self-righteous and mad at *me* for being upset that he's not bringing in enough money to keep our ship afloat."

"That's his self-defense." Sam shook his head. "It's easier than manning up and doing what he needs to do."

Her intended laugh sounded more like a choked cough. "Why can't all men be as smart as you?"

"It's not me. I've just always been surrounded by smart women. You, Cole, my mom…" His eyes crinkled slightly at the mention of his late mother.

Jill bit her upper lip, wanting to ease that painful reminder. "And now *Grace*."

"Yeah." He smiled. "Anyway, he stormed out."

"Right. I forgot about the empty cupboard and the fight for a few hours. Then at around six, he walked in the door carrying a paper bag. I thought maybe he'd brought home dinner, but he pulled out two six-packs and left the empty bag on the table. He went into the living room and plunked himself down in front of the TV. I couldn't believe it."

Jutting out his jaw, Sam shook his head. "Did you say anything to him?"

"No." She covered her face with her hands, then drew her fingers down to her chin. "I'm such a coward. I just shared a can of soup with Riley, and put him and Emma to bed."

"Jill, I'm telling you." He kept his voice hushed, but firm. "Nothing's going to change if you don't talk to him."

"And I'm telling *you* that talking to him is about as useful as talking to that wall." She waved a hand at the exposed brick next to them.

"Yeah. I get that." He looked away, then at her again. "So what happened next?"

"Well, I decided I needed to do something besides sitting around feeling like Old Mother

Hubbard, so I went into the kitchen and sorted my coupons. Then I made a menu and a shopping list for the rest of the week."

"Sounds productive."

She nodded. "Then I went to grab the grocery envelope from behind the cookbooks. I knew I had about fifty bucks left in it." Her shoulders stiffened. "Or I *thought* I did."

"The money was gone?"

She gave a slow blink. "All of it."

"So he drank your grocery money." Leaning back, Sam folded his arms. "What did you do?"

"Well, normally I would have gone upstairs and cried myself to sleep. But last night, something snapped. I hit the roof."

"And made him leave. That part he told me, but he wouldn't admit to the reason why." Sam ran a hand through his short-cropped dark hair. "So, you need grocery money."

"Yeah, but that's not all." She reached into her purse and removed the shut-off notice.

He took it from her. Disgust filled his dark

brown eyes. "Unbelievable."

"Yeah." A lump started to form in her throat. "I called this morning. I have to pay at least half to keep them from shutting off our power."

He folded the paper and put it into his shirt pocket. "Don't worry about it."

"But I can't expect you to—"

"This is between Caleb and me now." He rescued Emma's giraffe as it teetered on the edge of her tray. "You have enough on your mind."

Relief came out in a sharp breath. "Thanks, Sam."

"You're welcome. And about the grocery money…" He pulled his wallet out of his back pocket.

"Oh…I couldn't—"

"Consider it a loan." He slipped her a wad of bills. "Which I'll happily take out of your husband's hide."

"Thanks." She tucked the money into her purse, grateful that she wouldn't have to count pennies at the Peach Basket Market in order to buy dinner tonight.

"So…" He put his wallet away. "What happens now?"

"Well, for starters I'm not letting him back in the house. Would you change the locks for me?"

"That sounds serious. You sure about that?"

"I'm done, Sam. This is the absolute last time." She let out a breath. "Now I have to focus on finding a job."

"A job?"

"Right." She cleared her throat. "That new factory is interviewing today."

"Yeah, I heard. You sure you want to work there?"

"I think. I mean, why not?"

He shook his head. "It's just that you're not the one who should be looking for a job."

"I've given up hope that Caleb's going to do it. That leaves *me*. But, I need someone to watch the kids for a little while this morning.

Since you're already babysitting Caleb, maybe Grace's mom—"

Sam shook his head. "Mrs. Fontaine is coming in here to take over for Grace so she can start packing for New York. Don't worry. I'll take the kids."

"Thanks, but I really don't want them to be around Caleb."

"Dad can keep him busy at the hardware store. I've got a bunch of paperwork I can do at home. The kids can stay with me."

"Thanks, Sam."

His gaze hovered over her for a moment, as if some major and obvious piece of the puzzle needed to be pointed out. "Jill, you know I'm happy to take the kids today, but what are you going to do with them once you get a job?" He scrunched up one eye. "Have you thought about asking your—"

"I'll work something out." The words sounded sharper than she'd intended.

He held up a hand. "Okay, so your mom's not an option."

"You know my reasons." Straightening her spine, she shifted forward in her seat. "This is hard enough as it is."

"Right." Scooting his chair back, he reached for the diaper bag. "Call me when you're done. I'll change the locks when I bring the kids home." He stood, shouldering the bag. "And don't worry about Caleb. I'll make sure he stays out of trouble."

Rising to her feet, she nodded. "You're a good friend, Sam."

"He'd do the same for me."

"I didn't mean to Caleb." She dipped her chin. "I meant to me."

He let out a breath. "You know you're like family. Just relax and focus on your interview."

Suddenly lightheaded, she pressed her fist to her stomach. "I don't know if I can really do this."

Sam placed a comforting hand on her shoulder. "Just have faith. God will give you what you need."

Faith. She let the thought settle as she lifted Emma out of her seat. It made sense for Sam, but how was *she* supposed to have that kind of faith when her life had just completely jumped its tracks?

A muffled groan underscored the notion that she was about to enter into completely unchartered territory.

Chapter 4

As the turnoff to the falls grew smaller in Jill's rearview mirror, her feeling of exploring new territory took on a more literal meaning. Even though she'd lived in Madison Falls her entire life, she'd seldom had reason to come out this far on the old highway. Few people did. Once you passed the Tastee Freez and the picnic area, there wasn't much to see but mountains and an occasional glimpse of the river for a good twenty miles.

She slowed as the two lanes ribboned between rising blankets of deep evergreen, accented with intermittent matchsticks of fall color. She let out a soft groan. Normally, an autumn drive would have been rejuvenating, but today the reminder of the normal life she was setting aside only augmented her anxiety.

Just ahead, she spotted the sign for the turnoff to the old mine. A big banner hung from the bottom edge of it and she squinted to make out its precise lettering. *Nyland Enterprises. Interviews Today.*

A disquieting feeling settled like a fog. She'd nearly turned back four times in the twenty minutes since leaving Madison Falls, but she had attributed her hesitancy to her lack of job qualifications. The idea that there might be something more to it seemed irrational. She was here now. She might as well go through with the interview.

As she took the hard right onto the dirt road, images filtered in from the crevices of her memory. Her father bringing her along to pick up a friend of his who had worked at the mine and had been stuck with a flat tire in the parking lot. *Ugh.* As her old Honda bumped along up the road-less-traveled, the last thing she wanted to dwell on was the possibility of a flat.

The only other time she remembered going up this way, she'd been happily jostled up and down on a seat of the school bus, laughing with her friends in anticipation of their day of learning about sapphires, and missing math class.

That was where her personal experience with this place ended. She sighed as a lingering resentment percolated to the surface. The high school memory of her then-boyfriend Caleb recounting his antics with his friends. Driving up here on a pitch-black Saturday night. Scaling the fence and smashing a window to get into the main building. They'd bragged about breaking into the mine itself, but Jill had chosen to believe that part was more bravado than reality. Not even Caleb and his buddies were that stupid.

A car came from the opposite direction and Jill maneuvered as far to the side of the road as she could to accommodate it. People were leaving already. The thought that she might be too late came as both an annoyance and a relief. Maybe fate would let her off the hook.

Going even slower now as a precaution against the possibility of oncoming traffic, she rounded a curve. A tall fence came into view, and she couldn't help but picture Caleb and his renegade friends hauling themselves over it. She squirmed at the sight of the barbed wire rimming the top edge. Maybe those boys were braver than she'd given them credit for.

The road leveled out, and an imposing gate appeared. She passed through it, noting the rusty old lock and the ancient *Warning* signs on either side. She ignored a dull throbbing in the pit of her stomach.

Beyond the gate, cars filled in the spaces between the edge of the road and the woods.

In her memory, the parking lot still beyond the trees was huge. Could it really be full? She kept driving, not seeing a safe place to stop. Besides, the last thing she wanted to do was to hike the rest of the way wearing Colleen's heels. Why hadn't she kept her comfy—and practical—ballet flats?

As the car came around another bend, the trees thinned and she let out a little gasp. Her memories came to life before her eyes. Except for the cars packing the lot and the people milling about, this place looked exactly the way she remembered it.

On the far end of the dirt parking area, the main building loomed large against the side of the mountain. The first-floor windows stretched at least two stories high and there was another floor above that. It looked like solid concrete, but the carved trim at the base of the flat roof, and corners jutting out like Roman columns gave it detail. It made sense that she remembered it as both utilitarian and ornate. Whoever designed it had taken some care to make it interesting.

She skirted the edge of the lot, half looking for an empty space and half ogling the remnants of what once had been one of Madison Falls' most auspicious places of employment. A path led up to a wooden structure which she vaguely recalled learning the purpose of on that field trip. Closer to the building, she saw a smattering of old wooden picnic tables, which conjured up a memory of eating a peanut butter sandwich at one of them.

A couple of women crossed in front of her car, eying her like they might be sizing up the competition. Jill watched as they walked toward the main building and the swarm of humanity in front of it. Clearly, she *wasn't* too late.

A set of tail lights popped on up ahead, and she paused as an SUV pulled out of a spot. She slipped into it, grateful that she would have a relatively short walk, and on ground that was level if not exactly smooth.

After gathering her purse, Colleen's bag, and what remained of her nerve, she stepped from the car and scanned the area, then started walking. Along the edge of the hillside to her right, the construction crew had set up a couple of industrial trailers, some serious-looking equipment, and an imposing row of porta-potties. A pile of broken chunks of wood and tangled metal gave evidence that the renovation was well underway.

Stepping carefully over a web of electrical wires, she studied the faces of a small group of safety-orange-vested workers, hoping to see Bob or some of his men. Disappointed, she skimmed the crowd of would-be employees, thinking that a friendly face right about now could make the difference between her boldly carrying on or running like a scared rabbit.

Seeing no one who looked familiar, she rustled up her courage and melded into the end of the line anyway. Colleen was right. This was a great opportunity and she had to give it her best shot. Besides, there was no way she was going to run like a rabbit wearing these shoes.

The adrenaline rush that had propelled her all morning settled into a queasy chill. Folding her arms across her midsection, she tipped her head back and caught a bit of warmth as the sun peeked from behind a cloud.

She studied the building towering next to her. From this vantage point, she could see how time-worn the walls were. Bits of concrete had crumbled away, giving the surface a pockmarked texture. Paint flaked from the edges of the tall window near her. Leaning in a little closer, she peered through the dirt-encrusted glass. Debris strewn across the floor indicated that this particular room hadn't been cleaned up yet. Still furnished, it looked as though the people who owned the mine hadn't bothered to take anything with them when it closed. *Fascinating.* Her imagination started to run wild.

Since she and Caleb had never had money to buy new things for the house, she had developed a knack for repurposing old furniture and items that could be salvaged for a new use. That was why her coffee table at home was an old window on a spindle, and Riley's headboard was a wooden bench she'd found at a swap meet. Her love of repurposing had become both a practical skill and a creative outlet.

A voice pulled her attention as a young red-haired man walked down the line. "Please have your résumé ready when you get to the front." He thrust a brochure at Jill and she took it by reflex. "Remember, we can only see as many people as we have time for today."

As she unfolded the slick piece of paper, she noticed that the line behind her had grown. She felt suddenly grateful to have secured a spot.

A couple of twenty-something men walked by, heading toward the end of the line. "This company is really green," one of them said in a chipper tone.

Green? Jill frowned. Was he referring to

the overgrowth of vines on the sides of the building?

A feeling of comradery started to form as Jill tuned in to the conversations going on around her. From what she could tell, people were excited for the opportunity to work and for the mission of this company. This could be something great, not just for the local community, but for the entire country. She glanced at the picture on the front of the brochure—groups of families and individuals with a globe motif in the background. A warm feeling shoved away the chill. This factory could be great for all of *humanity*.

The young man walked back up the line, still speaking to the group. "Stay in single file, everyone. Thank you for your patience."

"Um…excuse me." The woman in front of her waved a hand to get his attention. "How many people will you be hiring?"

He gave her a wide, practiced grin. "We're happy to be able to provide fifty new jobs for this community."

Fifty? Jill looked around. There had to be at least two hundred people packing this parking lot, and who knew how many other applicants they'd already seen. She didn't have a hope. On the other hand, if she didn't stand a chance anyway, she couldn't exactly blow the interview. She might as well just relax and enjoy getting to see the inside of this great old building.

"Fifty jobs?" A man behind her grumbled. "We woulda had more'n that if they'd gone and built that casino. They was promisin' upwards of a hun'ert."

"No kiddin'," another crotchety male voice responded. "That was what this town really needed."

Jill clenched her teeth, fighting the urge to set these men straight. The only reason Sam and his dad had even considered selling to that developer was that they needed the money to fund the cancer treatment for Sam's dad. Thanks to Grace, he had been able to afford the treatment and was on his way to making a full recovery, without having sacrificed the history and dignity of Madison Falls. John Roberts was a man of character. Selling out the town would have killed him, maybe even faster than the untreated cancer.

"Casino woulda brought tourist money into this town too."

That did it. Jill whipped around. "If you want to live in a tourist town, why don't you move to Las Vegas?"

Regret hit the instant she said it. The two men stared at her, their gruff faces suspended with surprise. Clad in dirty overalls and sport coats, both men looked like they'd come straight from the farm to the interview. And neither of them looked like anyone she'd speak to under ordinary circumstances.

One of them, a scruffy looking man in his fifties, spurted out a chortle. "Well now, that's an idea. Why don't I just pack up ever'thin' I own, and sell the house that's been in my family for sixty years and move to Vegas? Maybe I can get a job in one of them shows they put on there. Dance around with a feather plume on my head." Holding his fingers up like a rooster's comb, he backhanded the man next to him. When his friend failed to share in his mirth, he dropped his sassy smirk and cleared his throat.

The silent friend sized her up like a rattler ready to strike. Jill swallowed hard and grabbed her elbows, shuddering against a returning chill.

A rustling sound at her back clued her in that the line was moving, and she spun around to join it.

The voice she identified as the scowler rumbled behind her. "Some people are only here to take away jobs from the ones who are genuinely qualified."

Pretending to read her brochure, she tried to ignore them. Whatever sense of belonging she'd managed to rally was elbowed out by the reminder that more and more farmers around here were having to sell their places and look for work. Was it fair of her to even put herself in the running?

Maybe Scowling Man had a point.

Chapter 5

After what seemed like an eternity, Jill finally made it to the front of the line. As she mounted the cracked concrete steps, one of the Oz-size double doors scraped open and the young woman who had been shuttling candidates in and out emerged. She gave Jill the kind of broad smile you would expect from someone who *hadn't* been smiling broadly all morning.

"Your turn." She reached out to take Jill's résumé and, after giving it a quick glance, smiled again. "Hi Jill. I'm Kylie."

Her friendly approach eased Jill's frayed nerves. If they had hired this girl, who had to be just barely out of high school, maybe they wouldn't laugh Jill right out of the interview.

Kylie gestured for Jill to follow her, and they stepped into the high-ceilinged lobby area which, if memory served, hadn't changed much at all. Huge framed black-and-white photos depicting various aspects of the mining industry adorned the walls between tall, clouded windows. The thick drapes on those windows looked heavy with dust.

People stood around talking or looking over paperwork. Jill recognized a few of them from the line outside and assumed they must be waiting for the next step, post-interview.

"This way." Kylie dipped her head as she pivoted around and started toward an arched doorway on the far end of the lobby.

Jill hiked up Colleen's bag and fell in behind her, feeling even more unsure of herself in this cavernous space.

As they moved into the dim passage beyond the doorway, the hairs on the back of Jill's neck stood up. She attributed it to nothing more sinister than the creepy feeling of the long, windowless corridor they'd entered, which was eerily silent except for the echo of their footsteps.

It reminded her of the feeling she'd gotten when her class had been led into the mineshaft. They'd gone through a big door in this very building, and had been taken a short distance down the tunnel which cut into the side of the mountain.

Now, looking at the catacomb-like corridor with its faintly glowing wall sconces—the resemblance to the string of industrial lights in the mineshaft had to be intentional—she wondered what had become of those tunnels when the mine had closed. Did they generally fill those things in or just leave them? The thought of the pitch-black, empty tunnels sent another chill down her spine.

Shivering, she shifted her focus to the happy way Kylie's cinnamon-brown ponytail bobbed as she walked, taking comfort in the distraction.

They passed a door on their left then another on their right, leaving the one at the very end of the hallway as the only remaining option. Jill felt a sudden need to break the silence.

"What kinds of jobs are they hiring for?"

"All kinds." Kylie flicked the vague answer over her shoulder, not in a dismissive way, but like she wanted to offer encouragement. "They have Glenn and me helping with the interviews…" She pointed, Jill assumed, in the vicinity of the young, red-haired man who'd handed her the brochure. "They want to start training the office and production people in the next couple of weeks. The plant doesn't actually open for three months."

"Three months?" *Whoa.* That training period had better be with pay.

By the time they reached the end of the hall, Jill's throat felt like sandpaper. She wasn't sure if it was nerves or the dry, dusty air, but the thought of being asked to verbally sell herself made her knees go weak. Kylie gave the creaky old door a push, then stepped inside, motioning for Jill to follow.

"Wow, this place is great." Jill scanned the dimly lit office, feeling like she'd taken a step back in time to some unspecified but very cool era.

"Yeah. It's going to take a lot to renovate it though. Just between you and me, they have a budget of two hundred K just to furnish and decorate. Isn't that amazing? I mean, what I couldn't do to this place for that kind of money."

"Two hundred thousand dollars just to decorate? Wow." She had probably spent a grand total of a thousand furnishing and decorating her entire house over the years. Imagine what she could do with two hundred times that.

"Mr. Owens will be right back." Kylie fairly chirped as she crossed to a desk at the far end of the shadowy room and set Jill's résumé on it. She turned on her heel and hustled out of the room, leaving Jill wishing she could go with her.

As the sound of Kylie's footsteps grew softer, Jill shoved aside the unnerving suspicion that hers was the only soul present in this wing of the building. She pulled in a breath and looked around.

The high ceiling made the space appear larger than it actually was. The furniture—probably vintage 1920s to 1980s—was all coated in dust, as if the cleaning of this room had been rushed and not very well supervised.

She looked at the room's only window, which seemed tall enough to supply adequate light if not for the heavy taupe drapes covering it. What would be the harm in opening them and making the room a little less tomblike?

After straining her ears for a moment to make sure no one was coming down the hall, she moved quickly to the window. As she yanked at the velvet, a puff of dust bellowed up, launching her into a mini coughing fit. Blinking away the grit, she looked at the overgrowth of foliage outside and envisioned Caleb and his friends heaving a rock at the glass.

"So sorry."

Gasping, she reeled around to face the possessor of a deep voice. A thirty-something man in a light-gray suit stood just inside the door, eyes fixed on her.

"I had to take a quick break." He shifted his gaze from her to the window, then to the table next to it. "Would you like coffee?"

She glanced down at a time-worn Mr. Coffee. The plastic encasing the stack of Styrofoam cups next to it had the same coating of grime as the coffee maker itself, giving the appearance that the entire set-up had been left behind when the factory had closed.

"Oh…" *Cough.* "No thank you."

The man—Mr. Owens?—gave her a small

smile, which she took to mean that he had chosen to ignore the less-than-inspiring first impression she'd no doubt made. He entered the room then clicked the door shut, adding to the no-going-back-now inevitability of the actual interview.

As he crossed to an ancient-looking office chair behind the desk, Jill surmised that he wasn't from around here. Most local men, even the ones who worked at the bank, never bothered with a suit jacket. Mr. Owens looked Big City right down to the pocket square in his jacket and his stylish dark-framed glasses.

"I'm Dean Owens." He reached out a hand. "Please call me Dean."

"Dean." She nodded as she stepped closer and shook his hand.

"And you're…" He glanced at the résumé still waiting on the desk. "Miss Martin?"

"*Mrs.* Martin." Her voice came out in a nervous croak. "Please call me Jill."

"Jill." He gave a polite smile as he drew back his hand. "Won't you, uh…" His sentence drifted to a standstill as he picked up the résumé. The expression on his face confessed that he wasn't any more hopeful about this than she was. "…sit down?"

Clearing her throat, she moved toward an olive-green upholstered chair with chrome arms and legs, noting that as old as it looked, it was probably the newest item in the room. She lowered herself, and he did the same.

He kept his eyes on the page as he spoke. "You've…uh…looked over the brochure about our company?"

"Yes." She lifted her copy from the outside pocket of Colleen's bag, as if keeping it handy might win points in her favor. "It sounds fascinating."

"We have great plans." He looked up at her. "You've never worked in a technical field?"

"Oh…well, no. But I'm a quick learner. Plus, I type fast." She'd had to develop that skill if she'd ever wanted to finish writing an email while keeping Riley quiet in the library.

"And I ran the electric fryer at the Tastee Freez." *Ergh.* Way to underscore her pathetic lack of job experience.

Giving a polite smile, he returned his attention to the résumé. After several seconds, he looked up again. "What was it that attracted you to this company?"

"Um...well, I find the fact that you're hiring very attractive."

He nodded, his expression remaining expectant.

She swallowed. "I...n...need a job. And when I found out about the interviews today, I thought I should jump on the opportunity." *Ugh.* That sounded lame, even to her.

"I see." He eased back in his chair. "From everything you've read about our company, tell me how you feel you could make a contribution."

"Oh, well...I...don't know exactly what positions you're hiring for, but like I said, I'm a fast learner. And I move fast too. I have to, to keep up with my three-year-old." She accented her answer with a little laugh, which came out more pathetic than worldly.

"Mmm." He nodded, jotting something on her résumé.

Craning her neck in a futile attempt to make out what he was writing, she went for a save. "I really like everything I've heard about this company's forward thinking. I've lived in Madison Falls my whole life, and I would love to be a part of something that's focused on making it better."

He looked up, his expression shifting just enough to offer encouragement.

She went on. "And who wouldn't love to work in this great old building? I mean, its history is so…you know…historical."

"Yes." He glanced around the room, the corners of his mouth lifting slightly. "Tell me, how would you rate yourself as a team player?"

"As a team player? Well, let's see." She clutched her fingers together in her lap. "I think it's important, as a member of a team, to know the rules and to follow them."

"I see. And what kind of guidance do you see your ideal boss providing?"

"Oh. Well. Strong leadership of course. I mean, I like to be clear on what the expectations are."

"So…" Clasping his hands together on the desk, he leaned forward. "Would you say you're more of a follower than a leader?"

"No, I wouldn't say that. Necessarily." She scrambled, trying to figure out what he was going for. An employee would need to take orders, but a "follower"? That didn't sound good.

"Uh-huh." He scribbled out another note on the bottom of the page.

Jill's heart started to race. She had pretty much zero experience with job interviews, but even she could tell that this one was not going well.

Just as she was about to reach into her purse for gummy worms, she remembered Colleen's advice. *Your goal is to convince them that hiring you will benefit them.*

She slid forward in her chair. "Like I said, I'm a quick learner and whatever you need me to do, I can deliver great results. I will fit in with your team and get into the spirit of…" She flicked a quick glance at the brochure. "*Nyland Enterprises*. And I can tell you that whatever it is you're looking for in an employee, I will be as good as any candidate out there." She let out a breath.

He tipped his head, as if considering what she'd said, then stood and stuck out his hand, signaling an end to their conversation. "Thank you for coming today, Miss…*Mrs.* Martin."

"Jill," she said numbly.

"Jill." Rounding the desk, he lifted a hand in the direction of the door. "We'll be in touch."

Disappointed, she trudged self-consciously across the room and out the door. The arc of light at the end of the gloomy hallway seemed like a hundred miles away as she started toward it. She felt keenly aware of the fact that she would not be coming back.

She was about to pass one of the other doors leading off this hall when it swung open and someone stepped into her path.

"Oh!" She took a step backward, looking at the dark form silhouetted against the minimal light streaming out from that office. It took a moment for her to recognize him as Scowling Man.

As she caught sight of another man inside that room retaking a seat behind a desk, it struck her that Scowling Man had just received the same *we'll be in touch* message that she had. For a split second, she thought they might have a moment of shared condolences.

Instead, his dark eyes narrowed on her in a spiteful glare. Turning his body toward the arched doorway, he kept his steely eyes fixed on her. Finally, his head twisted to catch up with the rest of him, and he ambled down the hall, dragging one turned-out leg in a distinctive limp.

A cold wave moved through her. What exactly had she done to deserve that?

Jill Came Tumbling After

Chapter 6

"Hello, Vickie?" Bracing her phone between her cheek and shoulder, Jill stirred the contents of a pan on the stove. She had spent the entire drive back from the factory composing a mental Plan A of every potential babysitter she could think of and so far, she'd eliminated all but one. "This is Jill Martin."

Silence stretched, and she worried for a second that the phone company might have chosen that exact moment to disconnect her service.

"Oh, *Jill*." Vickie's game-show-contestant fervor fairly exploded in Jill's ear. "From that play group."

"Right." She grimaced. Vickie was last on the alphabetical-by-first-name Mommy and Me list from last summer, and Jill had to admit that she didn't even remember which mommy she was. Talk about feeling like a charity case.

After a quick accounting of her need for a babysitter that left out the part about her being suddenly single, Jill held her breath.

"I...don't know. My Trevor is still in diapers, and..."

"Oh, I understand. Thanks anyway." She stopped stirring and waited for Vickie to finish her thought. Apparently, Vickie subscribed to the philosophy that it was okay to say no, as long as you took ample time to explain how awful you felt about it. So much for Plan A.

The sound of her doorbell came as a welcome excuse to end this awkward phone call. Jill said a quick goodbye and flicked the burner off, then traversed the front hall as Riley's little voice filtered in from the porch. She set the phone in its stand on the table and opened the door.

"Hi Mama!" Riley darted inside followed by Sam, who carried a sleeping Emma.

Jill knelt down to give Riley a hug. "Did you have fun with Uncle Sam?"

"Yeah. We took'a Angel to the pawk." He held up a paper bag. "And we got'a the locks."

"You did?" Standing, she took the bag and set it next to the phone, then swung the door shut.

"They were both great." Sam handed over Emma, who made a contented gurgling sound as she nestled her head onto Jill's shoulder. "Emma took her morning nap, and then zonked out again on the two-minute drive over here."

"I bet somebody else is ready for a nap too." She ruffled Riley's curls, and ignored his protests as she encouraged him toward the stairs. "I'm going to put them both down. I'll be right back."

By the time she returned ten minutes later, Sam had brought in his toolbox and was testing a key in the lock of the open front door.

"You really wore them out." She tightened the string of the apron she'd pulled on after changing into jeans and a T-shirt earlier.

Sam smiled. "We had a good time." He shut the door. "This one's done."

"Great. I'm getting a start on dinner. You can keep me company while you do the back door." She moved toward the kitchen. "Did the kids eat lunch?"

"Steak and lobster." Sam's toolbox clanked shut.

She tossed a look over her shoulder as he stood and moved to follow her.

"I'm kidding." His usual upbeat attitude felt like sunshine as he entered the kitchen. "Riley had a hot dog and Emma downed one of the bottles you had in her bag." He set his toolbox on the floor next to the back door. "So, how did the interview go?"

"Uh…well…" Jill checked the pot on the stove. "Let's just say I didn't get the impression that my résumé is going to land in the short stack."

"Well, what can you expect?" He took out a screwdriver. "It was your first one."

"Right." She bit her lower lip. The thought of having to go through that process again was enough to make her want to run for the hills. Right now, she didn't even want to talk about it. "Thanks for keeping the kids long enough for me to go to the market."

"Not a problem." He started working on the doorknob. "I'm just happy to know you're not going to starve."

"We won't. Would you like to join us for dinner as payment for changing my locks?"

"Thanks, but I'm having dinner with Grace. She's going to be in Missoula all day tomorrow working with her vocal coach, so we're spending some time together tonight."

"Oh, of course." Her momentary lapse into life-as-it-used-to-be screeched to a halt. Of course he already had plans. Why wouldn't he?

"Another night, maybe." She took a spoonful from the pan and sniffed it, then crossed the kitchen and held it out to him. "How does this taste?"

"What is it?" Maintaining his focus on the doorknob, he allowed her to put the spoon into his mouth.

"Liver and beets."

He sputtered, nearly spitting it out. "What are you trying to do, kill me?"

She laughed. "That bad, huh?"

He grabbed a glass from the drain board and ran enough water into it to rinse his mouth. "Bad enough to make me glad I turned down your dinner invitation."

"This isn't our dinner." She chuckled. "I'm making baby food. I figure it'll save me some money."

"You're going to feed that to Emma?" He

resumed his work. "I thought you liked her."

She made a playful gasping sound as she retrieved a half dozen baby food jars from the drain board and set them on the counter. "I'm also making a chicken pot pie."

"Now *that* sounds good." He removed the old knob from the door. "You know, you and the kids are welcome to have dinner with Dad and me any time. It's the least I can do to save my goddaughter from the horrors of homemade baby food."

"Thanks." She started to pour the gloppy concoction into the jars. "But need I remind you that a certain banished husband is staying at your house?"

"Jill, you and Caleb are going to need to talk things out sooner or later." His voice held a tone of brotherly admonition.

"I realize that." She cranked lids onto the jars. "But you know how it always goes. Caleb does something awful, I get mad. He sobers up and turns on the charm again and I melt into a bowl of spineless Jell-O."

"If it's Jell-O"—an eyebrow arched her way—"it *never* has a spine."

"You know what I'm saying, smart aleck. I'm not strong enough to see him yet." Setting the jars in the fridge, she affected a nonchalant tone. "Has your dad said how Caleb's doing today?"

"Ah, you know Caleb." He took the new doorknob set out of its packaging. "Back to his old *charming* self."

"Of course." Why didn't it surprise her that Caleb had recovered just fine?

Sam no doubt detected her frustration. "Dad has a little too much sympathy for him, if you ask me."

"Really?" She tossed an onion onto the cutting board and started taking out her aggressions on it with a knife. "Your dad isn't on my side either?"

"It has nothing to do with taking sides." He positioned the new knobs in the door. "He just tends to fall for Caleb's woe-is-me saga. You know how it is."

She rolled her eyes, which had started to sting, thanks to the onion. Why did nobody understand what it was like being married to the guy? Even at church, all the advice she'd ever gotten was of the if-he's-not-violent-you-don't-have-a-problem ilk. *Some help.*

Except Sam and Colleen. They understood.

"That should do it." Sam set two keys on the counter next to the stove. "Put one of these on your ring before you forget."

"And you can keep the other one. I still need you to have a spare. But promise me you won't let Caleb know you have it, okay?"

"You think he's not smart enough to figure that out?"

"Good point." She continued to chop. "Maybe you should keep it someplace other than on your key ring, just in case."

"Fine." He pocketed the key. "I'll stick it in my mom's old jewelry box."

"Just be sure to tell your dad it's in there in case he ever decides to sell the jewelry and get rid of the box."

"He *gave* her most of that jewelry." He tossed the screwdriver into the toolbox. "He could never part with it."

"Are you sure? Maybe he's moving on better than you think. I mean, it's been over a year now."

"Nah." He shook his head. "He wouldn't even let Colleen take a necklace she wanted. Too many memories. Too much pain."

Blinking against the tears she could at least pretend to blame on the onion, she finished the chopping and went to the sink to wash her hands. He didn't have to say it, but she knew he was talking about the pain he still felt at the loss of his mom too. Losing a loved one was hard enough, but the abruptness of the rare respiratory ailment that had claimed her had left them all reeling. Mr. Roberts hadn't been quite the same since.

Truth be told, Jill really hadn't gotten over it either. As a kid, she had routinely pretended to be a member of Colleen and Sam's family as a defense against the chaos at home. In some ways, it had been harder to lose their mom last year than to face the death of her own father. And all the guilt she forced herself to feel about that did nothing to change it.

The lid to Sam's toolbox closed with an attention-snapping *thunk*. "Anything else need fixing?"

"You mean aside from my marriage?"

He tossed her a narrow gaze.

"Well, since you asked, the hall table has a severed leg. Do you have time?"

"Sure." He shrugged. "Should only take a minute."

"A minute. Right." She wiped her hands, then picked up her key from the counter and led the way to the front hall. "And if I'd waited for Caleb, the rest of the table would have rotted with age before he ever got around to fixing it."

"He's not exactly a handyman." Sam set his toolbox down next to the broken table. "But give him a fishing pole and it's a different story."

She grunted. "Even *that* sounds like a better way to spend his days than sleeping and drinking."

"At least fishing is productive." He turned the table upside down. "I always admired his patience with it."

Patience? Jill resisted an eye roll. How much patience did it take to sit by the side of the river all day? It hadn't bothered her so much when it had been a day-off activity for him, but after he lost his job, it had turned into another one of his ways of escaping responsibility. She would have given anything to be able to reel him back to reality with one of his own lures.

"We used to have some good talks waiting for the trout to bite." Sam kept his focus on the table as he spoke. "Maybe I should grab a couple of his poles and take him down to the river. That could be my best bet for talking some sense into him."

Crossing to the front door, Jill reached for her key ring and slipped her new key onto it. She sniffed. "His fishing stuff is all out in the garage."

"I should take some of his clothes while I'm at it." The glance he flicked her way registered as more of a reflex than a test of her reaction.

"S…sure." Her voice sounded weak as she hung up her keys. She was the one who had told Caleb to leave. Why did the finality of him moving his things out make her heart drop to her stomach?

Feeling suddenly lightheaded, she sat down at the bottom of the stairs. "I mean, of course."

"Tell me the truth." He regarded her from where he'd kneeled next to the table. "You don't really want him to be gone for good, do you?"

She swiped at a threatening tear with her sleeve. "I want sober, mature, *employed* Caleb to come back for good. There's not much I can do to turn him into that."

He sent her the sympathetic look she knew all too well. "There's always hope."

Hope. If the sentiment had come from anyone else, she would have smiled and acted grateful for the wisdom. With Sam, she could be real. "And I'm supposed to keep hoping that my husband will stop drinking, get a job, and start being around the way he should. Well, I'm sick of hoping."

"I'm sick of hoping too." He dabbed some glue on the base of the table leg. "But you know, sometimes God needs us to get to the end of our rope so He can start doing His work."

"Meaning...?"

"As long as we're trying to fix things ourselves, we get in our own way." He put the leg back in its place. "Rely on Him, and He'll never fail you."

Right. A tear rolled down her cheek and this time she didn't bother to wipe it away. The theory made sense when she was sitting in church. Why did it seem so impossible to apply to her actual life?

Maybe this would be a good time to start putting in a little more effort.

Sam's phone reverberated in his pocket, and he took it out to check the ID. "Mind if I take this?" A corner of his mouth lifted. "It's Grace."

"Oh." She pushed herself to her feet. "Of course." Feeling a little disoriented, she returned to the kitchen and to her dinner preparations. She took a bowl of chopped potatoes and carrots out of the fridge, drained it, and transferred the contents into a pan.

As she filled it with fresh water and put it on the stove to boil, she did her best to ignore what she could hear of Sam's muted end of the conversation. The last thing she needed was to overhear any romantic gushing that might make her feel lower than she already did. She was happy for Sam that he'd found Grace. They seemed so good together. It was normal to feel a little envious when her own relationship was falling apart, wasn't it?

After she had gotten out all the ingredients she'd need to make the crust for the pie, she realized she couldn't hear Sam talking anymore. She peeked through the door into the entryway and saw that he had finished his call and had gone back to working on the table. Something about his demeanor had hardened.

He glanced up at her. "Grace said to tell you that she and her mom can help some with babysitting until she leaves for New York. That should at least buy you some time."

"Great." She was pretty sure that Grace hadn't called just to tell him that, but whatever was upsetting him was none of her business. She took a step toward the stove.

"And it looks like I'll be available for dinner after all."

"Oh?" She moved back into the doorway. "Grace had to cancel?"

"Yeah. It's no big deal. It's just that her vocal coach can't work with her tomorrow like they had planned, so they're meeting this afternoon instead. She has to drive all the way to Missoula, so she'll be getting back late."

"Sorry."

He shrugged. "I knew things would be this way when she took this opera, but it's tougher than I expected."

"Really?" She paused. "How so?"

"It's not just about her being gone for the rehearsal and performance weeks. She's spending most of her free time now learning the music."

"Just because she's never done this role before. It won't always be this time consuming, right?"

"That's what she says." He grunted as the leg on the table twisted at an awkward angle. "She really wants me to go to New York for her opening."

Folding her arms, Jill leaned on the doorjamb. "Sounds like fun."

He cocked an eyebrow. "Seeing her perform would be fun, but *New York?* I think she hoped I'd change my mind about big cities when I went to LA for that songwriting competition." His jaw worked as he forced the leg into submission. "If I never have to face that traffic and the smog and the crowds again, I'll be a happy man. Grace, though…" He shook his head. "She really loves the excitement. New York, Chicago. She might even have a chance to sing in Qingdao in a few years. I mean, I don't even know where Qingdao is."

She frowned. Neither did she.

"I guess it's just…" His voice lowered to practically a whisper. "…reminding me a little of Becky."

Jill's stomach clenched. Becky had been Sam's high school sweetheart. Everyone had assumed they'd get married someday, but they had broken up when her career goals had taken her away to Billings. As far as Sam had been concerned, that was "big city" enough for him to choose not to go with her.

"I'm sorry, Sam."

"It's okay. I'm just feeling a little frustrated." He set the table upright and gave it a nudge.

"Would you say you're at the 'end of your rope'?" She gave him a slight smile.

As he put the rest of his tools into the box and shut the lid, his features softened. "Are you saying I need to get out of the way and let God do His thing?"

"Sounds like good advice." She took a couple of steps toward him.

"You know something? Sometimes…" Standing, he made a show of looking around as if someone might be listening. "…I think you're the only person I can really confide in."

Caught off guard by the sentiment, she felt slightly awkward. From where she stood, it seemed like he had plenty of people he could confide in. Was she really that special to him?

He started for the door. "So, what time do you want me to show up for dinner?"

"Oh, uh…" She fumbled, feeling an unexpected warmth move up her cheeks as she kept pace behind him. "Around six is good."

"Six it is."

As she stood in her doorway watching him walk down her steps, a strange sensation of loneliness took her by surprise. Shutting the door, she pondered. She was just adjusting to not having Caleb around, that was all. Sam had always been like a brother to her, nothing more. Well, that wasn't exactly true. He'd been like a brother who was also a close friend.

She gave herself a mental shake. With the kids both asleep, she shouldn't waste her time standing around thinking. She had things to do.

Back in the kitchen, she checked the pot on the stove. The veggies looked done, so she took them to the sink to drain.

She grabbed her big skillet off its hook, then set it on a burner, cranked it up to High, and tossed a chunk of butter into it. As she waited for it to heat, her eyes moved to the imposing stack of bills on the table. She sighed. It just didn't feel right to go on welfare without at least trying to get a job first. Of course, that would be impossible to do with a baby on her hip and a preschooler getting into things.

She watched the butter sizzle and slide sideways. Straightening her shoulders, she scooped the chopped onion into the pan. She gave it a stir, feeling comforted by the savory aroma.

One thing was certain. She wasn't going to be able to lean on Sam for childcare. It was sweet of Grace and Mrs. Fontaine to offer to help, but that would only provide a partial solution. She had tried everybody she could think of.

That left her with no other option. Desperation had officially set in.

Jill Came Tumbling After

Chapter 7

Taking comfort in the familiarity of the dark tree-lined street, Jill pulled to a stop and shut off the engine. She looked up at the warm glow coming from the windows of her childhood home and thought about the last time she had been there. She'd stormed out, vowing not to come back without an apology from her mother. So much for sticking to her guns.

Rubbing at the knot in her shoulder that

had become more pronounced with each passing second of the two-minute drive over here, she checked the clock on the dash. Sam had been more than willing to stay with the kids for a while after dinner, especially when she had told him what she intended to do, but she didn't want to keep him too long. That was as good a reason as any to make this quick. Not that she was dying to linger.

She got out of the car and pulled her jacket tighter around herself to fend off the evening chill. Even though her mom's house was just a couple of blocks from her own, she hadn't come around a lot after getting married five years ago. She'd avoided even driving past the place for the last few months. As she started up the walk, all the memories of childhood came flooding back to her. Good ones, followed by not-so-good ones.

Losing her nerve, she nearly did an about-face. What was she thinking? Nothing was going to be any different. This was only going to add to her humiliation.

No. This was her last shot. She had to get a job, and she had literally eliminated every other possibility for childcare. It would do her no good to wait for an apology that would never come, and besides, didn't being a grandmother imply some sort of obligation, at least in an emergency?

Leaves crunched under her feet as she stepped up onto the porch and glanced toward the front window. Her mother sat in her chair crocheting and watching TV, just like she had most every night of Jill's childhood. Only back then, Jill's dad would have been sitting in his chair too.

The chair that now sat empty.

Ignoring the voice in her head that urged her to leave while she still could, she raised her finger to the doorbell. Before she could press it, her mom looked up and saw her through the window. Her face brightened for the briefest second, then fell to an indecipherable neutrality.

Feeling the sting of that reaction, Jill

waited, lifting a smile and a small wave. Her mom hesitated, leaving Jill trapped in an awkward moment of wondering what to do. Should she just walk in?

The answer came as her mom set her crocheting aside and rose to her feet. Jill lost sight of her momentarily as she moved from the living room to the entryway.

A moment later, the door opened and Jill saw the face of the woman who had raised her, cared for her, been there for her in times of need, made her lunches every childhood morning and sent her off to school. The face of the woman who had told her that if she married Caleb, her life would be ruined, and then turned her back when that had proven to be true.

Invisible tension charged the air between them.

"Well, you're here," her mom finally said. "You might as well come in."

She turned to go back to her chair and Jill followed her in, shutting the door behind herself.

"Place looks nice." Unbuttoning her jacket, she looked around at the house that, apart from a little paint and some new throw pillows, hadn't really changed much in her lifetime. The small space seemed even smaller than she remembered, crowded as it was with memories.

Jill shook off her jacket and laid it across the arm of the sofa before perching next to it. "Aren't you glad I talked you into repainting last summer? And it's amazing what a few new pieces will do to give a room a whole new look."

"There was nothing wrong with the way the place looked before."

"No, there was nothing wrong with it. It's just that everything had been the same for so long. I thought it would cheer you up to have something new to look at."

"I didn't need cheering up. I was fine. Still am." The brusqueness of her tone seemed to undermine the reassuring words, but that was the way her mother had always been.

Jill gave a slow nod. "Good."

They sat in silence for a moment and watched a contestant on the TV ponder her answer, then get it wrong. The drawn-out sound of collective audience disappointment grated on Jill's nerves as she glanced at the clock on the mantel. She shouldn't take advantage of Sam's kindness for too long. If she was going to do this, she'd have to just bite the bullet.

She pulled in a deep breath. "Mom, I have something to ask you."

"What is it, dear?" The endearment seemed clipped, almost automated, and her eyes didn't stray from the TV screen.

"Well, I just—"

She was cut off by the sound of shrieking on the TV as the other contestant jumped up and down, having apparently just won the round.

Jill rolled in her lips. "Can I turn this off for a few minutes? This is really important."

Her mother flicked her a look that said *nothing* could be more important than the final round of *Wheel of Fortune*, before picking up the remote and clicking Mute.

She appeared to transfer her full attention to her crocheting, but Jill figured that was probably the best she could expect.

Jill swallowed hard and pushed her voice past the tennis ball that had formed in her throat. "I'm going to get a job."

Her mother raised a questioning look tinged with disapproval. "Oh?"

"Yes. I plan to work during the day and I really need you to watch the kids for me."

"What about Caleb?" The words shot out like arrows. "Why can't *he* do it?"

She shifted in her seat. "Mom, you know how it is."

"Did he get a job? Is that why he's unavailable to watch his children?"

"No...I mean, sort of." All rational thinking seemed to shut down, the way it always did when she tried to talk to her mother about anything even remotely contentious. "He's working with Sam at the hardware store." Well, that was partly true. *Partly.*

"Oh?" That apparently caught her mom's attention, because her gaze cut toward Jill. "I thought they had all the help they needed. I know John mentioned not long ago that he wished they could afford to hire more help to take some of the burden off Sam."

Jill felt her shoulders tighten again. She'd forgotten that her mom chatted about things like that with Sam's dad whenever he waited on her in the hardware store or they ran into each other in the market. They'd both grown up around here and had known each other for years.

She tried for a save. "They haven't hired him full time but he's helping out."

"For free?" A sharp-edged unspoken *gotcha* trailed behind the question.

"No. Not for free, exactly." Jill's brain started to twist into the customary knot it wound itself into whenever she tried to avoid giving complete information to her mother. "They're just helping him out, that's all."

"Well, are they helping him, or is he helping them?"

"Both. Look, Mom. I just really need a sitter, so can you do it?"

"Jillian." Her mother put her crocheting in her lap and leveled a hard look that stabbed at Jill's core. "You haven't come to see me or even given me a phone call since that day you shouted at me about that husband of yours."

"Mom." It was true. She'd been so angry at her mother that day. Emma had been tiny still, and Jill had felt weak and vulnerable. Fatigue and the lack of emotional support from Caleb had driven her to the brink of what had felt frighteningly close to a breakdown.

She had gone to her mother's that day because she'd felt like she would lose her mind if she stayed in the house with a newborn, a toddler, and an unemployed husband who was sleeping off yet another hangover. Instead of sympathy, she'd gotten an earful about making her bed and having to lie in it, or some such sentiment.

And anyway, who was her mom to tell her how she should handle Caleb's drinking? She hadn't done any better herself with her own husband. Jill glanced at Dad's empty recliner, her stomach burning at all the emotions dredged up by the sight of it.

"I've seen you intentionally avoid me in the market, Jillian. How do you think it makes me feel that you only come around here now that you need something?"

"I'm sorry, Mom. I…" She faltered. That was true too. What did she have to say in her own defense?

Her mother gripped the arms of her chair. "Something's happened with Caleb, hasn't it? What is it?"

Jill closed her eyes, wanting to shut out the ugly truth. But there was no way to avoid it. She had to just say it.

She opened her eyes, but kept her focus on the muted TV, where a cat cha-chaed on his hind legs in exchange for canned food. "I asked him to leave."

"Leave…your home?"

"Yes." Would she actually receive some support and sympathy from the one person who should understand? The one person who should know how it felt to live in a desperate marriage where there was no hope for improvement? "It just got to the point where I couldn't take any more."

Her mother returned her attention to her crocheting, the yarn seeming to take on a life of its own in her hands. "I could have told you that would happen."

"Yes." Jill sighed. "I'm sure you could have."

Bitter disappointment washed over her. Why would she have expected any other response? Her mother had, after all, stuck by Jill's father without complaint for all those years, no matter how outrageous his behavior got. It was hard to see that as admirable, considering how bitter she had become.

"It doesn't matter." Her mother's eyes and mouth seemed to pinch closer to her nose. "You wouldn't have listened to me."

"Mom"—she toyed with a loose thread on the arm of the sofa—"let's not do this."

"I told you he was just like your father. I told you that from the start."

"I know—"

"But you married him anyway. You sealed your fate." By now her hands were working so fast that Jill questioned if she was actually taking stitches or just moving the yarn back and forth with the hook. "You could have married anyone. When I think about how close you always were with Sam."

Jill's intended response caught in her throat as she replayed that last sentence in her mind. Had she understood her correctly? Her mom had never suggested Sam as a boyfriend for her. Why was she bringing it up now?

"And you had absolutely no right to tell the man to leave his own house. It's your job as a wife to remain silent and comply with your husband's wishes."

Jill narrowed her eyes. "You don't really believe that, do you?"

Her mom tossed her a quick, condescending look. "The truth is the truth, Jillian. Young people just want to make up their own rules. You're defiant. And now Caleb has to suffer because of your selfishness."

"Selfishness?" Jill felt herself rise to her feet. "Is it selfish to expect him to support his family? To come home at night to spend time with us instead of getting plowed with his buddies at the Spur?" Her voice thickened and she dug her nails into her palms. "I'm really sick of everybody telling me I'm supposed to feel bad for poor Caleb. Right now, I'm a little too busy feeling bad for poor me!"

"Jillian—"

"I'm sorry to have bothered you." Her throat aching, she bolted for the entryway. "Forget I even came here tonight."

Behind her, the TV blared back to life as

Jill flung open the door. Cold air nipped at her skin, reminding her that she had left her jacket behind, but she didn't care. No way was she turning around now.

Outrage burned in her chest as she hurried down the front steps toward her car. It was bad enough that her mother had basically told her she should have gone down with the sinking ship, but she hadn't even had the decency to dwell on Jill's dramatic exit before returning to her game show.

That was it. Jill would just have to go on welfare and make that work. Lots of women did it. That way, she could be there for her kids until they were both in school.

She got into her car and started the engine, resisting the urge to scream. To think that her own mother believed that a woman should continue to submit to a man who had stopped supporting his family and was being devoured by his addiction. The thought repulsed her, but it came as no surprise. It explained why her mother had stayed with her father, in spite of everything. And even though Jill really hadn't seen it until it was too late, her mother was right. Jill had married a man who was just like her dad.

She shifted to Drive and pulled away from the curb. One thing was for sure. There was no way she was going to turn into her mother. She owed that much to her kids.

Jill Came Tumbling After

Chapter 8

Jill held her phone a few inches from her ear to give herself a break from the relentless crackle of hold music. The welfare office was supposed to open at eight, but she'd been waiting for twenty minutes already and had started to wonder if anyone even knew she was there.

She pictured an office full of people sitting around swigging coffee and joking that anyone on hold could just wait. After all—

they would say—without a job, what else did they have to do?

She sighed. After leaving her mom's house the night before, she had been so upset that she'd gone straight to Colleen's apartment. From there, she had called Sam and asked him to stay with the kids long enough for her to calm down and put in her welfare application online.

Then this morning she'd gotten up before the sun and had finally tackled the stack of bills. Now, having written up a tally of her monthly expenses, she faced the moment of truth. Would the number exceed what she'd be able to bring in if she went on welfare?

She looked at the clock. Eight twenty-two. She really wanted to get this done before the kids woke up, and they'd be stirring any time now. In her mind, the people in the welfare office laughed at the blinking red light signaling her call, and poured another round of coffee.

Her stomach did a little break dance as she

looked again at her rough budget. She had cut every corner she could think of with their living expenses. There was nothing she could do about the mortgage payment, but if she kept the heat as low as they could stand and traded in their standard size trash can for the smallest one, she could cut her utility costs. If she got on the food stamp program and qualified for the food bank, that would help with groceries.

Of course, she'd need to cut everyone's hair herself, including her own, but how hard could that be? And she'd have to stick to thrift shopping for clothing for the kids and borrow whatever she needed for herself from Colleen. And they wouldn't be seeing the inside of a restaurant in the near future unless someone else offered to treat.

She looked at the number on the page. Sixteen hundred dollars a month seemed like a fortune, but it didn't actually stretch that far. How had they managed to survive the past several months? Caleb had obviously brought in more from the odd jobs he'd done than she'd realized.

She crossed to the coffee pot and refilled her cup. It would do her no good to feel sorry for herself. This was one of those "times of trial" people always talked about in church when the difference between falling apart and keeping it together depended on having the right attitude. It was time to make the necessary mental adjustment.

Leaning against the counter, she looked around her cozy kitchen. Sure, she wished she had the funds to paint and make a few updates, but they had everything they needed. As long as she could draw enough welfare to keep up with the bills and put food on their plates, it wouldn't be so bad. When the kids got older and went to school, maybe she could get a job. At least then it wouldn't be out of desperation.

It was good that she had realized this before wasting any more time going on fruitless interviews. That weighed heavily on the plus side. And with zero childcare options, she had no other choice, anyway. She'd have to make this work.

Pressing the phone to her cheek, she took a long, comforting swig of coffee. This felt like a good plan.

She ambled across the room and paused in the doorway between the kitchen and the dining room, which had turned a soft pink with the morning sun filtering in through the windows. Being on such a tight budget didn't sound like much fun, but if they couldn't afford to go anywhere, at least they had a comfortable place to live. As long as she had her home and her kids, things couldn't be that bad.

She looked through the dining room into the living room which, aside from the master bedroom, was her favorite room in the house. She'd managed to score an antique Persian rug at a yard sale that covered most of the hardwood floor in that room. One of her neighbors had given her a camelback sofa and matching chair when she'd redecorated her own house, and Jill had made a few throw pillows to add some color and breathe new life into them. The bookcase she'd found at a garage sale and painted the shade of sea-foam green that was in the rug, made a perfect storage unit for toys. She loved the homey feeling that gave the room.

Leaning her back against the doorjamb, she closed her eyes and tried to relax. With everything she was taking account of these days, this would be a good time to get back into the habit of thanking God. It seemed like her prayer life had shifted from a balance of gratitude and requests, to mostly asking for things, to outright pleading. Then lately it had disappeared altogether. She let out a long breath. Maybe that was why things had gone so wildly out of control. She had forgotten to turn to God for guidance.

Holding the phone next to her shoulder, she dropped her head, lulled by the muffled sound of the hold music. Then something else stole her focus and she opened her eyes. A scratching sound…but where was it coming from?

She lowered the phone and strained to listen. It was definitely coming from the kitchen. She took a few careful steps, honing in on the lower cabinets right next to the back door, where she kept her larger pots and lids. A few more steps…then she knelt next to it. Yes, there was a distinct scratching sound coming from the cupboard.

Oh no. She leaned back on her heels. *Rats.*

Panic rose in her throat. How could she have rats? And why now—now that she didn't have a man around to deal with the problem?

The thought of rodents—or to be more specific, rodent droppings—terrified her. An image of Sam's mom being taken to the ER was still all too prominent in her mind. The last time Jill had seen Mrs. Roberts, the woman could barely breathe and her eyes had been filled with terror. Who would have thought that something as simple as cleaning out a barn could kill you?

But, there was a big difference between a

verminous old barn and a kitchen cupboard. She was the head of the house now and, like it or not, she'd have to learn to face the hard problems. If she had furry intruders, she'd deal with them somehow, but the first step was to confirm their presence. She reached out her hand, then yanked the cupboard open.

"Department of Public Health and Human Services. How may I assist you?"

The sound of a woman's voice next to her cheek startled her, and she fell onto her backside.

"Oh…uh…" She fumbled with the phone, trying to refocus on her reason for making the call while scanning the cupboard for evidence of unwelcome boarders.

"Ma'am? Are you there?"

"Yes, I'm here." Confirming that there was no evidence of critters among her pots and pans, or at least not that she could easily detect, Jill got her feet under her. "I applied online and I'm calling to find out how much I can qualify for."

"I see." The words came out sounding clipped and vaguely impatient. "Social?"

"Not really." Jill sat on her haunches. "I have kids."

A drawn-out breath sounded in her ear, and Jill realized she'd misunderstood the question. Grimacing, she quickly recited her social security number.

The woman muttered under her breath as she typed the numbers in. "Can you hold?"

Could she? Hadn't she already proven her ability to hold for the past half hour? "Yes, of course." She tried to sound obliging, but the music started again before she'd even gotten the words out.

Making use of her time, she poked around in the cupboard and saw nothing suspicious. Then the scratching sound started up again. She stuck her head inside the cupboard. It was clearly coming from underneath. She frowned. Under the house?

Great. The source of the sound was obviously something that wasn't supposed to be there. How could she possibly afford an exterminator?

She would have to call Sam.

Sam. She'd been pushing back thoughts of him all morning. The memory of his nice words had combined with her mother's comment, creating a hot mess of confusion in her mind. How could she call for him to rescue her again and not feel like some kind of scheming female?

The answer was that she couldn't. She'd have to face this on her own. At least figure out what exactly she was dealing with before she played the damsel-in-distress card.

Keeping the phone as close to her ear as she could stand, she used her free hand to wedge the baby monitor under her arm, then grabbed a flashlight from the drawer next to the back door. She stepped outside, trying to recall everything she had ever heard about rodent control. If they had gotten in under the house, maybe all she needed to do was block their entryway. She hurried down the steps, then lowered herself to her knees.

Still hearing the sound, which was louder now and much harder to assign some acceptable explanation to, she shined the light in through the lattice work that edged the underside of the porch. At least if anything was under there, she had an illusion of a barrier between it and her. The sound grew more urgent and she wedged the flashlight through one of the openings.

The beam caught a pair of eyes from deep under the porch. She gasped, jarring back and nearly dropping the light. Then the sound became something more complex. More like a whimper.

She focused her light again, catching the eyes looking out at her from a cute little face. She didn't have rats. She had a puppy.

An involuntary laugh escaped her throat. What a relief to not have rats. Or more to the point, not to have to pay to execute the rats. A puppy was so much better.

A puppy. Poor Riley was going to be so

happy, then so disappointed when she told him they would have to either figure out who had lost this little guy or find a home for him.

She shone her light around to make sure there weren't any more. No litter and no mama. Where in the world had this little fella come from?

The whimper grew into more of a pained plea for rescue. Thanking God that at least the source of the sound was under the porch and not in the no-man's-land crawlspace under the house, she set down the light and looked for an access point. On the end of the porch next to the house, the lattice seemed to be pulling away. She tugged at it and removed the piece on the end.

"Come on puppy. Come on."

The pitch of his whimpering went up a notch, as if to say, "No way, lady. You come in and get me." *Great.* That meant that he was probably hurt, stuck, or scared. And she could either search the kitchen for some kind of treat to lure him out with or go in after him.

Considering that the closest thing she currently had to a dog treat was raw hamburger, she decided to go with option B.

She quickly clipped the baby monitor to the side of her waistband and held the light in one hand, then stared at the phone. Since she really didn't want to have to start over with this call, she decided to take it in with her. She tapped the Speaker button, then got onto her stomach and used her free arm to pull herself toward the puppy.

Cooing softly, she managed to grab hold of the warm, trembling little critter.

"Ma'am." The voice on the other end demanded instant attention.

Nothing like rotten timing.

"Oh...hi." She pushed herself backwards with her elbows, trying not to sound like she was crawling on her belly carrying a flashlight, a baby monitor, and a puppy. "Can you tell me if I qualify for welfare?"

"We no longer call it 'welfare.'" The woman snorted. "It's Temporary Assistance to

Needy Families."

"Oh…I'm…*sorry*." Kicking her way out of the confined space, she chastised herself, as if pleasing this woman might factor into her eligibility for funds.

"Yes. I see you here. Jill Martin. Two children. Sep-ar-ate-ed." She stretched out the last word as if it gave her some sort of morose pleasure to rub it in.

"Yes. That's me." She managed to sit up. The puppy licked her chin, and she fumbled to take the phone out of Speaker mode.

"And you have no current means of financial support. Is that accurate?"

"Very. My husband lost his job." She stood. "And now he's lost me."

"I see. And *you've* lost your income." It was as if the woman used the word "income" as a substitute for "gravy train." Jill wanted to protest, but it wouldn't help her any. The woman must be used to dealing with people who tried to work the system.

Struggling to keep the dirty brown-and-white puff ball from wriggling out of her arms, she hurried up the back steps and into the house, listening for any indication that Riley might be awake.

"Mrs. Martin, I see that with a combination of temporary assistance funds and food stamps, if you qualify, you will receive twelve hundred a month."

"Twelve hundred?" She dipped down to set the flashlight on the counter, then went to the table and looked at the paper with her budget written on it. Twelve hundred wasn't enough. She needed at least sixteen hundred, and that was if she made her own laundry soap and kept her driving to a minimum. "Oh. Well, do you have any other programs I can apply for? My mortgage payment alone would take up most of that."

"Have you spoken with your lender?"

Her lender? That must be the bank. "No, I haven't."

"They might be able to recommend something."

"Great. I'll look into that."

The woman went on to talk more about "qualifying" and terms, but the squirming puppy made it hard to follow what she was saying. "Get back to me as soon as you find out about the mortgage payment so I can update your information. Then we can continue the processing."

Demonstrating a sudden burst of canine tenacity, the puppy twisted out of her grasp and landed with a thud on the floor. He scrambled in place for a moment, his claws clacking against the tile. Then just like a prison inmate with a precisely mapped-out escape plan, he took off running through the open baby gate and into the dining room.

The woman hadn't stopped talking. "My name is Angela Hoyt and I'm your case worker, so if you have any questions, you should call me." She began to recite the number, obviously assuming that Jill was seated with pen and paper at the ready.

"Oh." Jill vacillated between chasing after

the dog and finding a pen. Figuring that Angela Hoyt wouldn't be very sympathetic to her plight, she opted for a crayon and a torn envelope. How much damage could an unsupervised puppy do in the time it would take to jot down a phone number?

"The recording will prompt you to add my extension."

Jill's hand hovered over the envelope, waiting to write down the promised extension. The sound of Riley's feet *clunk-clunking* down the stairs accelerated her sense of urgency. Why wouldn't this woman talk faster? She grabbed the paper and tried to write in the air as she walked into the dining room.

"Extension two-oh-seven. I'll expect to hear from you ASAP."

"Yes. Thank you." She clicked the phone and hurried into the living room.

"Puppy!" Riley plunked down in the middle of the rug, and the puppy climbed him like a tiny tree. "Mama! You got'a me a puppy!"

"Oh, Riley. He's not—"

Riley shrieked with glee just as Emma squawked on the monitor, which was still clipped to Jill's waist.

"Stay right there while I go get your sister." As Jill headed for the stairs, she remembered what Sam had said about having faith.

Oh Lord, help me.

Chapter 9

Jill positioned Emma in the sling at her waist, then lifted a box with the puppy in it from the backseat. She'd considered leaving him at home, but with no way of containing him, that hadn't seemed wise. The same went for leaving him in the car. And since she had to act on the refinancing option as soon as possible, she'd decided to bank on the kindness of her friend Joanne, who worked as a teller and loved kids and dogs. With any luck, business would be slow, and the puppy wouldn't create much of a stir.

"Come on, Rile." With the box secured under her arm, she reached out her other hand to Riley, who gripped the *Found Puppy* flyers that Jill had quickly created with construction paper and crayons. She knew he didn't fully comprehend their meaning, and she hadn't been as bold as she'd wanted to be in explaining. She just couldn't handle a heartbroken preschooler on top of everything else she had to deal with right now.

She swung open the door to the bank and trailed Riley into the high-ceilinged, old-fashioned lobby. To her relief, there was only one customer, and she was being served by Nick, the second teller.

Joanne looked up, her smile broadening when she saw them. "Good morning, Jill." Her voice echoed across the quaint little lobby.

Hoisting the box higher on her hip, Jill scooted Riley toward the teller windows. "Hi, Jo."

As they neared, Joanne leaned over to peer into the box. "Who do we have here?"

"We got'a a puppy," Riley announced proudly.

"Oh?" Joanne raised a questioning look at Jill.

"Actually, we *found* a puppy." Jill set the box down on the marble counter and shook out her arm. Now we're trying to find his owner. You haven't heard of anyone losing one, have you?"

"No." Joanne reached into the box to pet the little fella, who wagged his tail in delight at the attention. "I'll keep my ears open though."

"Great. We made flyers." Jill handed one across the counter. "Is Mr. Stanley in? I have a question about our mortgage."

"He sure is." She picked up her phone and hit a button. "I'll let him know you're here."

"Thanks." She glanced down at Riley, who was eying the colorful display of Dum Dums which sat on the counter just out of his reach.

Joanne replaced the handset on its base. "He says to go on in." She cast a look around the empty lobby. "I can keep an eye on Riley and the puppy for you, if you want."

"Oh, would you?" Jill had hoped for patience and understanding. An offer to babysit was even better. "I'd really appreciate that."

"I'd love to." Joanne moved from behind the bank of windows.

Feeling encouraged by the way things were working in her favor so far this morning, Jill got Riley and the puppy situated then headed for the open door at the far end of the lobby.

Mr. Stanley stood as she entered his office. "Good morning, Mrs. Martin. Thank you for coming in." His gaze trailed to the door behind her as she shut it. "Will…uh…*Mr.* Martin be joining us?"

"Oh, no." Jill pulled Emma from the sling to keep her from getting antsy. "I hope he doesn't have to."

"No…" Arching a thick gray eyebrow, he gestured for her to sit in the chair on the other side of the desk. "We can get started without him."

Her stomach clenched. *Get started?* She really didn't want to involve Caleb in this at all. Couldn't she just handle it on her own?

As Mr. Stanley retook his seat and started plunking at his computer, Jill sat, settling Emma in her lap. "The reason I'm here is that…well, I'm wondering if I qualify for refinancing."

"Refinancing?" He peered at her from over his glasses. "But that's not what I…" He stopped, looked away, then removed his glasses and gave a long blink. He let out a slow breath before speaking again. "I'm sorry, Mrs. Martin, but I'm afraid you don't qualify for refinancing."

"Oh." She allowed Emma to gnaw on her knuckle. "Well, what would I have to do to qualify?"

"I don't…quite know what to…" He

leaned forward, his gaze on her narrowing. "Haven't you been receiving the notices we've sent?"

Giving a slow shake of her head, she tried to recall if she'd seen anything from the bank in that stack of mail. "N…no…"

His eyes darted around his desk before settling on her again. "I'm afraid your house is in pre-foreclosure."

"Pre-fore…" Her heart jumped to her throat. "What does that mean?"

"It means that you're behind on your payments. The bank is going to have to take the house. I'm sorry. We've sent several notices. I assumed you knew."

"Take my house?" Her hands started to shake. "But, that can't happen. It belongs to us. Our names are on the deed."

"Yes, I understand that, Mrs. Martin, but you haven't paid the loan off yet, so technically it still belongs to the bank."

Jill felt the blood drain from her face, and for a moment she thought she might pass out.

How could he say that they hadn't paid for it? It had been their home for five years. No way could she just let someone take it. "What do I need to do to stop this from happening?"

"Well, if you bring the loan current, we could still stop the proceedings as long as the foreclosure notice hasn't been served."

A glimmer of hope surfaced. "How much would that be?"

He tapped at his computer keyboard. "Let's see, there hasn't been a payment made since…" He typed some more and studied the screen. "Since May."

"May? That can't be. My husband…" Her voice trailed off as she thought about it. What evidence did she have beyond her own naive assumptions that Caleb had been paying the mortgage? Or anything else, for that matter?

And now that she really thought about it, what had she assumed he'd been making payments *with*? The money from his odd jobs had barely been enough to keep food on the table. How could she have been so blind and trusting?

"Yes. So that's five payments that are owed. Your payments are nine fifty-two a month, so that means you are past due…" He worked his fingers over a calculator for what seemed like an eternity before coming up with a sum. "Roughly forty-seven hundred."

She sank lower into her chair, tears pooling in her eyes. *Forty-seven hundred dollars.* She couldn't begin to imagine how she could come up with even a fraction of that. "I see."

He consulted his desk calendar, the look in his eyes indicating that he wasn't enjoying this any more than she was. "Another payment will come due on November fifth. That's two weeks from now."

"Can we make a deal?" Emma started to fuss, and Jill bounced her on her leg to calm her. "If I can make that payment plus a little extra? I could do that every month until I'm caught up."

He started shaking his head even before

she'd finished. "I'm so sorry. If it were up to me.... The bank is very strict. I can't really advise you, but I'm afraid the foreclosure notice could get posted on your front door at any time."

"Any time?" Her mind frantically raced to come up with anything that might put the brakes on this runaway train.

"I'm so sorry. The process servers typically have other jobs. There's no guarantee of when they might find time to do their field work."

"So, day or night? Someone's going to show up at my door, and that's it?"

"Yes. I mean, you'll have a few weeks at that point to vacate—"

"A few *weeks*...?" Her voice trailed off as her thoughts raced. "Mr. Stanley, you know us from church. You know my husband's been out of work." She hated sounding so pathetic. "I'm sure he didn't mean to get behind."

His eyes started to glisten. "I'm really sorry, Mrs. Martin...Jill. I know this isn't *your* fault."

He said a few more consoling things, but Jill felt incapable of comprehending. Her mind jumbled with scattered fragments of possible solutions.

Mr. Stanley stood and walked around the desk.

Feeling numb, she got to her feet, then slid Emma back into the sling as she walked with him to the door. Her stomach burned. How could Caleb have done this to her?

She thought about the budget she'd calculated. Unless something miraculous happened, there was no way she could save the house on the amount she'd make on welfare. She hadn't even been officially approved and, judging by the way the phone call had gone this morning, that wasn't a sure thing.

Her mind whirred. If she could get the welfare, or at least part of it, then supplement it with a job, that might be enough. Would they let her do that? It was worth asking about. But she definitely had no time to waste.

"If you have any other questions—" Mr. Stanley placed a fatherly hand on her shoulder as she stepped out of his office and into the lobby. "—please feel free to ask."

She nodded dumbly.

Riley squealed from his place next to Joanne on the carpet in the middle of the seating area. Nick and a couple of customers had joined in the fun.

The smile fell from Joanne's face when she looked up at Jill. She stood and crossed to her. "Hey, are you okay?"

She nodded, grateful that Joanne didn't seem to know about the pre-foreclosure. "I just need to take care of something. Can I use your phone?"

"Oh, sure." Joanne gave her a look that let her know she was concerned but didn't want to pry. "Just dial nine to get out."

On her way across the room, Jill took the torn and now-crumpled envelope out of her purse. She turned her back to the participants of the puppy party and dialed the number with shaky hands.

When Angela Hoyt came on the line, Jill told her that the refinance wouldn't be an option, but didn't explain why. "So, I really need to pull together as much income as possible. Can I work if I'm on welfare?"

"*Can* you work?" Ms. Hoyt's pointed voice shot through the phone like a missile. "You would be *required* to work to remain eligible."

"What?" Jill shifted to keep Emma from grabbing at the Dum Dum display. Emma responded with a shriek, and Jill dug around in her purse for her keys to quiet her. "But isn't the point of welfare that it allows parents to stay home with their kids?"

She heard a huff on the other end that sounded like mingled disgust, irritation, and amusement.

"Mrs. Martin, wouldn't we all like to just stay home? But we can't, and that's why there are daycares." She cleared her throat, allowing time for her admonishment to settle.

Tears pushed at the backs of Jill's eyes. It wasn't like she was saying she wanted to sit on her couch all day. Being a stay-at-home mom was a full-time-plus job, and an important one at that. Because in her heart, even the best daycare was no substitute for her as a loving parent.

"*If* you qualify for assistance," Ms. Hoyt continued her explanation, "you would be required to work at least thirty-five hours a week."

"What?" That was almost full time. Besides, the only place in town she'd found that was hiring was the factory, and she'd already blown that opportunity. "But if I had a job for thirty-five hours a week, I wouldn't need to go on welfare."

"I'm sorry, but those are the rules. I can close your case, if you'd like."

"Oh, no. I still want to apply."

"Fine. I'll send your paperwork. You'll have to fill out a report verifying that you're doing an active job search each week."

"Does that mean I qualify?"

"I'll have an answer for you sometime next week."

Next week? She felt like melting into a ball of anxiety right there on the floor of the bank. Sam had loaned her enough grocery money to get them through the week, but what would she do after that? And she hadn't even looked to see if any bills were due in the next few days. This just kept getting worse and worse.

After completing the call, Jill gathered up the kids and the dog and went back outside, her heart sitting like a stone in her chest. Everything she thought she had was crumbling away, and there was nothing she could do about it.

Across the street, an engine roared to life, and Jill looked over to see Sam closing the tailgate of a pickup truck which was parked in front of his store, like he had just helped to load up a customer's order. The truck pulled away from the curb, revealing a second man next to Sam, who stood there wobbling like a guy who hadn't seen this hour of the morning from a vertical position in quite some time. *Caleb.*

Red framed her vision and if she didn't know better, she could have sworn steam started puffing out her nostrils. She felt like a bull ready to charge.

She tightened her grip on Riley's hand, and did her best to hurry him to the car. The last thing she needed right now was for him to see his daddy and make a fuss, or for Caleb to see them and come over to talk to her. Even in her fury, she knew it wouldn't be a good idea to have it out with him about the mortgage in front of Riley and potentially the entire rest of the town.

As they approached her car, she let go of Riley's hand so she could pry her keys from Emma's little fist. Emma let out a squeal of protest. Jill got a brief grip on the key fob, her finger compressing a button just as Emma yanked the keys away and the car alarm started to wail. Jill felt the keys leave her grasp and saw them go flying toward the street.

Sam and Caleb snapped their heads in her direction.

"Daddy!" Suddenly, Riley took off at a run, heading at a diagonal into the street.

As Jill turned to reach for him, a movement hooked the corner of her eye. A car was headed their way.

Her confused brain registered that the driver was looking not at the road in front of him but at her car, distracted by the blaring horn.

Her mind raced.

She needed to stop her son from charging out into the path of the car, but her voice froze in her throat.

Riley kept running.

Chapter 10

"Riley! Stop!"

Jill heard the words, but not in her own voice. Looking up, she saw Sam shouting and moving into the street.

Suddenly freed from her paralysis, she caught up with Riley and yanked him back by his tiny shoulder. The oncoming car slammed to a stop, and she glanced over to see Sam in front of it with his hand held up like a traffic cop.

She stooped down to give Riley a hug, followed by her usual admonishment about the dangers of traffic and disobeying her.

The car moved on, and Sam jogged the rest of the way across the street. He retrieved the errant keys and killed the earsplitting alarm.

"Are you guys okay?" When Jill couldn't choke out an answer, he knelt down to talk to Riley. "Buddy, we've talked about this. No running out into the street. Got it?"

Riley lifted a chubby arm in a point. "But'a my daddy!"

Jill stood, wrapping her arms tighter around Emma and fighting the urge to hurl herself at Caleb. He still stood in front of the hardware store, posturing in a lame attempt to look like he wasn't hungover. He appeared to be working up his nerve to join them, which was the last thing she needed.

But as much as she didn't want to see Caleb right now, she also didn't want to talk to Sam. Not when her thoughts and feelings about him were so jumbled. All she wanted was to go back to her house, bolt all the doors and windows, and crawl back into bed.

She lowered her gaze, doing her best to avoid meeting Sam's chocolate-brown eyes. "We just need to get home."

Sam nodded. "I'll get Riley into his seat."

As they both moved toward her car, a charcoal-gray Prius drove past, momentarily distracting her. She caught a glimpse of the driver. It was Dean Owens.

She opened the door to her backseat, watching Dean pull into a spot up the block and get out.

Her thoughts raced. This was her chance to talk to him again. She had to do it.

"Jill…" Sam had opened the door on the other side of her Honda. "Why is there a dog in your car?"

She watched Dean enter the diner, then blinked and looked at Sam standing there waiting for an explanation.

Riley—who, in the excitement of remembering the dog, had apparently forgotten he wanted to see his daddy—willingly climbed into the backseat. "Mama got'a me a puppy!"

"She did?" Sam raised an eyebrow at Jill. "You *did?*"

"Can you watch them for a minute?" She quickly transferred Emma from her sling to her car seat. "I have to go do something."

"Okay." The look on Sam's face conveyed a suspicion that her thin thread of sanity was rapidly unraveling. "But what—?"

"I'll be right back." Before he could ask any more questions, she started toward the diner, having absolutely no idea what she was going to say when she got there.

The bell dinged above the door as she marched in and scanned the room. Somewhere deep down she knew that this was probably a really bad idea, but she didn't care. Desperate times called for uncharacteristically bold and potentially self-destructive measures.

The breakfast crowd had thinned, with only a few people seated at scattered tables.

Dean sat in a booth with his back to her, studying a menu.

Before she lost her nerve, she slid into the seat across from him.

He looked up, eyes widening behind his designer frames.

"Mr. Owens. *Dean*." Her voice didn't even sound like her own. "Do you remember me? You interviewed me yesterday."

"Right. Mrs...."

"Martin. *Jill*."

He started to nod, as if putting up a polite pretense that this was normal behavior and not something that verged on psychotic. "Yes. What can I—"

"I don't want to waste your time. I know you interviewed a lot of people yesterday, but I need a job."

"Mrs. Martin." He patiently set down his menu. "We would love to give a job to everyone in the community who needs one. But we're operating on a very tight budget."

Her mind whirred. "But what if hiring me

could actually save you money?"

He stared at her. "I'm not following."

Neither was she, but the words kept coming out of her mouth, propelled by desperation. "I can help get the building ready."

He shifted in his seat, looking around as if hoping someone would rescue him from the town crazy lady.

She continued. "I'm really good at repurposing. Like those things that are used for...you know..." She spun her hand next to her face as she searched her rambling brain for the right words. "You use them for storing papers..."

"File cabinets?"

"Yes!" She pointed at him, like he'd guessed the right answer in a game of charades. "Those rusty old file cabinets are probably ready to disintegrate. But I noticed a bureau in that office we were in that would work great for that. I could refinish it for just a few dollars."

"I see where you're headed with this, but we won't be needing file cabinets. We're aiming to be a primarily paperless company."

"Oh. Well, there are lots of other things. Like those old drapes. They're so dirty and some of them are torn."

He drummed his fingers on the table. "I'm sure we'll replace them with new ones."

"But that's going to cost more than it would to clean and repair the old ones. Plus you'll be maintaining the historical aspect of the place if you keep some of the original decor. And this company is all about utilizing resources and saving the environment, right?"

He angled his head. "That's true…"

"You wouldn't have to hire me permanently. It could be like a…like a trial run. Look…" She leaned so far forward that he shrank back a few inches. "I just lost my husband."

"Oh…" His self-protective stance seemed to relax a notch. "I'm so sorry."

"Yes."

She looked out the window, to where Caleb stood supported by the front wall of the hardware store. He squinted, like he was trying to see her through the window of the diner. She scooted a little away from the window, appreciating that at least he hadn't followed her in.

"I mean, not *lost*." She gritted her teeth. "He's standing right over there."

Dean's look of sympathy flipped back to one of impatience. "Mrs. Martin—"

"*Jill*. Please. I'm losing my marriage and if I don't get this job, I'm going to lose my house too."

He let out a breath. "I'm sorry."

"But I—"

"We'll keep you in mind." He gave her a concerned but dismissive smile just as the sound of a vibrating phone drew his attention. Looking thankful for the interruption, he reached into his jacket pocket. "If you'll excuse me…"

Realizing that this was a lost cause and that

any more talking she did would only make things worse, she scooted out of the booth and skulked toward the door. She stepped outside, avoiding eye contact with Caleb, even as she felt his inquisitive glare burning into her. The last thing she wanted to do was face him right now.

Sighing, she walked slowly toward her car.

Sam stood next to the passenger side, leaning an elbow on the top, with his hand on his hip. He studied her as she neared, and she half expected him to offer to take the kids for the day so she could get the rest she obviously needed.

"Is everything okay? You look a little upset."

Finding her voice, Jill fought back tears. She couldn't go into this right now. "I'll tell you all about it later." She reached out for her keys. "Right now, I just need to be home."

"All right." He continued to eye her with concern as he handed over the keys. "I've got plans with Grace tonight, but why don't I come by tomorrow and pick up some things for Caleb. We can talk then."

She nodded, still not sure how much she should lean on him.

She watched him cross the street and say something to Caleb. Caleb threw another look her way before following Sam into the store.

"Mrs. Martin!"

She turned and, much to her surprise, saw Dean hurrying toward her.

"Things have changed. That phone call…" He seemed to collect his thoughts. "What I'm trying to say is that if you're still interested, I'd like to hire you after all."

Jill gasped. Was she dreaming?

"Can you start tomorrow?"

"Tomor…?" Her mind whirred, as her mouth opened to form a "yes." If Grace and her mom could watch the kids tomorrow, just as a stopgap till she could find a better solution, this just might work. But she'd have to get that confirmed *after* she latched on to this opportunity.

She extended her hand. "Sounds perfect."

A relieved smile graced his face as he shook on their agreement, then proceeded to give her a few more details. Jill glanced over at the hardware store, confirming that both men were still inside. Part of her wanted to call Sam and tell him the news, but the thought brought on a burst of butterflies fluttering in her gut. Better to ask Grace to tell Sam for her.

She said goodbye to Dean, then gave a curious-looking Riley a little victory gesture as she started around the car.

Finally, something had gone right today. Maybe things were going to turn around after all.

Jill Came Tumbling After

Chapter 11

After reading three bedtime stories and explaining a dozen times that the puppy would sleep better in his box in the kitchen than in Riley's room, Jill finally made her way downstairs. She paused at the bottom step, listening to the quiet. No sound came from the baby monitor in her hand or from the kitchen. She considered checking on the puppy but decided against it. Riley had worn him out running around in the backyard earlier, and it was probably best to let sleeping pups lie.

She went into the living room and collapsed onto the sofa. This was the first time all day that she'd been able to stop and really process everything that had happened. Yes, they had gotten behind—*way* behind—on their house payments, but she had managed by some miracle to land a job.

Dean had explained that some people from the government organization that would grant the factory the certifications they needed to start production would be coming next Friday—a full month earlier than expected. That meant they had just a week and a half to get the building ready for the inspection and he needed someone to coordinate that.

And that someone—Jill's stomach tingled—was *her*. Starting tomorrow, she would be the new Solutions Strategist for Nyland Enterprises. They hadn't talked about her salary yet, but she did know it would be a full-time position. With benefits.

Not only that, but because he had admired her persistence and the nerve it had taken to corral him in the diner, he promised that the job would morph into something more permanent once they were in production. In other words, she had job security.

Plus, since she was technically a single mother, she stood a good chance of qualifying for welfare on top of that. She would have to file the paperwork to make her separation from Caleb legal, but it gave her hope that there would be a way to save the house. All she had to do was make a plan and stick to it.

And if that plan was going to work, it had better be in writing. She grabbed a piece of paper and a colored pencil—green seemed like an appropriate choice—from Riley's art bin. Easing herself back into the cushions, she wrote *Save the House Plan* across the top of the sheet. She sighed. It wouldn't be easy, but it wouldn't be impossible.

Tapping the pencil against her cheek, she pondered. It was pretty clear that she had two options. She could either try again to make a deal with the bank, or she could borrow the money. A personal loan. People took those out all the time, didn't they? When she thought about it that way, her situation didn't seem quite so pathetic.

She wrote down *Option One: Bank*, then thought some more.

Her only hope there would be to tell Mr. Stanley she needed to speak to someone higher up who could strike a deal with her. There had to be someone with enough authority to make that decision. She would just have to utilize her newfound persistence.

In the meantime, she could focus on option two. She wrote that down and let out a sigh. Who did she know who had that kind of money, and would be willing to let her borrow some of it?

As she pondered that question, a *clunking* noise cut through her thoughts. She froze, her heart pounding. It sounded like someone was walking up her porch steps. She held her breath. Would the person in charge of posting foreclosure notices really be so sneaky that they'd creep around after dark? And if she caught him in the act, would there be any way she could talk him into giving her more time? Bribe him with gummy worms, maybe? Or a puppy?

Standing, she grabbed the baby monitor, then quietly made her way to the front door. Would the person knock, or just post the notice and leave? Gripping her upper arm, she held her breath. This was all just too much.

A rough strategy began to take shape in her mind. What if she opened the door and explained that she was making a plan and everything would be fine if he could just give her one more week. Then she could get it all worked out and save everyone the trouble of doing the foreclosure. Wouldn't the bank appreciate not losing money on her house?

Taking in a strengthening breath, she reached for the doorknob but, to her surprise, it jiggled in her hand. She jumped back, staring at the door. The knob moved again, with the scraping sound of a key. Someone was trying to unlock her door.

Her head spun. Did the bank own some sort of skeleton key that fit every front door in town? Were they going to come in and claim the house right then and there? She carefully reached up and engaged the chain lock, as if that would actually provide an impenetrable barricade.

Realizing how unlikely the whole skeleton key thing was, she stood on her toes and peeked around the curtain that covered the window in the door.

She let out her held breath at the sight of Caleb.

As she stood back on flat feet, relief flushed out the adrenaline from her system, leaving her a shaky mess. It wasn't someone from the bank stealthily delivering an after-hours portent of doom. At least she still had time to save the ranch. One more night, anyway.

The knob rattled again and relief quickly dissolved to annoyance. So he had found his keys. Terrific. What was he doing here?

The extended *ding...dong* of the doorbell jolted her annoyance into flat-out anger. She undid the chain and whipped open the door.

"Caleb!" She stage-whispered his name as she clipped the baby monitor to her waistband and slipped out onto the porch. "Don't you have any sense? The kids are asleep."

"Well, I wouldn't have to knock but my key's giving me trouble."

"Your key's not 'giving you trouble.'" Making a quick check that the house remained silent, she shut the door behind herself and stood in front of it with her arms folded. "I had the locks changed."

He creased his brow, then subtly inflated his chest. "You can't do that. It's my house."

"Not for much longer, it isn't." As she drew in a breath to support the speech she'd spent the day mentally composing, she studied him. He was wearing nice jeans and one of

Sam's dress shirts with a denim jacket, which hung slightly looser on him than it did on Sam. His hair needed a trim, but it was combed and he'd obviously shaved before coming over. She sniffed. He'd even put on cologne, which he'd probably borrowed from Sam's dad, since it wasn't a scent she recognized.

Before she could speak, he gave her his best Don Juan smile and held up a bouquet of flowers.

She clenched her jaw. This was so like him. He'd get drunk and act terrible. Do and say awful, destructive things that ripped at the fiber of their relationship. Then when she was feeling beaten, he'd turn around to offer "comfort." It was sick.

Then her part was always to forgive him. Things would be good for a while and she'd live under the delusion that he had actually changed and that this was the way it would be from then on out. But it never lasted. Reality would set in. He'd get stressed, usually about money and his inability to do what was necessary to hold down a job. Then the pressure would build and he would work his way up to another drunken episode.

This was the horrible, exhausting pattern they'd been going through for years. It could last anywhere from a day to a month, but he always cycled back around eventually. It was about time she caught on that nothing was ever going to be different with him.

"Here." He took something out of the pocket of his jacket and held it out to her. "Sam said you were feeling down. And I know how much you love chocolate."

She looked at it, more annoyed than appreciative. She loved *dark* chocolate, but he never remembered that. He'd buy her milk chocolate even though it always wound up sitting in the cupboard until he ate it himself.

"Caleb." She gritted her teeth. "Please don't bring me presents. It's not going to work this time."

"Come on, Jilly. You know you can't stay mad at me forever."

"Oh yeah?" Shifting her weight onto one foot, she refolded her arms. "You want to bet?"

He lowered his hands to his sides. "You really have no right locking me out, you know. I'm the man of this house."

She flapped her hands like she might just reach out to strangle him, landing them on her hips instead of around his neck. "What does that mean, anyway?"

"You know what that means. I'm in charge. I'm the provider."

She spurted out a sardonic laugh. "And you're providing what, exactly? A roof over our heads? Because in order to do that, you'd have to keep paying the mortgage. Did you know that's how it works?"

"Of course." His look turned suspicious. "Why do you say that?"

"Because you haven't exactly kept on top of the payments."

He shrugged. "I've been under a lot of pressure lately."

"It's not going to do you any good to make excuses for yourself this time."

Looking down, he scuffed a wayward leaf with his toe. "So, I missed a couple of payments."

"A couple? Try five. Try, enough to put our house into pre-foreclosure."

He furrowed his brow, then worked his jaw and looked away.

"You didn't know? What, you didn't bother to read the notices from the bank?"

"Look, I'm sorry, Jilly." He met her eyes again. "I'll fix it. I promise."

"Oh yeah? And how are you going to do that? Because unless you've got five thousand dollars in your pocket, you can't fix this."

His eyes widened. Yeah, he'd really had no idea how far behind he'd gotten. What had he done with the notices? They weren't in the stack of bills, because she'd checked.

Anger filled his features. "You think it's so easy to get a job?"

"I know it isn't easy, but it's completely

impossible if you don't even try."

"I was just taking a break from looking." His voice had assumed that hard edge she'd become so accustomed to. "I was going to get back to it."

"Oh really? When were you going to do that? When we were all living in our car?" She let out a breath. She didn't want to get into this with him. It was pointless. "Just don't even worry about it, Caleb. I'm taking care of us now."

His eyes slitted. "What are you talking about?"

She paused. When she had talked to Grace earlier to ask if she and Sam might be able to help her out with the kids and the dog until she figured out a more permanent solution, she hadn't mentioned whether or not Sam should tell Caleb her news. Now, judging from the look on Caleb's face, she knew that he hadn't.

She drew back her shoulders. "I got a job."

He made a sour face. "What kind of '*job*'?"

The sarcasm lacing that last word grated on Jill's nerves.

"I'm working in the new factory at the site of the old sapphire mine. I'm sure you've heard about it." She almost added that they were still hiring, but thought better of it. No point in starting a fight over something that wouldn't amount to anything anyway. There was pretty much no way that Caleb was going to put in his résumé there. If he even *had* a résumé.

"What did you go and do that for?"

"Because the kids and I have this crazy habit and we don't want to break it. It's called 'eating.'"

His eyes filled with something Jill wanted to interpret as guilt but was more likely just plain anger at her for hurting his ego. Moving on to actual guilt would involve too much painful self-awareness, and she was pretty sure he wasn't willing to expose himself to that.

His look softened back into his I'm-going-to-charm-you-now mode. "It's just the way it is right now, babe."

"Don't call me 'babe.' And what I don't understand is, why didn't you tell me how far behind we were on our bills?"

He drew in a breath. "I didn't want you to worry."

"Seriously?" She rolled her eyes. "If you were actually concerned about *me*, you would have gotten a job digging ditches to keep this from happening. You didn't tell me because you knew you had messed up. It had nothing to do with looking out for me."

He paused for a moment, clearly realizing he had no defense against the truth. "At least let me come in and get some of my stuff."

"I don't want you to come in, because I know what will happen. I'll have to threaten to call the sheriff to get you to leave, and I really don't want to go through that again. Just tell Sam what you need, and he can come pick it up tomorrow."

The edges of his nostrils flared and his

eyes sharpened. "I came here to be nice to you. I was all set to forgive you, and you can't even let me in the front door? What kind of Christian woman are you, anyway? Ever hear of the fruit of the Spirit? What about kindness, huh? What about forgiveness?"

She shook her head. *What about longsuffering?* She bit back the thought, not wanting to yell. She pretty much had that one mastered.

He grabbed her left hand. "What about this? I thought this ring symbolized commitment. For better or worse."

Guilt sucker punched her as he released her hand, leaving it hanging limply at her side.

Stomping down the porch steps, he pitched the bouquet of flowers into the yard. He started in the direction of Sam's house, then paused and stormed off in the other direction, toward Main Street.

Jill took in a breath. The only things that were open downtown at this time of night were the sheriff's office, the diner, and the Spur. It didn't take a genius to figure out which one he had on his radar. She was pretty sure he wasn't headed off to get a slice of pie.

She gritted her teeth. Should she go in and call Sam? He'd retrieve Caleb before he could do any real damage.

No. She couldn't go running to Sam every time she needed to be rescued. It was time she learned to take care of herself.

Chapter 12

The next morning, Jill stood with Dean in the doorway leading to the factory's production floor, which was currently buzzing with workers in the throes of a massive renovation. This space took up almost half of the building and rose to its full two-story height. It could easily have been used as a basketball court if it weren't for the massive machinery and tree-like pillars positioned around the room.

He had told her they couldn't enter the construction zone without protective gear, and she had declined his offer of a hard hat. Since nothing in that area would be her responsibility, she didn't feel a need to risk injury or bad hair just to get a closer look.

"You'll have a better view from the upper level anyway." He indicated a balcony-like area above their heads. "That's the regular observation deck, and that"—he pointed to a row of second-floor windows that stretched across most of the far wall—"is Mr. Nyland's office. He'll be able to keep an eye on everything that goes on down here."

He had already given her a quick tour of the rest of the main floor with an overview of what he wanted her to accomplish in each room. It was a good thing she always kept a small notepad in her purse because, so far, her to-do list had filled up eight of its pages.

Clearly, the building still needed a lot of work. Her job this week would be to focus on cleaning, safety issues, and functionality. The aesthetic improvements would come later.

The thought both thrilled and terrified her. Was she really capable of taking the lead here? What had she gotten herself into?

She followed Dean back out to the lobby and they continued the tour.

"We're not so concerned just yet with things like refinishing the woodwork." He waved a hand over the splintery but ornate wooden banister as they started up the wide stairway to the second floor. "Once we pass all the inspections, we can take our time with things like that."

Jill nodded, making a note of it anyway.

She coughed a little as she adjusted to the dusty air, which seemed even muggier up here than downstairs. With no air conditioning yet, she could see that the first order of business would be to buy some fans. She added that to her list of things she'd need to order from Sam.

The buzz of a saw echoed from the lower level as they progressed to where the stairs opened up to the second floor.

"Oh, wow." She stopped a few steps from the top and looked around.

Most of this level was a big open space with light streaming in through several tall windows in the wall to her left. The facing wall had no windows because, as Jill remembered, that part of the building was embedded in the side of the mountain.

The floorboards groaned beneath her feet as she took the last couple of steps and moved toward the observation area about fifteen feet from the top of the stairs, where half of this level was open to the production floor below. Dean was right. She did have a much better view from up here.

"You said that's Mr. Nyland's office?" Jill gestured directly across from them to the bank of windows with blinds covering them that Dean had pointed out earlier. A narrow set of stairs led from that end of the production floor up to a closed door, which was also accessible from a catwalk overlooking the front side of the production area. "Is he the owner?"

"Yes." Dean lowered his voice, as if to underscore the importance of not disturbing the boss. Although with the blinds drawn, it was impossible to tell if he was even in there. "Harvey Nyland *is* Nyland Enterprises."

Dean paused, reverently, then made a broad gesture toward a couple of doors that opened up to the catwalk. "The center door leads to Mr. Steele's office, and the one closer to us is mine."

"Oh. And Mr. Steele is…?"

"Mr. Nyland's right-hand man. And I'm Mr. Nyland's second assistant. You and Kylie report to me."

Nodding, she continued to take in the details of the space.

She remembered being brought up here on that field trip, only they hadn't climbed the stairs back then. They'd been transported in a big cage elevator. Funny, she hadn't noticed it in the main room downstairs, but with all the construction, maybe it had been covered over.

She twisted around and saw the elevator behind her, next to the far wall. Back then, it had been considerably more inviting than it was at the moment. Now it seemed like something she'd prefer to avoid.

Another cough tickled her throat. She tried to suppress it, which made it come out sounding all the worse.

"Sorry it's still so dirty up here." Dean looked a little embarrassed by the condition of this level. "We hired a cleaning company last week to prepare the offices and the spaces downstairs that we used for the interviews. Apart from that, not much has been done yet."

Jill had a sudden terrible image of cleaning this vast space all by herself. That wasn't what she'd had in mind when she'd offered her services. "And this cleaning company…" She coughed again. "Will they be coming back?"

Dean nodded. "First thing tomorrow."

She breathed out relief, along with a little dust. "I'm glad I won't be doing all the work myself."

"Well, like I said we're on a tight budget. Do what you can and let me know if you think we need to call in more outside help. Kylie's job this week is to set up final interviews for the rest of the new positions, but she should have time to assist you as well."

She smiled at that. It would be great to have the help, not to mention a bit of female companionship. As much as she loved this old building, it was a little overwhelming, and parts of it were downright spooky.

But in spite of the stale air, the watermarked walls, and overabundance of cobwebs, this space was really pretty intriguing.

The lights flickered just then, adding to the room's eerie ambiance and sending a chill up her spine.

"Sorry about that." Dean took a couple of steps toward the windows and lifted his arm in a point. "The contractor said that the drilling company we hired is working near those old power lines and that we should expect that to keep happening till they're done."

Jill nodded. She was about to ask when that might be, when something skittered across the floor between them. She jumped back with a little shriek and looked down to see a tiny mouse run behind an old file cabinet.

Dean apparently noticed her jump. "So, obviously we have a rodent problem." He cleared his throat. "You're not afraid of mice, are you?"

"Oh…well…"

She thought about Sam's mom, and how she'd died from inhaling dust from rodent droppings. Stuart Little and his friends could be more than just a minor annoyance. She really couldn't work in a building with an unchecked rodent population.

Mustering a weak smile, she muttered, "Maybe a little."

Dean mimed a writing motion in the direction of her notepad. "That should probably be taken care of before anything else."

Relieved, Jill wrote *Call Exterminator!* at the top of the first page in her notebook, then added *face masks* to her list of supplies she needed to order.

"And over here…" Dean moved further toward the wall of big windows, making a presentational sweep with both hands. "…is your office space."

Jill pulled in a breath. Two antique-looking school teacher desks sat on either end of this part of the area, facing each other.

"This is my office?"

He angled a nod. "Yours and Kylie's."

Pleased that she would have company up here, she moved in for a closer look. One of the desks had been personalized with framed photos, and a lime-green hoodie hung from a row of hooks on the wall behind it. Kylie had clearly settled in.

"This is your desk." He indicated the other one. "We're having computers delivered tomorrow, and they'll all connect with the printer over there." He gestured to a long wooden sideboard between the windows. "It serves as a copier too, although you shouldn't need to use it much. We're doing our best to go paperless."

As Dean continued to talk about the benefits of "going green," she looked out the splintery-framed window at the tall pines and glimpses of valley beyond the parking lot. If she had to have a job, she'd been blessed with what had to be one of the most magnificent views in the whole state of Montana.

Dean checked his watch. "Why don't you get started on your list? I'll be in my office if you need me." Punctuating that with a small nod, he did an about face and left her on her own.

Jill studied her desk for a moment, then pulled back the vintage wooden chair that looked like something Atticus Finch would have sat in while pondering Tom Robinson's defense. She contemplated the thick layer of dust covering the cracked Naugahyde seat. All it needed was a good cleaning and a new cushion, and she'd be ready to take on the world.

Feeling a little like she was snooping, she jimmied open the narrow drawer in the center of the desk. Since she had no idea what she expected to find, the random collection of office supplies it contained gave her pause. It didn't look as though the desk had been stocked for her, but more like the last person to use it had just left without emptying it. The thought gave her a weird feeling, like she was intruding in someone else's workspace. What had happened here that had made the workers leave without taking the time to clean out their desks?

Trying to ignore the unsettled feeling that thought left her with, she decided that giving her immediate area a good cleaning would help her to feel more at ease. But before she could do that, she'd need to locate the cleaning supplies. Should she bother Dean with such a rudimentary question or just start poking around on her own?

Before she could decide, the sound of someone taking the stairs at a rapid clip sent her heart racing. She held her breath, waiting for whoever it was to appear in the stairwell. To her relief, a familiar-looking cinnamon-brown ponytail bobbed into view.

Almost at the top, Kylie turned, saw her, and flashed that ray-of-sunshine smile she apparently hadn't worn out the other day.

"Hi, Jill." Swinging a book bag off her shoulder, she skipped straight to Jill's desk. "Remember me? I'm Kylie."

"Of course. Hi." The feeling of reassurance she'd gotten from her before the interview washed over her again like a cold sprinkler on a scorching day.

Removing one arm from her denim jacket, Kylie bounded to her own desk. "I was so happy when Dean told me he had hired you."

She put her bag down and finished removing her jacket, which she then hung next to the hoodie. "You and I are the only women here so far, so that means a lot."

As Kylie continued to fill her in on her experiences there so far, a warm feeling of comradery rushed through Jill. Maybe this would start to feel like her new normal sooner than she'd expected.

Jill Came Tumbling After

Chapter 13

By the time Jill thought to check her watch, she was surprised to see that a couple of hours had passed. She'd succeeded in thoroughly cleaning and organizing her desk, scheduling an extermination crew to come out the next day, and placing her order with Sam. She'd also given him her work phone number, which he had promised to pass on to Grace, who had her kids for the day.

After crossing each of those items off her list, she leaned back and looked at the door to Dean's office, which had remained shut all morning. Although the sound of the ongoing construction reverberated through the building, she hadn't seen anyone else around.

Rolling her head from side to side to encourage the kinks out of her neck, she looked over at Kylie, who had spent the morning sorting résumés and making phone calls. Jill sat forward, causing her chair to let out a loud *screech* that made Kylie giggle.

When Jill opened her mouth to laugh—more at Kylie's response than at the chair—a yawn came out instead. "I could really use some coffee."

Kylie's eyes lit up. "I saw the break room when I was prowling around earlier in the week. You want to go check it out?"

"Sure." Jill stood, grateful for the opportunity to stretch her legs and to get to see more of the building. She met Kylie at her desk and together they headed for the stairs.

"I'm so glad you're here. I wouldn't have the nerve to go exploring on my own. This place kind of gives me the creeps."

Kylie shrugged. "It *is* a little spooky. I hope they fill the rest of the positions next week so we don't have to feel like we're all alone. Just us and the ghosts."

"Ghosts?" She eyed Kylie as the steps creaked under their feet.

"Oh, sure. I grew up in Blue Crest, just on the other side of the mountain. I've heard stories about this place my whole life." Her ponytail bounced like a show pony as she trotted down the stairs. "You from around here?"

"Madison Falls."

"So you must have heard the same stories then."

She had heard stories, of course. Miners dying in the tunnels, and their ghosts walking the halls of the building. She'd never paid much attention to them, but the thought sent a shiver through her, just the same. "I don't believe in ghosts."

Kylie tossed her a narrow-eyed glance. "Not even at Halloween?"

"Especially not then. My kids and I like to focus on the lighter side of things this time of year."

"You've got kids?" Kylie's tone got even perkier. "How many?"

"Two. A boy and a girl."

"I hope to have kids someday too. If my boyfriend ever gets around to proposing, that is." Kylie landed at the base of the stairs on both feet, like a gymnast sticking a landing. "You're so lucky to be married."

Jill offered up a polite smile, not wanting to explain that "lucky" wasn't exactly the word she'd currently use to describe herself. Best to avoid that topic, at least until she knew Kylie better. "Do you do anything fun for Halloween?"

Kylie crinkled her nose as they took a left, toward the back part of the building. "I'll probably just stay home with my mom and hand out candy. Blue Crest is so small. The younger kids are all done by seven and the older ones stay out making trouble. Fun times."

"You should come to Madison Falls." Jill followed Kylie's lead down a hallway that she had seen that morning with Dean. "The whole downtown area is one big party. There's live music, and all the businesses give out candy. Everyone dresses up, even the adults. The whole town turns out."

"That sounds like so much fun. Maybe Jackson would want to go with me."

"That's your boyfriend?"

"Yeah." Her face softened into a dreamy smile. "He's the best."

Kylie stopped, her demeanor subtly shifting as she looked from where they stood at the end of the hallway into the small lobby-like area it opened into. There were no windows in this part of the building, so the only light came from more of those wall sconces that were in all the hallways, and a couple of old fashioned glass bowl lights hanging from the ceiling. Kylie dipped her chin toward the focal point of the room—an imposing set of huge metal doors with a big chain threaded through both handles and secured with a large padlock. A sign above the doors warned in no uncertain terms to "Keep Out."

"That"—Kylie's manner shifted to something resembling a tour guide in a haunted house—"is the mine entrance."

Jill nodded. Dean hadn't even stopped when they'd passed through this way earlier, but the memory of entering the mineshaft as a child had sent both a chill and a thrill through her that hadn't quite left her all morning.

They moved forward, eyes fixed on the doors, and stopped at the center of the room.

Jill wouldn't have put it past Kylie to walk boldly up to that padlock and try to jimmy it open. "You haven't gone in there, have you?"

"No way." Kylie's head retreated a little into her neck like a tortoise with a ponytail. "Honestly, I'm grateful for that lock. I like the idea of no one being able to get in." She twisted a look at Jill, then added, "Or out."

An odd sensation skated across Jill's skin. She assumed Kylie was referring to the aforementioned "ghosts," but that didn't make sense. Weren't ghosts supposed to be able to move through walls?

Before she could point that out, Kylie pivoted around and headed for a smaller door at the other end of the room. Following, Jill tried to recall what, if anything, Dean had told her about this door. She must have been so focused on the mine entrance as they'd passed through that she hadn't even noticed it. The place was so huge. What else had she missed?

Kylie heaved the door open, revealing a set of stairs. "Down this way." She pushed a switch, summoning a dim overhead light in the stairwell to pop to life, then bounded down with the same carefree enthusiasm she seemed to approach everything with.

Jill hesitated, looking past Kylie into the shadowy space below. "The break room is in the basement?"

"Yeah." Kylie slowed a little, speaking over her shoulder. "I got bored one day and decided to check it out. But don't worry. It's really cool down here."

Jill twisted her mouth, wondering if she wanted coffee badly enough to embark on a *Ring*-like quest for it. But since Kylie clearly knew where she was heading, Jill's curiosity won out over her urge to bolt back to the relative safety of her desk.

"Have you met the other bosses yet?" Jill daintily tested each step before trusting it with her full weight.

"Mr. Steele is harsh." Kylie underscored each word with a firmly raised palm. "Totally no-nonsense."

"And Mr. Nyland?"

"Oh. He's not even here yet." She shrugged. "I guess he lives in, like, Florida. Dean said even *they* don't know when to expect him."

As odd as that seemed, Jill felt a sense of relief. If the owner wasn't in a hurry to get here, he must really trust the men he'd put in charge.

At the base of the stairs, Kylie took a left and Jill trailed a step or two behind. The wide hallway they were in was shadowy and cavernous, reminding Jill of the ones upstairs, only plainer. A couple of bare bulbs hanging from the ceiling lit their way, but even more fixtures held dead bulbs or none at all. It brought to mind the kind of passageway you'd find yourself walking down in a bad dream, and later wonder at the symbolism of it.

Kylie stopped at the first doorway they came to, much to Jill's relief. She reached inside and flicked a switch, illuminating a series of long fluorescent tubes suspended from a high ceiling with exposed pipes. The buzzing sound from the ancient-looking bulbs made Jill wonder if they were safe. How long had fluorescent bulbs been in existence, anyway?

Kylie moved between the rows of long tables with attached benches, like old Formica picnic tables, and spread her arms. "Isn't this place totally retro cool?"

Jill nodded in agreement as she entered the room and took it all in. The walls were lined with old vending machines that looked like they'd been collected over a stretch of several decades. If it weren't for the thick coating of dust on everything, the place could have passed for a museum of American break room artifacts.

"Wow." Jill eyed a couple of machines that offered *Candies* and *Cold Soda*. "Do any of these still work?"

"The other day, I got some gum out of this one." Kylie moved around the tables to get to a dusty powder-blue cube that looked like it had come straight out of a 1950s Doris Day movie.

"Really?" Jill frowned. "Could you actually chew it?"

"It softened up after a while." She pointed to another machine, her expression shifting. "I don't know about that one, though."

Jill followed her gaze to a friendly looking little box that promised *Hot Meals*.

"Ew. I don't even want to think about what might be brewing inside there."

"Speaking of 'brewing,' here's your coffee." Kylie raised her hand to a cute little apparatus that was about a foot shorter than her. The sign on the top of it said *Coffee—Piping Hot*.

"It's only fifty cents." Kylie started digging in her front pocket. "Got any quarters?"

Jill moved next to her. "I don't—"

A resounding *bang* cut her off, and the lights flickered, then went out. The hum that had been hanging in the air went silent.

Surrounded by absolute darkness, Jill felt the blood drain from her face. She reached out, found Kylie's arm and grabbed hold of it.

"Oh, man." Kylie clung to Jill too, clearly rattled. "The lights have been flickering all week, but they never went out before."

"It's okay." Jill told herself to stay calm, but her heart pounded like a drum. Dean had warned her about the flickering, but the possibility of losing power altogether hadn't really occurred to her. It *would* have to happen when they were down in this dungeon. All she wanted right now was to get out of this basement and go hug her kids. Why had she ever thought that getting a job was a good idea?

She held an arm out in front of herself, alarmed that she couldn't even see her own hand. "We just have to make it back out into the hallway..." Afraid she sounded as freaked out as she felt, she let her sentence trail off.

Just as they both took a careful step forward, a light flashed on the other side of the doorway. Jill froze, feeling Kylie move closer and grip her arm even tighter. They both stood rooted to the spot.

Suddenly, a blinding beam shone into the room, illuminating the outline of a man in the doorway. Panicking, Jill tried to take a step back, but her leg hit one of the table benches with a dull *thwunk*.

"Oh, sorry, ladies." The man lowered his flashlight to the floor between them. "I didn't know anybody was in here. I was looking for a breaker box."

Jill let out a breath. "Bob?"

"Yeah…." Taking a step into the room, he raised the beam, thoughtfully keeping it below her eye level. "Is that…*Jill?*"

"Yes." She felt like hugging him, but held back, gripping Kylie's arm tighter instead as they both inched closer to him. "You startled us."

Relief washed through her, leaving her shaking. Bob Branigan was married to her friend Lucy. They were about a decade older than her, and she'd known them pretty much forever. She remembered now that he was the contractor on this project.

After Jill introduced Kylie and explained her own presence there, the three of them followed the beam of his flashlight back out into the hallway.

"Do you know why the power went out?" As they headed for the stairs, Kylie sounded a little shaken, but no less perky than usual.

"It's just an unavoidable consequence of the construction work. Nothing to worry about. Might be a good idea for you ladies to keep flashlights on you just in case this happens again."

"Noted." Jill could hear the quiver still in her voice. Since Dean hadn't mentioned the basement as part of her responsibility, she wasn't likely to be coming down here again, even if she wrapped herself in lights like a Christmas tree. "We were just looking for some coffee. I guess from now on we should bring our own."

"We've always got a pot going over in the trailer we use as an office. You're welcome to help yourselves."

"That's awfully nice of you." The reminder that there were other people on the premises—familiar faces from her old life before everything had gone haywire—warmed her even more than a good strong cup of coffee would. She exchanged a smile with Kylie and felt a little silly for being scared of the dark. "I think we'll take you up on that offer right now."

Jill Came Tumbling After

Chapter 14

Jill and Kylie had just made it back to their office carrying lidded Styrofoam cups filled with piping hot, super-potent coffee, when the loud creak of ancient hinges pulled their attention to the door of the center office. It swung open to reveal a man of around forty wearing a sleek gray suit and a pinched expression. This had to be Mr. Steele.

His eyes darted around like a pinball, pinged off Kylie, and landed on Jill. "You there." He snapped his fingers at her.

She jolted, tossing a quick glance at Kylie for support. "Yes, sir?"

"Get me a shredder. ASAP."

"A shredder?" She took a step closer, on the verge of asking if he meant for vegetables or cheese. But before she could speak, her gaze latched on to several bankers boxes on the floor inside his office. Her mental fog cleared. "Oh, for *paper?*"

Mr. Steele's narrow-eyed look told her she'd gotten off on the wrong foot with him— the boss's right-hand man. "Get it to me as soon as you can."

The door groaned shut behind him, leaving Jill with more questions than she had courage to ask.

Letting out a breath, she cast a look at Kylie. "You haven't seen a shredder around here, have you?"

"Nope." She shrugged. "And I wonder what's in those boxes. I saw them stored down in the basement last week. At least I assume they're the same ones. They looked new, not like something that was here before." Her eyes widened, like she'd just remembered something. "Hey, the computer guys are supposed to be here anytime to set everything up for us. Good thing too, because one more day without internet would make me want to scream."

Setting her cup down on her desk, Jill sighed. She was going to have to face the learning curve of the new computers now too.

Nothing could convince her that there was a harder job in the world than parenting and housework, but at least she'd mastered that. This was turning out to be a whole different kind of challenge.

Balancing Emma on her hip, Jill fit her new key into the front door lock. She said a little prayer of thanks that there had been no foreclosure notice on her door, in her mailbox, or anywhere else. And hopefully, the bearers of bad home-ownership tidings had better things to do with their evenings.

It had taken two trips from the car to the front porch to get the puppy—who now resided in a borrowed crate, compliments of Grace and her cat, Trouble—and both kids up to the porch. Now Jill hoped she had it in her to get them all fed and put to bed, then pack up some of Caleb's things to give to Sam before she collapsed from exhaustion.

"Then Miss Gwace took'a us to the beasto, Mama." Riley continued to chatter happily, as he had all the way from Grace's house. "She gave'a me hot cocoa."

"I'm so glad you had a good day with her, Rile." The front door opened with a *whoosh*, as if the house was relieved to have them home. The warm air inside felt good but reminded her that she'd better lower the heat during the day from now on if she wanted to keep her electric bills down.

"She a nice wady."

"Yes, she is." Jill put her keys on the hook, then went back out to the porch to haul the carrier in. "Did Angel get along with the puppy?"

"Yep. They fwiends now." Riley poked a finger through the bars, then sniggered when the puppy licked it.

"Oh, that's good." A pang of anxiety prodded her as she set the carrier down in the entryway and closed the front door. Grace had kindly offered to help with the kids again tomorrow, but Jill hated the feeling of taking advantage of her. She knew how busy Grace was, tying up loose ends with her businesses before leaving in two days for her upcoming opera in New York. The childcare solution was still the big missing piece to the puzzle of Jill's life.

Riley removed his coat. "Can I pway'a with the puppy?"

"You can open up his crate, but only if we keep him in the kitchen with the gate shut. Promise?"

He nodded. "Pwomise."

"And hang up your coat, please." She grabbed the handle of the carrier and started for the kitchen.

A quick glance at the phone as she passed the hall table told her that there was no blinking light, which meant no responses to the puppy flyers she had put up before work that morning. She heaved a sigh. What was she going to do if no one called to claim the little guy?

After putting Emma down in her kitchen playpen, she removed her own jacket and hung it in the hall closet, then went back into the kitchen and secured the baby gate behind herself. When she opened the door to the carrier, the puppy scampered out, his tail wagging like he'd been imprisoned for a year.

Riley dissolved into a fit of giggles as the puppy tackled him to the floor.

Jill grabbed an apron from one of the hooks by the back door and tied it while she studied the contents of her freezer. As worn out as she was, she really wasn't up to cooking from scratch tonight.

"How about lasagna, Rile?" She pulled the box out as Riley cheered. Pasta of any kind always met with his approval.

As she turned on the oven to preheat, the sound of a vehicle pulling into her driveway caught her ear. She crossed the room to look through the house and out the living room window.

Sam's truck. Her stomach did a little flip. She hadn't expected him so soon. She'd really wanted to avoid having him come over at all until she sorted out these confused feelings she was having, but at least this was better than having Caleb pack his own things.

"Watch the puppy for just a minute, Rile." She put the lasagna in the oven. "Uncle Sam's here."

"Unca Sam!" Riley wavered between looking toward the front door to confirm that Jill was telling the truth and allowing the puppy to continue licking his cheeks.

"Don't let the dog get into anything. I'll be right back." She scooted through the baby gate and into the entryway.

When she opened the front door, Sam was on his way up the steps, clad in his usual workday uniform of faded Levi's and a casual brown shirt. He held something under his arm that looked like a cake box.

"Hey." He smiled the way people do when they're trying not to let on how tired they are at the end of a long day. "How was your first day of work?"

"Busy." Shivering in the early evening air, she stepped to the side so he could enter. "But it should actually be fun once I figure out what I'm—"

"Unca' Sam!" Riley called out from the other side of the gate, where he and the puppy appeared to be having a relay race.

"Hey, buddy." Sam waved, then chuckled as boy and dog scampered out of view. He set the box on the table by the door. "I brought you all the face masks we had in stock and I ordered another case. I have some fans in the truck that I can load into your car before I go. I'm glad you're being careful, but you know I'm worried about you."

"I know." Shutting the door, she tried to ignore the flutter in her stomach at the sound of that. "I have the exterminators and the cleaning crew coming tomorrow." She nodded at the box of masks. "We'll feel better having these till they get things under control."

"One more thing." He reached into his jacket pocket and produced a candy bar. "I thought you could probably use this after the last couple of days you've had."

Recognizing the label, she smiled as she took it from him. *Special Dark*. Her favorite. "Thanks, Sam."

"My pleasure." Removing his jacket, he lowered his voice. "Don't let Riley know you have it."

"No way." She slipped it into her apron pocket. "This is mine."

He hooked his jacket over the end of the banister. "So, is now a good time?"

"A good time?"

"For me to grab Caleb's things?"

"Oh. Right." How was it that she'd practically forgotten his reason for coming here? "I just haven't packed anything yet. Between starting work, and the puppy—"

"I'm here to help." He held up a silencing hand. "What can I do?"

The sound of Riley's happy squeal from the other room turned their heads.

"It would help if you'd watch the kids for a few minutes while I go up and pack. I really don't want Riley to see Caleb's suitcase leaving the house."

He nodded in understanding. "What have you told him?"

"Just that Daddy's staying at your place for a little bit. I haven't figured out what I'm supposed to say."

He shrugged his eyebrows. "I'm sorry that lunkhead put you in this position."

"Me too."

As Sam went to join the kids in the kitchen, she started up the stairs. At least she'd be able to get this task she'd been dreading over with before dinner.

Once in her room, she opened the closet and took out Caleb's suitcase. She drew in a deep breath, then set it on the bed and flung it open. Her throat tightened. They hadn't used it since their honeymoon in Glacier. She huffed out a sad chuckle. She could have sworn he'd gone on that trip as much for the fishing as to spend time with her. He'd always loved fishing.

Blinking back tears, she opened his top dresser drawer and let out a little grunt. As hard as she worked to fold his laundry and put it away neatly, he always managed to get it all stirred together in a disorganized heap. Why had she been working so hard while he hadn't even managed to do the basics to keep up his end?

A bolt of frustration surged through her as she grabbed a handful of socks and drew her arm back to pitch them into the suitcase. But something stopped her from following through. A sigh pressed at her throat as she set them back in the drawer and dutifully matched up a pair. This wouldn't be her problem after tonight, but she was still his wife and she owed him her best effort.

As she dug through the pile with the goal of reuniting another pair, something pointy grazed her finger. She sifted through the socks and saw what appeared to be the crisp white corner of an envelope. Funny, she'd put Caleb's things away in this drawer for years and had never noticed anything in it besides socks and T-shirts. The thought that he might have tucked something away at the bottom piqued her curiosity.

She moved the laundry to the side, revealing an unruly stack of envelopes. Guilt prickled, but she read the return address on the top one anyway. Someplace called A-Plus Collections.

A cold jolt of betrayal crash landed in the pit of her stomach. He'd been contacted by a collection agency? And he hadn't bothered to tell her?

She picked up the pile, its jagged corners shooting out in all directions, and read the next one. *American Express*. She frowned. They didn't have an American Express card, at least not that she knew of. So why did this envelope say that their statement was enclosed?

Whatever guilt she'd felt for snooping melted away as the fire of indignation grew. She flipped to the next one and her heart caught in her throat. It was from the Madison Falls Bank. Marked *Urgent*.

One by one, she looked at the unopened envelopes. All of them were bills of some sort and about half were from the bank. The postmarks indicated that the bank notices had been coming regularly for months and he'd just shoved them into his drawer. Hiding them from her. Like he thought that covering them up would make the problem go away.

Pressing her eyes shut against threatening tears, she sank onto the bed. Why hadn't he trusted her enough to let her in on what was happening with their finances? If they'd been able to face this together, to pray about it and weigh all of their options, it would never have gone this far.

She stared at the open drawer. The notices had been right there every time she'd put away the laundry she'd washed and folded for him. She'd been doing her part to keep this family running, while the evidence of his betrayal had been right under her nose. And right under his clean socks. She'd been so trusting.

What kind of idiot was she?

Jill Came Tumbling After

Chapter 15

Ten minutes later, she hoisted the packed suitcase down the stairs, hearing Riley's and Sam's laughter interspersed with high-pitched puppy yelps. Such a contrast to the darkness of her mood. She left the suitcase on the porch just outside the door so Riley wouldn't see it, then drew in a deep breath and joined them in the kitchen.

Sam looked up from where he sat next to Riley on the floor. "Look, Riley. Your mommy's back."

Riley, who was down on all fours apparently pretending to be a canine himself, barely seemed to notice, but Emma let out a happy squeal from her playpen.

As Jill crossed to the cupboard to grab some plates, the spicy aroma of lasagna made her knees go weak. Her surge of emotion upstairs had left her feeling drained, and it had been a while since the brown-bag lunch she'd eaten at her desk.

"Is everything okay?"

Sam spoke close to her ear, and she almost jumped, not having realized that he'd stood and crossed to her.

"I'm fine. I put the..." She cast a quick glance down at Riley, then lowered her voice. "...the *thing* out on the porch." She opened the cupboard and attempted to resume a normal tone. "Are you staying for dinner?"

What was she thinking? Hadn't she told herself she needed to spend as little time as possible around him right now? Especially with him being so perceptive about her emotions. Caring about her when her own husband didn't. No, dinner together was not a good idea.

"It's hard to say no to lasagna." He tapped the empty Stouffer's box on the counter. "But I should get home. Dad's making burgers, and Caleb will wonder what's keeping me."

Jill tried not to show her relief as Sam said his goodbyes to the kids. She stepped through the gate and waited for him in the entryway.

Sam shut the gate and they started toward the door. "Grace said the puppy was great today."

Jill glanced back to make sure Riley wasn't listening. "No one has called to claim him." She kept her voice low. "What am I going to do? I can't take him to the pound."

Sam took his jacket from the banister and started to put it on. "Why don't you give me one of your flyers and I'll make some copies to put up around town. In fact"—he reached into his back pocket and pulled out his phone—"if you take a picture of him, I can add that to the bottom."

"Great idea." Grabbing the phone, she nodded toward the living room. "The flyers we have left are sitting on the coffee table."

As Sam went to get a flyer, Jill moved to the kitchen doorway and focused the phone camera into a tight close-up of the puppy, who was now lying in the middle of the floor like he needed to recharge.

"What ya doin', Mama?" Riley looked up at the click of the camera.

"Oh, I'm just taking a picture for Uncle Sam."

"Me be'a in it too." He threw his arms around the puppy's neck and pressed his face into his fur.

Not wanting to explain why she'd needed the solo shot, she went ahead and snapped this one, then gave Riley a smile. On her way back to the front door, she examined the images. The one with the two of them made her throat tighten. They were so cute together. How on earth was she going to tell Riley the dog wasn't staying?

"What's this?"

Looking up, she saw Sam standing in the archway to the living room, holding up a piece of paper. She assumed it was a flyer at first, but when she saw the writing at the top, her heart started to race. *Oh no*. Her *Save the House Plan*.

"Oh, that's…nothing." She grabbed it from him, then handed him the phone and folded the paper in half like that might convince him to forget about it. But he was too perceptive to be dissuaded.

"You're behind on your mortgage?" His brown eyes were filled with concern but edged with anger. "By how much?"

"You don't need to worry about it, Sam." She took a step toward the door. She was on the verge of tears again and she didn't want to fall apart in front of him.

"I can't believe Caleb did this." He put a comforting hand on her upper arm. "You know I'll do whatever I can to help you. I'd loan you the money myself, but—"

"Don't even think about that." Feeling ill-at-ease, she pulled her arm away with the pretense of wanting to reach for the doorknob. "You have to finish paying for your dad's treatments. In the big scheme of things, that's way more important."

"There must be somebody. The church could—"

"I called the benevolence coordinator. She said they can give me three hundred dollars, but that's about it." She let out a sardonic chuckle. "Three hundred dollars. That wouldn't even put a dent in what he…I mean, what *I* owe. The bank won't stop the proceedings for anything less than the full amount."

"It should be his responsibility, Jill."

"Well, considering that it *should* have been his responsibility to prevent this from happening in the first place, I'm not exactly waiting for him to submit a plan for fixing it." She shook her head.

"How much time do you have to come up with the money?"

"The notice could show up on my door any time. I keep expecting it."

"Great." He looked at the door, then at her. "Like you need to be worried about that right now."

"I'll get it figured out. In the meantime"— she pulled the door open a few inches and leaned with both hands on the knob—"I just want to try to keep things as normal as I can for Riley. It's hard enough trying to ease him into the idea of Caleb not coming back. I don't know how I'm going to break it to him if we have to move."

"Just remember, you can call me if you need anything." Looking like he'd wanted to say more but had stopped himself, he reached out and pulled her into a hug.

She held her breath, feeling the roughness of his shirt against her cheek and smelling the lingering scent of his aftershave. Her heart fluttered in a way it hadn't since high school, and never as a response to anyone's proximity but Caleb's. This was crazy.

After a moment of vacillating between putting her hands on his shoulders to accept the friendly hug like she would normally do, or pretending she smelled their dinner burning, she remembered the suitcase.

"I…um…set his things out on the…" She jerked awkwardly toward the door, which had remained open a crack. When she gave it a tug, she gasped at the sight of her mother standing there with her hand hovering near the doorbell and her mouth agape.

"Mom." Feeling her face heat, she glanced down to see the jacket she'd left behind the other night draped over Mom's arm.

Mom's look of surprise very quickly morphed into a more familiar one of silent disapproval as she pursed her lips at Jill, then gave Sam a subtle once-over.

Jill struggled for something to say. Mom had obviously witnessed what must have looked like more than just a show of friendly support on Sam's part. "Sam was just…" She hesitated.

"Picking up a few things for Caleb." Sam sounded so natural, like the situation hadn't registered as awkward to him. "He's staying with Dad and me until he gets some things straightened out."

"I see." Mom's pinched expression softened just a touch as she daintily pointed from Sam to Jill and back again. "I don't mean to interrupt."

"You're not." Jill hated the quiver in her voice that came from nerves but sounded like guilt. "Sam was just going."

"Yes." Picking up on the cue, he stepped back a little to allow Jill's mom to enter. When she shifted backward instead, he wasted no time moving out onto the porch. "It was nice to see you, Mrs. White." He tipped a nod and grabbed the suitcase handle, then gave a final reassuring glance at Jill. "Call me if you need anything."

As he made his way down the porch steps and toward his truck, Jill turned her attention to her mom. "We're about to have dinner. You're welcome to join us."

"No, thank you. I've eaten." Her pinched look returned. "I just came to give you this." She held out the jacket.

Jill took it from her. "I appreciate that. I'm sorry I left…" She was about to say *in such a hurry*, but since that wasn't really true, she concluded with, "…it behind."

Sam's truck roared to life, and Mom tossed a glance over her shoulder. When she looked at Jill again, it was with an accusatory glare.

"What are you doing?"

"What do you mean?"

"You know what I'm talking about, Jillian." She folded her hands in front of her in the manner that had always preceded punishment or condemnation. "Why was he here?"

"I told you, Mom." It had been a long day and Jill was in no mood to defend herself. "Besides, it's nothing unusual. We have him over a lot."

Mom arched a graying eyebrow. "Without your husband present?"

"Mom. Sam is my friend." Jill moved closer to the doorjamb, pulling the door with her to help prevent their conversation from carrying to the kitchen. "He's always been my friend. There's nothing wrong with him being here."

"Does Caleb know he's here?"

"Well, I would imagine so, considering that Caleb is staying at Sam's house."

"I see." Mom's chin jutted out. "You've made a real tangle of things, haven't you?"

Jill gave a slow blink, praying for the strength to gracefully end this pointless conversation without having to be rude to her mother. "Thank you for bringing my jacket, Mom." She took a half step back and started to shut the door.

"Have you gotten that *job* yet?"

Jill paused, then re-opened the door a few inches. "Yes. In fact, I started today. The old sapphire mine is being turned into a factory, and I'm working there."

"I see." Her mother's head bobbed in acceptance, if not approval. "You'll be working every day, I suppose."

"Monday through Friday."

"Well then, I won't keep you." She adjusted the strap of her purse on her forearm. "What time will you be bringing them by tomorrow?"

Jill stared. Growing up as she had in a home where passive-aggressive conversation left everyone constantly on edge and doubting their own perception, she hesitated to trust anything left half said. "Wait. Are you saying you'll—?"

"I'm not doing it for you. I'm doing it for those kids. Do you think I want my grandchildren to grow up not knowing me?"

Giddy relief momentarily edged out all her lingering resentments. "I can bring them by at eight fifteen."

Her mother nodded primly and turned to go.

Jill stood in the doorway, watching her walk down the steps. Then she recalled the other half of her daycare dilemma. "Mom?"

Her mom stopped, paused, then turned. "Yes?"

"I hate to ask, but…how do you feel about watching a puppy too?"

Both of Mom's eyebrows shot up this time, and Jill could sense another lecture about the mess she'd made of her life coming her way. Instead, Mom threw her hands up and shook her head as she turned again. "Just pack a bag of kibble if you want the creature to eat."

Jill let out a long, slow breath and thanked God for help from unexpected sources.

Chapter 16

When Jill pulled into the factory parking lot the next morning, several people were already there for interviews, walking from their cars to the building. She picked a spot opposite a van with the words "Simply Clean Restoration and Janitorial Services" on its side, and a white truck that said "A-1 Pest Control."

"Hallelujah." She shut off her engine, then grabbed her purse and her work bag, thanking God that the troops had arrived.

She went around to the back of her car, hoisted out the box fans she'd gotten from Sam, then shut the trunk and managed to grab one fan with each hand.

A clanking sound in the distance drew her attention to the curious-looking structure off behind the trees to one side of the factory. The cooling tower, Bob had explained. The drilling crew was now busy constructing an imposing razor-wire-topped fence straight out of *Shawshank Redemption* around it.

As she started toward the main building, she noticed a man of about fifty or so dressed all in beige, crouched next to the foundation and jotting things on a clipboard.

"Hello," she called out as she veered in his direction. "Are you the exterminator?"

He looked up, squinting into the morning sun. "That's right." He pulled himself to his feet, as though that movement wasn't as easy for him as it had once been. "Name's Hal."

"I'm Jill Martin. I'm the one who called you."

"Ms. Martin." He nodded. "You got yourself an infestation."

"Yes." While she appreciated the professional confirmation of what she'd already seen with her own eyes, it was almost nine and she didn't want to be late on her second day of work. "So, what do we need to do about it?"

"Well..." He scratched his cheek and took in a long breath, like the question both fascinated and befuddled him. "We can set some traps inside, of course. But more will keep coming in. It's the time of year for it. Getting colder out here. I'd imagine you've got the heat turned on inside by now."

"Yes. We do."

"Uh-huh." He eyed her, as if she'd just admitted to a grievous wrongdoing. "Might as well hang up a sign that says 'Mouse Hotel.'"

She let out a little chortle at what she assumed was exterminator humor but bit her lip when he failed to so much as crack a smile in return. "Can't we do something to stop them from coming in?"

"Mmm…" He rubbed his chin. "You've got all kinds of things working against you." He pointed at the foundation of the building. "See that opening right there?"

Jill set the fans down and bent at the waist, grateful that she'd decided to wear her durable cargo pants today instead of going for a more professional look. She noticed an opening in the cement, so small she doubted she could even stick her finger through it. Not that she was about to try. "You mean that tiny one?"

"You got more of those than I can count. Those rascals can slide their way through them like toothpaste out of a tube."

Shuddering at the vividness of his description, she scanned what she could see of the foundation through the overgrowth of weeds. He was right.

"And look up there." Stepping back a few feet, he pointed skyward. "Those tree branches touching the roof? That's like an open invitation for varmints to climb on over. Then once they're on your roof, if there's a way in, they'll find it."

"You mean we have holes up there too?"

"I haven't been on the roof yet, but judging from the condition of things down here, I would imagine it's got its share of weak spots." He shook his head. "I'll have to get on the cherry picker and check your eaves. You got problems along there too, I guarantee it."

"I see. But you can close up the openings, right? So no more mice can get in?"

"I can fix what I can, but you got an old building here."

Historic, Jill wanted to correct him. As if that would change the situation, or at least his attitude toward it.

He scratched his head. "It won't be cheap.

Her stomach buckled a little. As if it weren't enough that she had to fret about her own budget, now she had the company's to consider as well. "Let me know when you have an estimate. We'd like to get this taken care of as soon as possible."

Leaving him to complete his inspection of the exterior, Jill headed inside. She was a little surprised to see Dean wearing a bright-yellow hard hat and leading a group of a dozen or so men and women—also in hard hats—through the lobby. A few of them looked her way when she walked in, and she very quickly realized that they must be the first batch of second-round job candidates, receiving a factory tour.

She observed—with guilt-ridden relief—that Scowling Man and his buddy weren't among them. Those poor men needed jobs, but the thought of having them as co-workers made her shudder.

"In order to tap into the steam deep underground"—Dean spoke as he walked—"we're drilling a well over a mile deep."

A collective expression of awe rose from his audience as they followed him, then formed a crude half circle around the double doors leading to the production floor.

"That steam will power these turbines." He pushed one of the thick double doors open and pointed into the huge space that was still a construction zone. "Which will in turn be linked to electricity generators. We're projecting that this plant will be able to produce enough clean energy to power a third of the state of Montana."

Jill slowed her steps, straining to hear more of what he had to say as she started up the stairs, but the sound of power tools and occasional shouting from the construction workers made it very difficult to catch a full sentence.

As she neared the top of the stairs, the smell of cleaning products buoyed her optimism. The janitorial crew had gotten to work, and this floor looked brighter already.

At the top step, she looked around, picturing the colors she'd like to use up here when it came time to paint, and wondering how to calculate how many gallons she'd need to order. It didn't matter. Sam would know.

She grimaced. Why was "Sam" always the first answer that popped into her head? She was going to have to get over that.

Kylie looked up from her desk. "I'm glad you're here." Standing, she grabbed one of the stacks of résumés that she'd spent a good portion of the previous day sorting, and tapped it on her desk to align the edges. "I've got to get downstairs to greet this morning's job candidates."

As she made her way into their office area, Jill contemplated whether the bedazzled message on Kylie's shirt—*If You Can Dream it, You Can Be it*—would offer the applicants encouragement or just plain annoyance.

Letting out a sigh, Jill put her lunch sack in her desk drawer and cast her gaze past the stairwell to the other large open area on this floor. Dean hadn't said anything about what he wanted to do with that space, but it would be a shame to let it go unused. Maybe she could gather some eclectic seating. Or use it as an open conference room.

She could even put together a photo retrospective of the history of this factory and the mine along that wall. Hang some interesting relics she'd found too, just to add interest.

The possibilities got her creative juices flowing.

Jill Came Tumbling After

Chapter 17

A few hours later, Dean had done tours and interviews with two more groups of hopefuls and had long since returned to his office. Mr. Steele had emerged a few times between long stretches of—Jill assumed from the intermittent shrieks of the shredder—making serious headway on the contents of those boxes she'd seen earlier. Each time he'd appeared, it had been to give instructions about various things to Kylie, who had spent the better part of the day carrying them out.

Jill herself had made what felt like remarkable progress on the checklist in her notepad. All the drapes in the entire building had been taken down and hauled away by the Madison Falls dry cleaner, who had been more than happy to promise a quick turnaround for both cleaning and mending. Jill had then gone around to each room, matching her list of needs to her inventory of furniture and other items that could be repurposed to meet those needs. She was pleased to wind up with a relatively short list of items they'd have to buy.

Hal had shown her the condition of the roof and was currently out on his cherry picker inspecting the eaves, while the cleaning crew had practically *sandblasted* the decades-old grime off the walls, ceiling, and floor in the main area of the second level.

After the computers had been delivered, Jill had set up an email account and had updated Angela Hoyt on her employment status. Angela had immediately and unceremoniously sent yet another form for her to fill out. This one included all the details about her job, serving as a personal reminder for Jill that she still didn't know how much she was going to be paid.

Now, she sat at her desk pondering. This was Thursday. If she didn't get the form back to Angela today before five, chances were good she'd have to wait until after the weekend to find out if she'd be able to count on any welfare funds.

She looked up at Dean's cracked-open door. This was probably as good a time as any to risk interrupting him. Rising from her creaky old chair, she gathered her nerve.

Kylie looked up from her screen, which had held her attention for the hour since lunch. "What are you doing?" She reached her arms up in a stretch, sounding hopeful that she might be able to tag along if Jill's plans sounded like fun.

"I have to ask Dean a question." Chewing on her lower lip, she looked at his door again. "I hate to interrupt him, but it's kind of important."

"Would you mind giving these to him?" Kylie held out a stack of forms that the interviewees had filled out. "If I go over there, I'm afraid Mr. S. will give me something else to do. I have to be out of here by five today."

"Me too." The last thing she needed was for her mom to threaten to go back on her promise to babysit just because Jill couldn't get out of work on time. She took the forms, eying them with curiosity. "Hey, they didn't call in that guy who interviewed right after me, did they?"

"You mean Lenny Simpson?" Kylie made a face that said she knew exactly who she meant. "The guy who looks like he belongs in a movie with the word 'chainsaw' in the title?"

"Ew." The image sent a shiver through Jill that only added to her current state of unease. "I guess so."

"They haven't had me call him." Her forehead creased. "He didn't do something to bother you, did he?"

"No, he just gave me the creeps, is all. I could do without running into him."

"Yeah," Kylie nodded. "You and me both."

Clutching the papers with both hands, Jill approached Dean's door. As she neared, the six-inch opening gave her a clear view of his desk, and the accompanying awareness that he wasn't sitting at it. She raised her hand to knock, but the sound of voices, too muffled to be coming from that room, stopped her. Moving her head slightly to the right, she could see that the door connecting this office to Mr. Steele's was ajar too. Judging from the distant quality of the voices, she surmised that the two men were in there talking to each other.

"...really sensitive negotiations...foreign investors..." Mr. Steele's voice was the louder, and more urgent, of the two.

"…take care of this now…" Dean seemed calmer, but his voice still held a distinct edge. "…before things get dicey…"

She lowered her hand, not wanting to eavesdrop but not quite able to step away.

"I need to be there, but…" The next part of Mr. Steele's sentence sounded jumbled.

But *what?*

"You don't…worry about that…I can take care of things here…" Dean spoke as though part of his job was to quell Mr. Steele's anxieties while reminding him of his own competence. "...won't be a problem..."

"If we don't prove that this was a one-time oversight…"

Jill found herself straining to hear. What were they talking about? What oversight?

"You and I know that we can successfully meet the power demand." The intensity of Mr. Steele's voice rose along with his volume. "And that our plant design poses no public risk…"

Jill held back, feeling awkward at the prospect of hearing something she shouldn't. She made a snap decision to leave the papers now and to come back later to talk to Dean. She pushed the door open and scooted inside, then dropped the forms in the center of his desk and turned to make a quick and stealthy exit.

"Did you need something?"

The sound of Dean's voice from behind her stopped her cold. She whirled around to see him standing in the doorway, with one foot in his own office and the other in Mr. Steele's. He looked stressed, but not angry at her for trespassing, thank goodness.

She gulped in air. "I was just…" She lifted a hand in the direction of his desk. "…leaving those forms for you, and…" She wanted to add *I didn't hear anything*, but of course that would be like admitting that she actually had, even though she wasn't sure what any of it meant.

The tension on his face seemed to ease. "Oh, thank you." He shot a glance into the other office, then moved fully into his own, leaving the door behind him open. "How are things going out there?" He was either trying to act as though everything was fine, or everything actually *was* fine and what she had heard was just standard conversation for them.

"Oh…great." As she watched him cross to his desk and start to finger through the papers she'd placed there, she felt a little less awkward. Maybe this would be a good time to ask, after all. She cleared her throat. "Do you have a minute?"

He glanced up then lifted a hand, inviting her to take the chair opposite his desk. As she moved to sit, the grating of papers being turned into shreds started up from Mr. Steele's office—the same shrill sound she'd heard sporadically all day, but was considerably louder in here. A flash of irritation crossed Dean's face as he reached over to shut the door, dulling the sound only slightly.

He crossed back to his desk to sit, giving her his full attention. "What can I do for you?"

She scooted to the edge of her chair. "I'm just wondering if you've had a chance to think about my salary."

His eyebrows shot up. "I'm so sorry for not getting that settled." He started tapping on his computer keyboard, then stopped and studied the screen.

Waiting, Jill toyed with the notepad in her lap. The sound of the shredder mingled with the motor of Hal's cherry picker outside as it seemed to move closer to this part of the building.

"I see we haven't categorized your position yet. I'll need to get with William…" He jabbed a thumb toward the wall behind him. "…Mr. Steele. But let's start with this." He took his eyes off the screen and intertwined his fingers, looking directly at her. "What would you like to be paid?"

The question caught her completely off guard, and her stomach did a somersault the way it had the day of her interview. She thought about the budget she'd written up and left sitting on her kitchen table. Welfare might still be a possibility, and she didn't want to seem greedy.

She pulled in a breath. "Well, I *need* sixteen hundred dollars a month." She felt herself wince a little after the words came out. That was so much money.

Dean drew back a little. "A *month?*"

Great. He probably thought she was trying to take advantage of them. She nodded, not really knowing what else to add.

He tapped something into his computer. "Let me talk it over with Mr. Steele, and I'll get back to you as soon as I can."

As she nodded and moved to stand, the shredding sound contorted into a loud screech, followed by Mr. Steele calling out a curse word. He had probably tried to feed more than a few sheets through at one time and had jammed the thing. Jill bit her lower lip and Dean winced, then cast a look of apology her way.

The muffled sound of a ringtone was followed by a few more select curse words. Jill took that as her cue to excuse herself and return to the relative peace of her own office.

Back at her desk, she had just started compiling a list of supplies she'd need for her furniture projects when Mr. Steele burst out onto the catwalk. She glanced up, expecting him to bark out an order at Kylie. Instead, he snapped his gaze—and his fingers—at *her*.

"You there."

"Uh…" She jolted to her feet. "Yes, sir?"

"Come here." Pivoting around, he seemed to notice Kylie, and lifted a snap at her as well. "You too." With that, he disappeared back into his office.

Feeling unnerved at the notion of being summoned into the lair of her boss's boss, Jill grabbed her notebook. Kylie, who was used to this routine by now, slumped her shoulders as she stood and joined her.

At the door to his office, they could see

Mr. Steele pulling on a trench coat. He gave them a cursory glance, then snapped his fingers again and pointed at the boxes stacked in a semi-circle around the shredder, which sat on a small table next to the wall. "I need you to get all of that shredded and out of here by tonight."

Jill stared at the boxes, her hopes of getting anything else done that afternoon dwindling. Two of the boxes stood empty next to their lids and a couple of large black trash bags, which she assumed now held the shredded remains of the papers they'd once contained. She made a quick count of the rest of the boxes, which appeared to be untouched. *Ten.* That was a lot of paper yet to be cut into ribbons with a shredder that was intended for home use. And he wanted it done *today?* So much for getting anything else checked off her list that afternoon.

Dean entered through the adjoining door, also pulling on his coat as he spoke. "I made a dinner reservation at the Cattleman's Club in

Victor. That should give him a good impression of this state, and the condition of our—"

"Yes." Cutting his gaze toward Jill and Kylie, Mr. Steele seemed to communicate that there were things the staff shouldn't be privy to. "We'll take my car."

He picked up an expensive-looking leather laptop bag with one hand and started thumb-tapping at his cell phone with the other. As he charged toward the door, Jill and Kylie stepped backward to avoid being run over or knocked down.

He barked out a few more commands—either to them or into his phone, it was unclear which—as he advanced toward the stairs.

Dean arched an eyebrow and shut the door between the offices. "Sorry for the abrupt change of plans." He shifted his own laptop bag from one hand to the other and moved toward them. "The inspector from the Department of Energy is flying in from D.C. today instead of next week. That changes our priorities somewhat."

"Seriously?" Kylie crinkled her nose. "They can *do* that?"

"Apparently." Dean shrugged. "They're a government agency. They make the rules."

Jill's stomach tightened. "Does that mean he'll be here at the factory tomorrow?"

He nodded. "But don't worry." He looked at the boxes. "Everything will be fine, as long as we get this cleaned up."

Something about that statement seemed strange. "Really...?" Jill walked toward the boxes and Kylie followed. "It's that important?"

He nodded. "Part of what the DOE will be checking on is whether we meet the qualifications to become certified as 'environmentally friendly.' The factory is up for a significant grant from the state if we pass their 'Green Factory Standards.'"

"Oh."

"And as I've stated, we're striving to become a primarily paperless company. Since all these documents are no longer needed, we want to get them off the premises. That will help us make a good impression."

"I see." She really didn't, but she nodded anyway. If they were getting them "off the premises," why the urgent need to shred them first? "So after they're shredded, what would you like us to do with them?"

"Well…" Adjusting the collar of his coat, he seemed to consider the question. "Just continue to put them in those trash bags, then empty the bags into the recycling dumpster outside." He shifted his eyes to her. "What day is pick-up?"

"Oh…well…" She glanced back at Kylie, who looked as perplexed as she felt. "There *is* no dumpster. We don't have recycling pick-up here."

He stared at her for a moment, as if she'd just announced that they still lived in caves and hunted their food with clubs. "What do you do with recyclable materials?"

"There's a recycling center just outside of

Madison Falls. We don't have curbside pick-up quite yet."

A look of relief washed over his face that seemed disproportionate to the seriousness of the task. With everything else he'd given her to take care of before the inspection, why had this suddenly jumped to the top of the list?

"Fine then." Dean took a step toward the door. "You can take the bags with you when you go, then take them to the recycling center." Crossing the rest of the way to the door, he checked his watch. "I don't suppose they'll be open this evening?"

"No, they close at five."

"I see." He stopped in the doorway, working his jaw like he was debating possible solutions to world hunger. "Well, do what you need to do. Just be sure it's all out of here when you leave tonight."

"Yes, sir."

"Oh, and Kylie. Reschedule tomorrow's interviews. I'll be busy with the inspection, and I don't know how long it will take."

"Aye aye." Kylie gave a little salute as Dean disappeared out the door.

Jill Came Tumbling After

Chapter 18

After a few hours of taking turns manning the shredder with Kylie, Jill checked the time. "Oh wow…it's four o'clock."

Kylie looked up from where she sat on the floor, emptying the shredder bin for the umpteenth time into a trash bag. She groaned, glancing at the last untouched box. "We won't finish in time for you to get it to the recycling center, but I think if we keep going, we can make it with just enough time to load all the bags into your car."

Jill sighed, then pushed the lid off the box and took out one sheet, which was the most the weary machine could now handle without rebelling. "I think we'll be fine as long as we get it all out of here before the inspection tomorrow."

"What I'd like to know is…" Kylie popped to her feet. "…why was Mr. Steele wasting his time doing a menial task like this? Why didn't he have us do it to begin with?"

"I don't know." Jill ran the paper through before continuing. "Maybe he knows we have other things we need to be doing."

"I doubt it. I mean, he's had no problem having me run all over the building hunting for things, looking up statistics, making phone calls..."

Jill picked up another sheet, then raised her voice to answer as she pushed it into the slot. "Do you think he knows what our actual jobs are?"

Kylie grunted. "If he even cares." She matched Jill's volume. "To him, we're just nameless minions—"

A loud *bang* rattled the windows and made them both jump. The overhead lights flickered, then went out, leaving the only source of light in the room, the late afternoon sun streaming through the still-shaking panes. The shredder groaned to a stop with the top half of the page Jill had been feeding into it still intact.

"Not again!" Kylie grabbed the sides of her head. "We were so close to being done."

The construction sounds that had served as background noise for the past two days were replaced by the commotion of the workers venting their frustrations with some choice words. Jill and Kylie exchanged a glance, then walked out the office door onto the darkened catwalk.

They looked over the railing at the production floor below, which had previously been bustling with activity but now seem eerily still. Most of the men stood around with their hands on their hips, grumbling to one another. Jill felt for them. They were under a deadline that had been shifted ahead as well, and by the looks of things down there, they still had a long way to go.

At the far end of the room, Bob stood with his cell phone to his ear in one of the elongated streams of light that came through the tall windows and cut angular paths across the wide floor. Jill looked at Kylie as they both leaned on the railing, waiting for something to happen.

A moment passed, then Bob lowered his phone and cupped a hand to his mouth. "They hit the line again." He paused while the wave of disgruntled voices that followed his announcement settled. "No telling how soon it will come back."

"So much for finishing." Pushing away from the railing, Jill sighed. "I have to leave by five to get my kids."

"Time for plan B." Wasting no time, Kylie

sashayed back into the office, with Jill following at a slightly slower pace. "How about if we load the bags we have done into your car, and I'll take the last box." Kylie stopped, her ponytail swishing as she looked around, sizing up the situation. "Jackson has a shredder at work. I'm sure he won't mind if I go over there one day to finish up."

"I guess that's our only choice." Jill tugged at the half-shredded sheet, freeing it from the machine, then shoved it into the last bag and yanked the top corners into a knot. "I should take all the empty boxes too." The thought that they would come in handy if she had to start packing her house made her stomach ache. She couldn't think about that now. "I just won't have time to go to the recycling center until Saturday."

"I don't see what the big deal is." Kylie fit the lid onto the still-full box, then hoisted it into her arms. "So what if they sit in your garage for a few days. Mr. S. is never going to know the difference, right?"

Jill heaved in a breath. That seemed reasonable. It wasn't like Mr. Steele was going to stop by her house to pay a social call.

"Mama, I wanna be a pirate."

"Really?" Jill managed a distracted smile as she spooned bright-orange mac and cheese onto Riley's plate. "Interesting career choice."

"No." He grabbed his fork with his fist. "Dwandma says it's almos' Hall'ween."

"Oh…right." Placing a small bit of the pasta onto Emma's plastic Sleeping Beauty plate, she glanced at the calendar on the wall next to the back door.

What? Halloween was a week away, already. And she hadn't done anything about a costume yet. At least Riley was still young enough to think that anything she pulled together out of her fabric scrap box was a masterpiece. She'd better enjoy that while it lasted.

"…an' you, an' Emma." Riley continued to talk as he speared the macaroni onto the prongs of his fork. "We all be'a pirates."

Dishing up her own plate, Jill considered. "Emma and me too, huh?" Her throat tightened against a feeling of dread.

Why had she started that family costume tradition, anyway? It had been fun the last couple of years to include the whole family, but this year she'd hoped he'd be content to be the only one to dress up. Now he had the two of them cast as his back-up buccaneers.

"You know, Rile." She picked up her fork and shifted a piece of broccoli around on her plate. "I was thinking that maybe this year, since I'm busy working and everything, maybe Emma and I could just go dressed as ourselves."

"Nooo!" His little chin jutted out in protest. "You an' Emma an' Daddy too. We all be'a pirates."

Daddy too. Jill bit her lip. *Terrific.*

"Riley." She tucked a strand of hair behind her ear. "You know…Daddy's—"

The jangle of the phone cut into her half-formed response. Normally, she let calls go to voicemail during dinner, but under the circumstances she appreciated the excuse to table the conversation.

Scooting her chair back, she looked down at the puppy who sat next to Riley with hungry hope filling his big brown eyes, in spite of his belly being currently full of kibble. She raised a warning finger as she stood. "Don't feed him anything. I'll be back in a sec."

In the entryway, she reached across the bag of paper shreds she'd left leaning against the hall table when she'd dropped it off before picking up the kids. The rest of the bags remained in her trunk, but she'd hauled this one in so she could get to the car seats.

She looked at the caller ID. *Sam*.

Ugh. Her stomach did a flip flop as she considered not answering. But what would be the point of that? He'd only call back later.

She picked up the phone and tried to sound carefree. "Hi, Sam."

"Hey." His voice was like warm maple syrup. "You sound a little tense. Is everything okay?"

She squeezed the bridge of her nose. So much for *carefree*. "Oh, you know. As okay as it can be under the circumstances." She stole a quick glance at the kids, who were happily chattering at each other through mouthfuls of macaroni, then ducked around the corner into the living room. "I totally forgot about Halloween."

"That's not like you." Sam let out a chortle. "You *love* Halloween."

"I know, right?" Relaxing into the security of just being herself with him, she rested a knee on the overstuffed chair in a corner of the unlit room. "It's one of my top ten holidays."

"So, you've been preoccupied." His voice conveyed comfort, not the dismissiveness she would have expected from Caleb. "But it's not too late. You have a whole week."

"I know." Wrapping her free arm around her middle, she lowered herself into the chair. "I have a week to transform us into a family of pirates."

A beat passed and she heard Sam let out a sigh. "A *family*, huh?"

"Yeah. And to somehow let Riley know that Papa Pirate won't be setting sail on the Good Ship Trick-or-Treat this year."

"You could say you made him walk the plank."

"I'm serious, Sam." She chuckled in spite of herself. "What am I supposed to tell him?"

"Just enough for him to understand."

"He's only three. How can I expect him to understand *any* of this?" Leaning sideways against the back of the chair, she felt her chest tighten. "I know I have to be honest with him, but I don't want it to ruin Halloween." That feeling of panic that she'd been keeping at bay threatened to resurface. "Ugh. Then there's Thanksgiving, and Christmas—"

"Whoa. You're allowed to take this one major holiday at a time."

"Fine." Swallowing hard, she nodded. "I'll start with not ruining Halloween."

"That's the spirit." The lilt in his voice let her know that his pun had been intentional. "Hey, I have an idea. It won't exactly solve anything, but it might at least help make life seem more normal."

"I'm all for that." She toyed with the doily under the base of her thrift-store table lamp. "What is it?"

"How about if I take you and the kids to the pumpkin farm on Saturday?"

Jill's chest warmed at the suggestion. Holiday traditions had been hit and miss when she was a kid, so she felt adamant about maintaining them for her own kids. Then Caleb had only made things worse. Always promising to participate in family outings but rarely following through, either due to one of his gloomy moods or because he was too hungover to make good on his promise.

So for the past two years, Jill had taken Riley to the pumpkin farm on her own. They'd had a lot of fun, but it had been bittersweet. Seeing the other dads happily hoisting pumpkins and laughing with their families had made it almost unbearable.

What would it be like if they went with Sam?

She flinched at the hint of hopefulness that she couldn't quite suppress. "You don't want to spend your Saturday walking around in the mud carrying pumpkins for us."

"Believe me, you'd be doing me a favor. Grace leaves for New York tomorrow morning. I'm going to need to stay busy to keep from feeling sorry for myself."

Great. Just what she wanted to be. A diversion.

"Well, in that case..." A forced smile masked the resentment in her voice, or at least she hoped it did. "Riley would love it. And I wouldn't mind a little distraction, myself." She started to choke up, trying to ward off the thought that this might be the last time they'd put jack-o-lanterns out on the front porch of this house. Where would they even *be* by next Halloween?

A commotion in the entryway behind her cut through her thoughts. In an awful, drawn-out second, she remembered she'd left two kids and a puppy totally unattended for far too long.

She leapt to her feet and flew around the corner to find Riley standing next to the open baby gate waving his little arms over his head and squealing while the puppy spread paper strips across the floor. The trash bag was on its side, its top corners crinkled from the knot they'd formerly formed.

"Oh no! Bad puppy!" She reached for the wiggly mass of fur. "Riley!"

"Jill?" Sam's distant voice came from the phone, which was still in her hand but nowhere close to her ear. "What's going on?"

"Oh, sorry, Sam." Giving up on a single-handed snag of the doggy tornado, she moved the phone next to her cheek. "I'll have to call you back." Clicking the End button, she set the phone on the table then shifted her focus to her son. "Riley! You were supposed to watch him."

His lower lip quivered at her reprimand. "I sorry, Mama."

With a sigh, she cast her eyes down at the puppy, who looked up at her from a playful crouch with a mouthful of paper and a wagging tail. She scooped him up and carried him to the kitchen, as he fought for his freedom.

"Riley, close the gate." She released the puppy into the crate, then handed him the makeshift chew toy she'd created out of a knotted rag. "I should name you Wriggly." She closed and locked the door, ignoring his whines of protest.

"Are'a you mad, Mama?"

Letting out a breath, she straightened and looked at Riley, who stood in front of the closed but unlatched gate like a miniature sentry. His eyes glistened, and he looked so small and wounded that Jill had to resist the urge to throw her arms around him and grant a full pardon for his part in the incident.

She picked up Emma, who had been happily clapping at the puppy's antics from the safety of her highchair, and crossed to Riley, then knelt down and looked him in the eye.

"Listen to me, Rile." Resting Emma on her hip, she took Riley's little hand in hers. "I am a little mad that the puppy got out. You shouldn't open that gate by yourself, got it?"

He nodded. "Is'a Daddy mad too?"

"What?" The question hit her like a punch to the gut. "Why would you ask that?"

"A'cause he at Unca' Sam's. Is'a he mad at me?"

"Oh, Riley." She pulled him close with her free arm, wanting more than anything to protect him from the pain of their situation. She looked at his expectant face. "Daddy's not mad at you. He has to be away from home for a little while, but it doesn't have anything to do with anything you did, okay?"

He bobbed his chin, seeming to at least partially accept the answer.

"I know things are hard right now. But that means I need you to help me out, okay?"

His eyes brightened. "You want'a me to clean up the mess?" He lifted his arm toward the floor of the entryway, which now resembled the bottom of a gerbil cage.

She chuckled. "I appreciate the offer. But it's getting late. I can handle it this time, but what I really need is for you to help me keep the puppy from making any more messes, okay?"

"But how we do'a that?"

"By keeping this gate closed, for one thing." She studied the lock. Had he really figured out how to open it? So much for preschooler security.

He nodded decisively. "'kay."

"Come on, buddy." She pushed to her feet. "It's bedtime."

As they went through the gate and she reached back to securely lock it behind them, she said a little prayer of thanks. Riley seemed placated for now. But was her simple explanation going to be enough?

Jill Came Tumbling After

Chapter 19

A half hour later, Jill stopped partway down the stairs and groaned. She'd gotten so wrapped up in putting the kids to bed that she'd actually forgotten about the mess in her entryway. It was hard enough picking up after two kids. No way did she have the stamina to keep up with a furry whirlwind of destruction too.

It crossed her mind to leave it till the weekend, but she really didn't want to become that mom who let her house get into a shambles. She had to at least make an effort.

Rubbing her temple, she continued to the bottom of the stairs and bent to grab some scraps at her feet. Crumpling them in her fisted hand, she noticed the phone still resting on the edge of the table. Hadn't she told Sam she'd call him back? It would be rude of her to renege on a promise, leaving him in suspense as to what terrible catastrophe had cut short their previous conversation.

Kneeling next to the table, she fought back tears. Who was she kidding? It wasn't like her life was so interesting that anyone would be waiting with bated breath for the next installment of *The Jill Martin Chronicles*. Sam probably hadn't even given it another thought after she so abruptly hung up on him.

She bent down and shoved the fistful of paper into the bag. Besides, calling Sam wasn't the solution to her loneliness. Colleen was her best girlfriend. *She* should be the one on speed dial for venting frustrations and sharing funny stories. Not Sam.

She grabbed the phone and quickly tapped in Colleen's number, then braced it next to her ear as she knelt to gather up more shreds.

"Hey, girl." Colleen sounded apprehensive, like she might be waiting for Jill's second shoe to drop. "I've been thinking about you. How's everything going?"

"Oh, you know…" Her intention to share her "funny" story of puppy-meets-paper suddenly seemed superfluous. She had more pressing things to update her on. "Still no sign of a foreclosure notice."

"Well, that's good news." The tension in Colleen's voice eased a little. "Did Grace watch the kids again today?"

"No…" Seeing that the paper that had only gotten half shredded had dogged it all the way to the living room, Jill scooted over to retrieve it. "You're not going to believe this, but I wound up taking them to my mom's." Clinching the paper between two fingers, she slid back to the bag and waited for Colleen's response.

"You're serious?" She let out a little huff of disbelief. "So, desperation finally set in?"

"Well, I…" Jill dropped her gaze to the paper in her hand, fixating on the boldface, all-in-caps heading.

TOXICOLOGY REPORT

She frowned. Nyland Enterprises was supposed to be the epitome of environmental friendliness. Why would they need a toxicology report?

"*Yes…?*" Colleen drew out the word, directing Jill's attention back to their conversation. "What happened?"

Shaking off the momentary diversion, Jill dropped the paper into the bag and continued her cleanup. "She came to *me*, actually."

"No kidding. Did she apologize?"

"Not exactly."

"Still," Colleen said, "I think this is good. You can't avoid your own mother forever."

"No, I guess not." Securing the phone between her cheek and her shoulder, Jill punched her fist into the bag to condense its contents. She grabbed the top corners and tried to join them, but it was no use. The bag was too full. How had she managed to knot the ends together the first time?

She twisted her mouth. Obviously, she really *hadn't*, which was why it had opened so easily when the puppy had knocked it over.

Since the last thing she needed was a repeat performance of the carnival of confetti, she pushed to her feet and headed for the kitchen to get an extra bag.

"So…" Colleen went on. "How are things going at work?"

"They're hiring the rest of the staff." Keeping her voice down so as not to wake the tiny force of nature snoring away in his crate, Jill opened a drawer and yanked out a small white trash bag. "We should have new people starting soon."

"Well, let me know if they hire any single men. Maybe the factory will draw some of those country boys out of the woodwork."

"I'll be sure to keep you posted." Back in the entryway, Jill suppressed a shiver at what she'd seen of the "country boys" applying for factory work. She flicked open the bag, then transferred a handful of shreds as Colleen launched into a story about a matchmaking co-worker.

As Jill reached into the bag again, she felt the half-shredded sheet she'd stuffed in there a few minutes before and took it out.

"…tried to fix me up with her brother in Helena." Colleen continued.

"Oh, yeah?" Trying to sound more interested in the story than she actually was, Jill glanced at the partial report in her hand, which was mostly hard-to-decipher scientific data about geothermal energy. Then a portion of a sentence jumped off the page as if it had been highlighted.

…considerable alarm…

"I told her there was no way I was going to get involved in a long-distance relationship. Know what I mean?"

"Uh-huh." Jill's heart raced as she tracked back to the beginning of the paragraph so she could read the words in context.

Substantial amounts of the following substances seeping into the groundwater at the disposal site are cause for considerable alarm.

Her stomach jolted. *What?*

"...I mean, life's too complicated as it is, right?"

"Right..." Still attempting to split her focus, Jill continued reading.

...mercury, arsenic, boron, antimony, benzorine...

Frowning, she looked up from the page. She'd heard a lot about the negative effects of mercury. And arsenic...wasn't that a poison?

Then she remembered that conversation she'd overheard earlier between Dean and Mr.

Steele. Did this have something to do with the "oversight" they'd mentioned?

"I swear the only single men in this town either fall into the category of 'widowed' or 'divorced-and-I-can-see-why.'"

As Colleen's ongoing diatribe faded to the background, Jill continued reading.

...dangerous levels were found to be present in the drinking water in Nagosaka, Japan...

Japan? She huffed out a relieved sigh. So this had nothing to do with Madison Falls. Didn't she have enough to worry about without looking for more trouble? She shoved the paper to the bottom of the smaller bag.

"...dating in a small town. I swear, Jill. Be thankful you're not sing—" Colleen cut herself off, apparently catching the implications of what she'd been about to say.

Jill's focus snapped back to Colleen like a rubber band that had been stretched too far. For a long moment, her words reverberated through the phone lines. *Not single.*

"Oh Jill." Remorse cracked in Colleen's voice. "I'm sorry. I wasn't thinking."

"It's okay." She transferred more shreds. "We're both adjusting to my new status."

Besides, she really wasn't single. Not yet, anyway.

But the question remained…what exactly *was* she?

Jill Came Tumbling After

Chapter 20

By the time Jill got to work the next morning, the power had been restored and the construction crew was hard at work again. She somewhat reluctantly agreed to accompany Hal out onto the production floor so he could discuss evidence of mouse activity. Even though that space wasn't her domain, the rodent problem had managed to gnaw its way onto her list of responsibilities.

"So, you got a lot of entry points in this room." Hal dipped his head toward the wall near their feet, where holes had been cut for the pipes leading from the turbines out to the cooling tower. "The critters are taking this as an open invitation to come on in."

Struggling to hear him over the racket of sawing and drilling, she looked at the blue pipes he was pointing at and the quarter-inch gap between them and the wall. "I'll talk to Bob about sealing that up." She let go of the too-big hard hat that pressed down on the tops of her ears so she could make a note.

"See this over here?" Hal led her to the other end of the room, then pointed down to a deep crack in the back wall. "I suspect you might have a problem here too. Anything living in that mineshaft will come and go like it owns the place."

"Wait..." Frowning, she stared at the crack, reorienting herself to the layout of the room. "You're saying that crack leads into the mine?"

Hal shrugged, like he found that fact neither interesting nor unusual.

Jill stood there contemplating the idea of mouse-survival in that dark, creepy place. She was about to question the likelihood of that when the double doors from the lobby swung open and Mr. Steele entered with another man, both of them wearing hard hats and business suits. The man carried one of those handheld computer things that Kylie had referred to as a "tablet."

She tensed. This must be the DOE inspector.

As Hal continued to talk about the nature of rodents and what he would need to do to keep them from turning this space into their own personal vermin commune, Jill positioned herself so she could look just past Hal's shoulder and keep an eye on the inspector. Mr. Steele jabbed his index finger at various places around the area, and the inspector nodded and typed on his pad. As far as Jill could tell, their interaction seemed amiable.

Bob walked past and she sprang back to her more pressing concern. "Oh…Bob. Do you have a minute? Hal has some questions."

While Bob and Hal took up the discussion about the gap around the pipes, Mr. Steele and the inspector moved close enough to almost be within Jill's earshot. She took a couple of subtle steps sideways until she could more or less make out what they were saying.

The inspector pointed to one of the turbines. "So, this pipe takes the remaining steam to where, exactly?"

Mr. Steele had started nodding before the man even got his question out. "To the cooling tower, which is located a hundred yards from this building. From there it's reinjected into the earth via the injection well. This is the first geothermal plant to use this exact technology in the U.S."

"In the U.S?" The inspector continued to examine the pipes as he spoke. "It's been used successfully elsewhere?"

"Yes, there have been…"

Jill strained to hear as the sound of a drill cut into Mr. Steele's response.

"…Japan, among them."

Japan? Jill's stomach did a flip. Her crazy need to hear as much as she could of this conversation had just increased tenfold.

"And that was the…" The inspector turned his head, cutting off the comprehensibility of his sentence before he turned back in time for her to catch the ending. "…failed attempt?"

Mr. Steele's eyes darted around, like he was nervous that someone might be paying attention to their conversation. Jill quickly looked away, her hearing even more acutely tuned in.

"Not 'failed' so much as…" His voice trailed off again. "…inconclusive…pilot program still in the developmental stages…"

They moved around the turbines, till they were too far for her to make out their conversation unless she intentionally followed them, which she had to admit seemed like a bad idea.

Disappointed, she knelt down to get a better look at the crack in the wall. She looked up, intent on asking Hal some follow-up questions about mice in the mineshaft. But her words caught in her throat as, from across the production floor, Mr. Steele's steely gaze met hers. The inspector was talking to him, but his focus was fully on Jill.

Suddenly, Jill felt just like Jimmy Stewart in *Rear Window*, in that moment when Raymond Burr catches him spying on him through his binoculars. Like she should run if only she could.

Her blood felt like ice water in her veins. Why would he be glaring at her like that?

Apparently not noticing, the inspector gestured to something on the turbine as he continued to talk, and Mr. Steele turned his head to look at what he was pointing to. But he glanced back at her, confirming that she hadn't imagined his displeasure.

But with *what?*

She shook it off. It was probably nothing. Just her rattled nerves and clearly overactive imagination making something out of nothing. Mr. Steele could be frowning at her for any number of reasons.

Still, she stood, tucking her hands into her pockets to quell a sudden case of the shakes. And a serious disappointment that Jackson had already done Kylie the favor of pulverizing that last box of papers. What else might have been in there that was now lost forever?

Jill dragged herself up the walkway to her mom's house, anxious to get the kids and meet Colleen at the grocery store before heading home for dinner.

She opened the door and called in, "Hello!"

Her mom popped out of the kitchen, her eyes wide like she'd been taken by surprise.

"Hi, Mom." A tingle of nerves crackled through Jill as she shut the door behind herself. "Where are the kids?"

Her mom waved a hand in the air, as if to dismiss the question. "Oh…you know."

Jill frowned. "Actually, I *don't* know. That's why I asked."

They stood there for a moment in an awkward standoff. Was Mom trying to hide something?

The reassuring sound of Riley's happy squeals coming from the kitchen broke the silence. Jill cast another questioning look at her mom as she stepped around her toward the source of the sound.

Emma sat in the highchair that had once been Jill's. At the sight of her mommy, she slapped her hands down on the tray, launching a cascade of Cheerios into the air.

"Mama!" Riley sprang to his feet and hurled himself at her, a hammer dangling dangerously from his hands. The puppy lapped up a few Cheerios, then ran circles around her dad's big old red toolbox, which had been left open in the center of the floor.

And an all-too familiar-looking pair of legs stuck out from under the sink.

Jill gasped. "Caleb?"

Caleb's face appeared from inside the cabinet. "Well, hey, Jilly."

Jill felt her back go up. "What are *you* doing here?"

A goofy smile started to form as he gestured toward the pipes under the sink with the wrench he held. "So, it's not obvious?"

She started to speak but stopped herself. "Mom." She snapped the hammer from Riley's hand, ignoring his protests. "Would you take the kids and get their coats on? We need to go."

Her mom huffed like a bull, but she picked up Emma and shot a pointed look at Riley that directed him to follow his mother's instructions.

As soon as the kitchen door swung shut behind them, Jill put the hammer in the box and did her best to keep her voice controlled. "I'll ask you again." She folded her arms. "Why are you here?"

Letting out a long breath, Caleb pulled himself to his feet. "Everybody's gotta be somewhere."

"That's not an answer."

"It wasn't a reasonable question."

"I can't believe you came here." She fairly spit the words out. "You knew the kids were here, didn't you? Did my mom tell you?"

He took a couple of slow steps toward her, giving her a raised-brow look that implied only one of them was in control and it wasn't her. "You need to calm down, Jilly."

"Don't call me that. And don't tell me what I need to do."

He gave her his little condescending chuckle, the one that made her want to throw something at him. It was probably a good thing she'd already put the hammer away.

His look of pretend patience galled her further. "Why don't I put the kids and the dog in the car while you get it together."

Get it together? She stood there feeling like her chest had caught fire as he scooped up the dog and put him into the crate, then picked it up and left the room. Not wanting to scream at him in front of her mom and the kids, she trailed silently behind him, then stood there like a mannequin as he took Emma from her mom and led Riley out the front door.

The second it shut, she turned on her mom. "What is Caleb doing here?"

"He came here to fix my sink."

"Fix your sink? Since when do you call Caleb to do things like that for you?"

"Well, generally I don't." She folded her hands primly in front of herself. "I called the hardware store and he answered."

"Why would he—"

"I don't know why that would surprise

you, dear. You told me yourself that he's working there."

She let out a slow breath. "So he answered and you asked him to come fix your sink?"

"No. I asked him to have Sam come. Sam was busy, so Caleb came instead."

"And you let him stay? Knowing I don't want him around the kids?"

"How was I to know that? You didn't tell me."

Jill bit her tongue. She had her there. "Well, I'm telling you *now*." She fought to keep her cool. "Please don't let Caleb into your house when the kids are here."

Mom's mouth drew into a thin, white line. "They're his children too."

"I know that, Mom."

"Do you have some kind of legal order against him?"

"No, but—"

"Then I don't see how I can stop him."

"It's your house. You can just say no."

"Exactly how long are you going to play this ridiculous game, Jillian?"

"It's not a game. It's my life." Tempering her anger out of fear that she might lose her only option for childcare, she bent to pick up her diaper bag. She flung open the door. "And for now, I need you to just do this one thing for me, okay?"

When her mom finally gave a barely perceptible nod, Jill let out a little groan and stomped down the steps toward where she'd parked by the curb.

Caleb leaned on the car with his arms folded, kids and dog presumably buckled in position.

When she got out of earshot of her mom and any curious neighbors who might be lurking, she looked him in the eye. "I don't want to see you right now, and if you're going to be around the kids, I have to be sure you're not drinking."

"Don't you trust me?"

"Trust you?" It was all she could do, for the sake of anyone who might be watching, to maintain the appearance of an amiable conversation. "What have you given me to trust in?"

"I'm your husband. You're supposed to trust me. It's in the Bible."

"Oh really? Where? Where exactly in the Bible does it say that I'm supposed to blindly trust you? Huh? Where?"

He worked his jaw but said nothing.

"Right. I didn't think so."

She got in the car and shut the door, anger still brewing in her chest. Why did everything have to be so hard?

Chapter 21

Still simmering from her encounter with Caleb, Jill pushed the shopping cart with Emma in the seat and Riley sitting in the cart playing with his cars. Colleen strolled beside her, carrying a basket.

"I'm so mad, I could spit." It wasn't easy, but Jill kept her voice hushed and her expression controlled. "He honestly thinks I'm supposed to trust him after everything he's done. Like women should be stupid and blind and ignorant to all the bad things their husbands do. It makes me so mad."

"I'm telling you"—Colleen picked up a box of granola bars and waved it for emphasis—"that's one of the reasons I don't go to church. Religion messes everything up."

Jill let out a breath. "It's not God who messes everything up, Cole. It's people. People who interpret God's Word to suit their own purposes. That's not the way our church views marriage."

"Maybe not." Shrugging, she carefully placed the box in her basket. "But there are an awful lot of people *in* the church who believe that women are second-class citizens. That we should play dumb and act like a bunch of scared mice."

"Ugh. Don't say 'mice.'" Jill checked the price on a box of cereal and almost put it back on the shelf twice before finally setting it next to Riley in her cart. "I swear." She gestured for Colleen to follow her a few feet away from the shopping cart, just far enough to be out of

Riley's earshot. "I think my mom is trying to drive me crazy."

Colleen shook her head. "She never approved of Caleb. Now, suddenly she's on his side? I don't get it."

"She's just trying to prove a point to me." Jill pretended to be interested in the coffee grinding machine. "It's like she felt stuck in her marriage and she thinks I should feel the same way."

"You'd think your mom, of all people, would understand."

"That's Mom for you." She stepped back toward the cart. "Not exactly a model of supportiveness."

"What are you doing this weekend?" Colleen asked.

"What? Oh, um…we're going to the pumpkin farm with Sam."

"With Sam? Seriously? I don't think he's been to the pumpkin farm since we were in middle school."

"He says he needs to keep busy so he won't miss Grace too much. You should come with us."

"Sounds like fun."

A cart rounded the corner into their aisle and Jill was surprised to see Dean pushing it. Why should that surprise her? Obviously, the man had to buy groceries like everyone else.

He looked different…in a nice way, having changed into jeans and a sweater.

He noticed her, obviously a little taken aback himself. Then he smiled and pushed the cart to where they stood. "Jill. So nice to see you." He glanced at the kids. "And these are your little ones, I presume."

"Yes indeed. This is Riley and Emma."

Riley responded by running his car across the rim of the cart and making a *vroom* sound.

"And this is my friend, Colleen."

They shook hands. It struck Jill as odd, like her two worlds had unexpectedly collided in the cereal aisle of the Peach Basket Market.

"I thought you'd be off entertaining that inspector this weekend."

"Thankfully, no." He shook his head. "William…I mean, Mr. Steele didn't think we were both needed for that. And frankly, there are things I would rather do than play golf. So, I have the weekend off. Time to catch up on some computer work and personal time."

Without thinking, she glanced at the contents of his cart, which seemed to be filled mostly with fresh ingredients rather than the convenience foods she would have expected. "And to do a little cooking, it looks like."

"I try to do that when I can." He looked sheepish. "I'm pleased to report that the inspection went well."

"Great."

"I don't quite understand." Colleen flipped her hair over her shoulder. "Why did the inspection happen before the place is ready to go into production?"

Jill frowned. What had Colleen just been saying about "playing dumb"?

"Oh, this was just the first inspection." Dean cheerfully turned his attention to Colleen. "From the DOE."

"The Department of Energy?" Colleen's carefully shaped eyebrows scrunched together. "That sounds pretty important."

"Oh, it is. It just pales in comparison to the EPA inspection next week. That's the one we're really gearing up for."

"I should know this, but…" Colleen tilted her head, reminding Jill of the puppy—and that she didn't want to leave him in the car for too much longer. "…what's the difference between the DOE and the EPA?"

Jill frowned again. Funny that Colleen kept plying Dean with questions on the same subject that had practically put her to sleep when Jill had talked about it.

"*I* didn't even really know until recently," Dean responded patiently. "The DOE is the entity that will give the factory its certification of being environmentally friendly."

"That's why we had to get all that paper out of the building," Jill added.

"That's right. The job of the EPA is to help regulated entities meet federal requirements, and to hold them legally accountable for environmental violations. They protect human health and the environment."

"Fascinating." Another hair flip.

Edging her cart forward, Jill narrowed her eyes at her friend.

Seeming to get the hint, Colleen took a few steps. When Dean started forward also, Colleen hung back next to him, continuing the conversation that was now clearly just between the two of them. "So, how do you like Montana?"

"It's beautiful country. And our location couldn't be more perfect for the long-term vision of the company."

Looking back, Jill frowned. "Long-term vision?"

Colleen cocked her head like a curious collie. "What kind of vision?"

Jill couldn't help but stare. Was Colleen actually flirting with Dean? He was Jill's boss, for crying out loud.

"Actually, it's *my* long-term vision. But Mr. Nyland seems excited about it. It was his primary incentive for hiring me."

Jill looked at him, confused. "He hired you because you had a vision for *his* company?"

Dean smiled. "Actually, it's been a dream of mine for years. I was looking for someone to back it, and I came across Nyland Enterprises at just the right time. I guess you could say that's why I took this job. Because Mr. Nyland saw my vision as a perfect fit for his company's future."

"So what exactly is your vision for the company?" Colleen twisted a lock of hair around her finger, something Jill hadn't witnessed since high school.

Dean spread a hand as though he were painting a picture. "I want to transform the factory location into not only a working geothermal plant, but also an educational experience. We would offer tours and year-round activities for anyone who wants to come. Then in the summer, we'd have camps for kids of all ages. It would educate the next generation and get them excited about earth-friendly industries. We'd use it as a recruitment tool for young people who have an interest in pursuing some sort of career. Counteract the heavy hitters like Monsanto who go after our youth. We'd get them to want to work for the good of the planet instead."

"Wow, that's an amazing vision." Colleen seemed sincerely impressed, as was Jill once she got past her irritation with Colleen's coquettishness.

"And the best part is, we could do it working with the natural landscape. You'll be able to look out our windows and still see the forest and the view, but there will be an organic garden and a solar-powered dormitory. We'll use the existing structures as best we can. There are hiking trails all around the area that can be utilized. I've talked to Bob Branigan about it."

Jill pictured Riley having something like what Dean had described available to him when he was a little older. "The kids around here could really use something special to do in the summer."

"Right. And it wouldn't be just for youth who live in the area. I'd like to draw kids from all over. City kids who have no idea how to compost or do organic gardening. They'd come here to learn and get excited about it."

"So…" While not entirely dropping her flirty tone, Colleen at least regained a bit of her normal demeanor. "You must have some kind of degree in alternative energy."

"I have a master's in environmental science. I didn't know much about geothermal energy before I took this job. Mr. Nyland and Mr. Steele are the experts there."

While this was good information, all Jill wanted was to finish shopping and get her brood home. She rounded the corner into the canned goods aisle and scanned the shelves for the cheapest variety of soup.

Dean continued to chat as he and Colleen trailed along behind her. "I saw their ad and thought it might be a fit with what I wanted to accomplish. Turns out, I was right. It's just going to take some time to get there. Right now, the focus is on getting our EPA approval so we can start production."

Contemplating how many times this week she could get away with serving soup for dinner, Jill plunked a couple of cans of chicken noodle into the cart. "Well, we should let you finish up your shopping." Jill cast a half glance over her shoulder as she kept moving forward, hoping Colleen would take the hint.

Dean nodded, then turned to Colleen. "It was a pleasure meeting you." Giving them one last friendly smile, he turned and pushed his cart in the opposite direction.

The second he disappeared around the corner, Colleen whirled toward her. "Jill! Why didn't you tell me about him?"

"About Dean? I did. He's my boss. I told you everything."

"You didn't tell me how cute he is. Or that he doesn't have a ring on his hand."

"Oh…well, I—"

"And he's ambitious too. Did you know about his vision for the factory?"

"This is the first I've heard. Pretty impressive."

Jill pretended to listen as Colleen chattered on, but something else took hold of her thoughts. If Dean was so positive about the bright future of this company, that toxicity report couldn't have meant anything. She really needed to just put that out of her head.

Things had finally started looking up for her and the kids. Why would she want to cause trouble?

Chapter 22

Jill stood next to Colleen, bouncing the baby on her hip and watching Sam and Riley scour the orange-dotted field in search of the perfect pumpkin. There was nothing like being outside on a crisp fall day.

A sigh came out sounding surprisingly content. They had made it to the end of the week without a foreclosure notice. At this point, they would at least still be in their house for Halloween. That felt like a blessing.

But her moment of peace ended at the thought that they could still be forced to move before Thanksgiving and that they might not get another Christmas in their house. Taking in a faltering breath, Jill did her best to push that from her mind and just be in the moment.

"That one, Unca' Sam!" Riley pointed a chubby finger in the direction of a pumpkin the size of a basketball.

As Sam maneuvered the wheelbarrow, Jill squished through the mud, grateful to have him handling the physical labor. With Emma attached to her torso in the sling, she would have struggled to keep up with Riley and push that heavy wheelbarrow. Sure, she would have managed, but it was great to be able to relax and actually enjoy this excursion.

Sam bent to pick up the pumpkin under Riley's watchful eye, and a sense of security filled her. Like they were just another family on an outing to the pumpkin farm. Even though she knew that was far from the truth.

With Caleb, it always felt like family time

was what he did between bouts of "me time." Sam, on the other hand, spent time with her and the kids because he wanted to.

Why was she so conflicted? In her heart, she still held out hope that Caleb would step up to the plate. That his eyes would be opened and he would realize what was at stake. He was going to lose his family, and Jill wanted, more than anything, for that to matter to him.

She watched Sam with Riley, remembering her own childhood. When Jill would tire of playing dolls or jumping rope, she liked joining in on stickball games or playing pirate or safari with the boys. Caleb had been so mean to her. Pulling her hair or telling her she couldn't keep up because she was a girl. But Sam had never been that way. He had always been kind and protective of her, even when they were kids. So why, when hormones and teenage stupidity had kicked in, had she been drawn to the one who had never treated her very well?

And now, when she looked at Sam, she couldn't help but think about how much easier things would be if—

"Mama! Lookit!"

Jill realized that her attention had drifted long enough for Sam and Riley to hoist not one but two huge pumpkins into the wheelbarrow.

"We pick'a two, Mama." Riley pointed to the pumpkins as he trotted alongside Sam.

"I can see that." Jill smiled, hoping that no one had been perceptive enough to read her thoughts. "Is it up to me to decide?"

"We're getting both," Sam explained. "One for Riley and one for me."

"Oh? I was counting on you to help *him*."

"I can help him too. Now it's your turn. Tell me which one you want."

"Oh. I don't need one. This is going to get awfully expensive."

"Don't you worry about the money."

"Sam—"

"I can't fix everything, but this is one thing

I can do. Now go pick out your pumpkin."

"Hey, if Jill's getting one, I want one too." Colleen stepped daintily over a mass of vines, her sights set on a cluster of orange orbs several yards away.

Jill scanned the immediate vicinity in search of something a little smaller than the ones the boys had picked out.

"I help'a you, Mama!" Riley trotted ahead of them.

"Thanks for doing this, Sam. I don't know if I could have kept up with Riley in the corn maze if I had been here on my own. He had a blast."

"It's a rite of passage. I can remember when we were kids, coming here after dark. There's nothing like going through that corn maze with your best buddies and a flashlight."

"I'll bet that was fun." Mud squished underfoot as they stepped off the makeshift path. "I was never that brave."

With Riley's help, Jill located a slightly asymmetrical pumpkin that would present a creative challenge to carve.

Colleen returned and placed a small, perfectly round pumpkin next to the others and wiped the mud off her hands. "I'll catch up with you guys in the picnic area. I'm going to go to the gift shop to get some of Irma's huckleberry jam." She looked down at Riley. "Hey, buddy. You want to come with me? We can check out the homemade fudge." She looked up at Jill for her belated approval.

Giving her a helpless shrug of consent, Jill silently schemed to sneak some extra veggies into Riley's dinner tonight to counteract all the sugar he was getting today.

As Colleen and Riley headed for the gift shop, Jill and Sam started toward the stand at the end of the barn where they would weigh and pay for their pumpkins.

Sam glanced her way. "So, how are things with your mom?"

"I thought it was going pretty well. Now

I'm not so sure."

"Oh yeah? What happened?"

"She's having a problem with her kitchen sink."

"Yeah, Caleb told me. I guess he looked at it."

"Which is the problem." Leaves crunched loudly under her feet as if to emphasize her frustration. "I don't want him there when the kids are over, but of course my mom isn't going to cooperate with that."

"I'm sorry. I was helping a customer when she called. Otherwise I would have gone. He meant well."

"He always *means* well." She didn't even pretend to keep the sarcasm from her tone.

"He told me he adjusted some things, but he didn't sound too confident that the problem was fixed."

"Would you have time this week to help her?"

"I'll stop by on my way home today."

"Thanks." Jill stepped over a large root

that rose up across the trail. "Looks like staying busy to keep your mind off Grace isn't going to be a problem for you today."

"Yeah." He smiled lightly. "It's not exactly keeping me from missing her, but it's helping. I might take Caleb fishing tomorrow after I get back from church. That ought to do both of us some good."

"He's always loved to fish." She chuckled as they squished through the swampy area surrounding the pumpkin-washing pumps. "Do you remember that time we went to the falls and you two decided to try to catch fish with your bare hands, like the Indians used to do?"

"I remember Caleb actually caught one." Sam unloaded the pumpkins into the wooden platform. "I never stood a chance competing with him as a fisherman. The guy's good."

"He used to call himself a 'fish whisperer.'" She choked out a half laugh, hating the reminder of happy times that would never be again.

"Remember when he used to talk about wanting to open a fishing tackle store?"

"I completely forgot about that." Jill grabbed a wire brush, then pumped out water so icy she scrubbed extra fast to keep warm. "Now you pretty much have the market cornered in Madison Falls."

He shrugged. "We sell our share of tackle, but I always said this town could use a better supplier. The real serious fishermen go to Victor or all the way to Missoula."

"Too bad Caleb never tried opening his own place. Stopped talking about it altogether after Riley was born."

"Yeah." Sam placed the clean pumpkins back into the wheelbarrow. "It's important to go after what you're really passionate about."

"Like you. I mean, you're happier now that you're pursuing your music, right?"

"I've never *not* pursued it." He wheeled toward the checkout stand.

"I know, but there's a world of difference between singing your songs in the worship band at a small-town church and getting a recording deal."

"I don't have a recording deal. I didn't win that competition, remember?"

"Of course I remember, but you've had offers just the same."

"Yeah, I'm still weighing those." He started unloading the pumpkins onto the scale. "You know, I put Caleb in charge of the fishing department at the hardware store."

"Fishing department?" She sputtered out a little laugh. "Since when have a few poles and a bunch of tackle boxes been their own 'department'?"

He huffed as he took out his wallet. "Okay, so it's been an underdeveloped department. But Caleb did some special orders for a few of our customers, and he talked me into stocking a few more items. I gave him some extra shelf space in the back corner. It's keeping him busy."

"Oh. Well. Good. It sounds like he's had a productive week. Too bad you can't pay him."

"He's still working off his debt. Plus we're feeding him, so he can't exactly complain. And speaking of food…" He made a show of sniffing the air as he reloaded the wheelbarrow. "I smell roasting corn. Come on." He started to steer toward the exit gate. "We'll load these into your car, and then lunch is on me."

"Sam, you don't have to—"

"You know as well as I do that no visit to the pumpkin farm is complete without 'corn on the cobweb.'"

She sighed. "I can't argue with you there."

Jill Came Tumbling After

Chapter 23

A few minutes later, Sam directed the wheelbarrow through the puddle-strewn parking lot toward Jill's car. "Do you want me to load these into your trunk?"

"Yes. Oh, wait, you can't. My trunk is full. I'm supposed to take some big trash bags full of paper to the recycling center for work."

"I have to go out there anyway. Why don't I just load the bags into my truck?"

"You wouldn't mind?"

"If it was a problem"—he reached out to take her keys—"I wouldn't have offered."

Jill kept Emma entertained while Sam transferred the bags into the back of his truck and deposited the pumpkins into the trunk of Jill's car.

As they headed toward the snack shack, the smells of apple cider, corn, and mud hovered in the air, along with the happy sounds of kids as they rode the ponies and played on the playground. Jill scanned the nearby grassy area for an available picnic table.

"How about if Emma and I find a place for us to sit while you go get the food. But…" Her conscience pricked. Sam was doing so much for them already. "I don't need anything."

He started to say something but settled for a slight smile. Jill lingered, watching his back as he made his way toward the food line.

"Jill!"

She whipped around and saw a familiar form skip-stepping toward her. "Kylie. Hi."

"Aw! Your baby's so cute!" Kylie ran a hand over Emma's soft curls. "Are you here with your whole family?"

A complete answer seemed impossible to insert into the midst of Kylie's exuberance, so Jill just said, "Yes."

"Come on." Venturing into the busy table area, Kylie gestured for her to follow. "I want you to meet my boyfriend."

Kylie led the way through the maze of tables and happy families toward a clean-cut young man with glasses sitting alone at a long picnic table. He stood as they approached.

"Jackson," Kylie chirped. "Look who I found. This is Jill. She's the one I've been telling you about."

Jackson extended a hand, along with a welcoming smile. "Kylie's told me how much she's enjoying working with you."

"Why don't you sit with us?" Kylie waved a hand at the table, which was empty except for a tray of hotdogs, fries, corn on the cob, and hot apple cider. "We've got tons of room."

Jill looked toward the food stand, where Sam had taken his place in the line. "That sounds great. Thanks."

"I was just going to get some more butter for our corn-on-the-cobweb. I'll be back in a jiff." Kylie pivoted, then zigged her way toward the condiment table.

As Jill slid onto the bench kitty-corner from Jackson, he retook his seat. She tried to recall what Kylie had told her about him, but all she came up with was that he was "the best" and worked someplace that had a shredder.

"So." She smiled. "What do you do?"

He smiled back, like being left to make conversation with a virtual stranger wasn't unusual for him. "I'm just a drone for the UC."

"The UC?"

"Madison Falls Utility Commission."

Nodding like she should have known that was what he meant, Jill removed Emma from the sling and settled her onto her lap. "Sounds interesting."

"It's not." He offered her a fry, which she

turned down. "But it pays the bills. And it helped Kylie get her job at the factory."

"Oh?"

"Yeah. That guy…what's his name? Owens?"

"Dean Owens?"

"Right. He came into the office to apply for some permits. He mentioned that he needed someone to help get them organized. Kylie needed a job, so I called her and he interviewed her over the phone. She must have made a solid impression because he hired her on the spot."

Jill heaved a breath. If *she* had made such a "solid impression" in her interview, she could have avoided the whole begging part. "Well, that worked out well."

"Yeah. It's a good job for her, while it lasts."

Jill's stomach flipped like she'd just taken the plunge on a roller coaster. "What do you mean, 'while it lasts'?"

He lifted a shoulder and drew a fry through

the ketchup on his plate, as if he *hadn't* just dropped a potential bombshell. "It's just that their business model is fundamentally unsustainable."

A chill ran down Jill's spine. What was he saying, and why did he seem so nonchalant about it? "Wh…why?"

"Mama!"

Jill's attention snapped at the sound of Riley's voice and she caught sight of him running toward her, with Colleen struggling to keep up. She swallowed the question she'd been about to ask.

"Good job spotting your mom, Riley." As Riley hoisted himself up next to Jill, Colleen set a shopping bag on the bench by Jackson and plunked down beside it, casting a curious look at him.

As Jill made the introduction, she swallowed her dismay at the conversation with Jackson being cut short. What had he meant by "fundamentally unsustainable"? And would she have an opportunity to ask him?

This wasn't exactly a conversation she wanted to have in front of everyone.

Jackson's face lit up as Kylie returned, carefully balancing a paper bowl in her hands.

"Sorry that took so long." Kylie plunked down across from Jackson. "They ran out of butter and they had to go churn some more." She capped her little joke with an endearing titter.

As Kylie introduced herself to Colleen, Jill caught sight of Sam heading their way with an ambitiously overloaded tray.

Jackson's words still plagued her, but it was probably just evidence that Dean was right about the public's need for education about alternative energy. That thought comforted her, and she smiled as Sam set the tray down. It was full of hot dogs, steaming ears of corn wrapped in a paper imprinted with a cobweb design, and an assortment of donuts.

"Sam…" Jill lifted a hand in introduction. "…this is my friend Kylie from work, and her boyfriend, Jackson."

"Nice to meet both of you." Sam put a hot dog in front of Riley as he extended his other hand to shake Jackson's.

"Jill's a gem." Kylie gave Jill's arm a friendly tap with her elbow. "I'm so glad we're sharing an office."

Sam lifted a steaming cup from the tray and set it in front of Jill. "I knew you wanted a pumpkin spice latte. And look, they brought back your favorite. The hot Polish sausage." He waved it near her nose. "You hungry now?"

The spicy smells of pumpkin and sauerkraut made her stomach growl with gratitude. "Thanks, Sam."

"Mama, the crows!" Riley slid off the bench and waved his arms, shooing at the black birds who had landed a little too close to their table.

"Riley…" Jill started to stand, but Sam gestured for her to remain seated.

"I'll get him." Sam leapt to his feet and spoke over his shoulder as he moved toward the wayward Riley. "You relax and enjoy your lunch while it's hot."

Since it was too late to argue anyway, Jill leaned on the table and took a swig of the delicious, sweet latte.

"Pay attention, Jacks." Kylie reached across the table and playfully backhanded Jackson's arm. "That's what a good husband looks like."

Jill nearly choked on her coffee. "Oh, no. He's—"

"I've been telling Jackson what you said about Madison Falls on Halloween." Addressing Jackson, Kylie wagged a finger from Jill to Sam. "Jill says they go every year and it's the best."

"Come on, buddy." Sam swung the giggling Riley back onto the bench then sat on his other side. "It's time to eat."

As Kylie launched into a story about her all-time favorite costume, Jill decided to wait for a better opportunity to explain her situation. But Jackson's off-the-cuff comment wouldn't be as easily brushed aside.

Chapter 24

As Jill pulled into her driveway, she flicked a glance at her front door then exhaled relief at the welcome assurance that nothing was taped to it.

Shutting off the engine, she gave Colleen a sideways look. With the exception of an occasional comment inserted into Riley's ongoing monologue about jack-o-lantern ideas, her friend had been silent the whole way home from the pumpkin farm. Jill knew her well enough to recognize when something was bugging her.

Trying to sound casual, she reached over the console to retrieve her purse from the floor of the backseat. "Want to come back tonight to carve with us?"

"Actually…" Clearly distracted, Colleen pulled down her sun visor to check her hair in the mirror. "I have something going on tonight."

"You do? What?"

Colleen looked away, obviously weighing her answer. "It's nothing."

"Mama!" Riley impatiently swung his legs, kicking the back of Colleen's seat. "I wanna see the puppy!"

Colleen avoided making eye contact with Jill. "I can unbuckle him." In one smooth action, she snapped up her shopping bag and opened her door, seemingly happy to escape further inquiry. "Then we'll grab the pumpkins out of the back."

What's up with her? Jill grunted as she

opened her own door, then moved to get Emma. When she finally stood, cradling Emma's drowsy head against her own shoulder, she saw that Colleen and Riley had already transported all of the pumpkins up to the porch.

As Jill made her way up the walk, Riley bounced impatiently at the door, and Colleen stood there tapping the pumpkins with her muddy designer boot.

"So, you let Sam pay for all of these?"

Rolling her eyes, Jill trudged up the steps. She still felt wound up over her unnerving conversation with Jackson, and was in no mood for Colleen's obliqueness. "He just wants the kids to have a normal Halloween. He's being a good friend."

Colleen raised her eyebrows and sauntered toward the door.

Jill frowned as she fished her keys out of her purse. "What was *that* for?"

"What?"

She stuck the key in the lock and ignited

an excited-puppy bark fest from inside the house. "That look you just gave me."

Colleen flicked a glance down at Riley and didn't answer.

The second Jill pushed the door open, the high-pitched yips coming from the kitchen intensified. "Riley, go let the puppy out of the crate and open the back door for him. I'll be right there." As he happily obeyed, Jill turned her attention back to Colleen. "Something's bothering you. What is it?"

Colleen twisted her mouth as she slipped off her boots and followed Jill inside. "I wasn't going to say anything in front of Riley, but why did you let that girl think that Sam is your husband?"

"I didn't…." Her stomach did a flip. To be accurate, she *had* let Kylie think that. She shut the door and hung up her keys. "She knows I'm married, but I guess I didn't tell her my husband's name. So, she saw Sam with us and assumed." She headed for the kitchen. "It wasn't a big deal."

"But why not set her straight if it wasn't a big deal?" Colleen trailed behind.

"I will. It was just awkward in the moment, that's all." She slipped through the baby gate that Riley had left ajar. "Then Sam came back and I didn't want to embarrass him or anything."

Colleen nodded, one eyebrow still raised.

"It's nothing, Cole." Jill smoothed Emma's head and started toward the back door, also left open in the wake of child-and-puppy exuberance. "I should have said something and I didn't."

Following her once again, Colleen made a soft grunting sound. "It's just that sometimes you act like...I don't know...like you *own* him or something."

"I do not."

But it was true. She *did*.

Jill's stomach churned as she stepped to the edge of the back porch and watched Riley and the puppy take turns chasing each other. Colleen was her best friend, but she was also

Sam's sister. If Jill confessed her muddled feelings about Sam, it would only put Colleen even more on the defensive.

"You're reading something into this that isn't there. Besides..." She fumbled for a deflection. "I was distracted by something that Jackson said right before you joined us." Jill felt flustered. She hadn't wanted to mention this, but she needed to steer Colleen's focus away from Sam. "It just reminded me of this thing that's been on my mind. Something about work."

"Oh." Colleen unfolded her arms and leaned against the porch railing, her brow unfurrowing as her fit of pique morphed into curiosity. "What?"

"You remember I told you that we had to shred a bunch of papers?" Jill instinctively lowered her voice, as if there were a remote possibility that someone might overhear. "I noticed something funny about one of them."

"Funny, how?"

She let out a breath. "It said 'toxicology report' at the top. Then some scary stuff about chemicals in drinking water. And today, Jackson said he doesn't think the factory's plan is sustainable. It just has me thinking."

"What do you think it all means?"

"I honestly have no idea." She shrugged, feeling a sudden need to downplay her concern. "And I couldn't even see much of the report anyway because half the page had gotten shredded. It's probably nothing."

"Yeah, probably. But if it's bothering you, you should just show it to Dean. I'm sure he'd explain it."

Jill blew air between her teeth. It didn't seem wise to bring this up to anybody until she knew who she could trust. "I don't even have it anymore. I put it back in the bag. Which Sam is taking to the recycling center as we speak."

"Oh?" Colleen reassumed her judgmental stance.

Jill's back went up like a cat. "Because he was planning on going there anyway. Come on, Cole."

"Okay, okay." Colleen raised her palms in surrender, then jarred as she looked at her watch. "I need to go." She hurried back into the kitchen.

"You want a ride home?" Jill gave another look at Riley and the puppy, then followed Colleen inside.

"It's a three-minute walk. Two if I don't stop to say hello to Mrs. Henderson's cat." Colleen had already made it to the front door and was bending over to grab a boot. "Call me after you get home from church tomorrow. Bye." Abruptly, she pulled the door shut.

"'Kay, bye." Sighing, Jill gave a feeble wave to the closed front door. What was going on with Colleen today, anyway?

Shaking her head, she went back to the kitchen and checked on the frolicsome boy-and-dog combo in the backyard. If only she could be so happy-go-lucky.

Chapter 25

"**...a**nd we thank You, dear Lord, for Jill and her precious children."

Keeping her head bent, Jill peered from under her lashes at Mrs. Winger, who had blocked her into the row of pews, preventing her from exiting at the end of service until she was thoroughly covered in prayer.

"May You show this young woman what she needs to do to let Caleb know that he is loved and wanted."

Jill swallowed a sigh. Why did people assume that *she* was the one creating the problem? Like she was some sort of shrew who had forced Caleb to act like a rebellious teenager.

"May You give her the patience to wait on Your timing in guiding her husband back into their home."

She angled a glance toward the pulpit area, where Sam was helping to dismantle the setup for the worship band. A subtle shrug of his eyebrows told her he felt her pain.

"Amen!" Mrs. Winger lifted her head, her expression both triumphant and pitying. "He'll come back, dear."

Jill bit her tongue. This *was* Sunday, and she was standing in God's house. She couldn't exactly blurt out, "Come back? I was the one who told him to leave." Or, "I know, that's why I had the locks changed."

Instead, she gritted her teeth and muttered a soft, "Thank you."

Looking pleased with herself, Mrs. Winger gave Jill's hand one last surprisingly powerful squeeze and moved on to find the next soul in need of her aid.

Jill let out a long breath as she finally unfurled herself from the cramped aisle. She appreciated the thought. But being approached by people who insisted on inserting their personal commentary on her situation into a prayer was more a test of her patience with *them* than a lifting of her burden.

Coiling an electrical cord around his arm, Sam walked up to her and spoke softly. "Been prayed over, have you?"

She swallowed a half chuckle before it turned into a snort. "Put in my place, is more like it."

"She means well."

"I know she does."

"Too bad Caleb isn't here. She could pass on God's instructions to him too, not just you."

"Oh, but she'd only tell him that God wants him to be patient with *me*. Everyone seems to believe that Caleb is faultless and I'm the Jezebel who's led him astray with my non-submissive ways."

Sam just shook his head. "You know, I got him to come with me this morning."

"Seriously? Caleb hasn't come to church since I don't even know when." She cast a wary gaze around the now mostly empty sanctuary. "So where is he?"

"I told him he had to help the band set up. I thought once he was here, maybe he'd decide to stay for the service."

"Oh." She twisted her mouth. "Let me guess. He slunk out the back door so no one would see him."

"Yeah, he said he'd walk back to my place." He shrugged. "I thought it was at least worth the try."

"I appreciate the effort." She jolted, realizing how long she'd been standing there. "I need to go pry the kids away from the childcare room. They love it in there."

After making a plan for pumpkin carving later in the day, Sam returned to his band clean-up and Jill stepped out into the foyer. She put her head down to avoid catching the eye of any more well-intentioned prayer warriors and headed for the hallway that led to the classrooms and offices.

All the doors along this corridor were closed, except one that was cracked open just enough for her to see people moving around inside. An occasional burst of laughter accented the muffled sound of conversation, leading Jill to assume that this was some sort of social gathering, not a stodgy committee meeting. As she got a little closer, she cast a casual glance inside, vaguely curious about what it might be.

Since none of the people she could see looked familiar, she assumed it must be some sort of gathering that people would come from out of town to attend, like a reunion or a memorial. She continued past the door, then stopped in a stunned stare.

Through the small crowd, over near what looked like a food table set up by the window, a man stood with his back to her. She bobbed from side to side as people crossed her line of sight, trying to get a clear look.

Caleb?

But…that didn't make any sense.

Moving closer, she reached out to push the door open so she could see better. But just as her hand brushed the wood, an arm appeared in front of her face, shoving the door wide open. She jarred at the unexpected sensation of someone sideswiping her on their way out of the room.

She stumbled back, expecting an apology but instead meeting the cold hard glare of Lenny Simpson.

He barely hesitated, his mouth turning down in a scowl that revealed teeth that probably hadn't been within spitting distance of a dentist in quite some time. His glare held as he continued past her, doing his slow drag-step in the direction of the restrooms.

Jill planted her hand on her chest like her heart might beat right out of it. What would Scowling Man be doing at an event at her church?

It took her a moment to remember what she'd been in the middle of doing. When she glanced back into the room, the man who sort of resembled Caleb was nowhere in sight.

Shaking her head, she resumed her trek to the childcare room. She had to be imagining things. Of all the places she'd find her wayward husband, church would be at the bottom of the list. In fact, he was probably back on Sam's sofa at this very moment, sleeping a guiltless sleep.

Jill Came Tumbling After

Chapter 26

Jill sorted paint samples at one end of the large oak conference table she had relocated to the big open space on the other side of the second floor. Kylie had commandeered the majority of the table to put together information packets for the new hires who would be starting their orientation the following week. Jill had taken the opportunity to set Kylie straight on her complicated personal life.

"So, Sam's just a good friend. We've—" She paused to wait for a back-up sensor from somewhere down below to stop. After three and a half days of working above a construction zone, adapting their conversation to the ebb and flow of screeching saws and whining drills had become second nature to both of them.

The beeping stopped. "We've known each other since we were kids."

"Oh, Jill. I'm so sorry." Kylie finished distributing the last stack of papers to the fifty or so tidy piles she'd assembled, then leaned against the stair railing behind her to survey her work. "You two just looked so comfortable together. I assumed."

"It's no big deal." Jill held up a paint card, trying to visualize which shade of tan would look better with the green drapes—more toward the Devonshire Cream or more toward the Honey Bisque. "I should have said something at the time."

Kylie stepped back to the table, then leveled a stack of papers and positioned them in her three-hole punch. "I'm really sorry to hear about your separation."

"Thanks." Lowering the hand that held the paint card, Jill reached for her scissors. "That's why I really need this job to work out."

"Me too." The hole punch made a *crunching* sound as Kylie pressed down on it. "I plan on sticking around until Jackson gets a pay raise that will support a family. Assuming he's going to quit dragging his feet on that marriage proposal I keep waiting for." She slid the papers into a royal-blue cover, then clipped the new employee's name tag to the front.

As Kylie went on to describe her dream wedding, Jill's mind wandered back to her conversation with Jackson. Try as she might, she hadn't been able to get that out of her head. She'd even prayed about it yesterday at church. Left it at the foot of the cross. So why did she have to keep picking it back up again?

Or *was* she? Maybe God was actually answering her prayer for peace of mind by telling her she needed to walk through this problem instead of puddle-jumping over it. Maybe He wanted her to keep asking questions.

Setting down her sample cards, she swallowed hard. "Hey, Kylie?"

"Yeah?"

She moved around to Kylie's side of the table, glancing over her shoulder. Even though she hadn't seen either of their bosses all morning, she didn't want to risk being overheard. "Has Jackson ever mentioned anything to you about his concerns about this company?"

"Did he say something to you?" Kylie blew a tuft of hair away from her face. "Don't listen to him. He overanalyzes everything. And he's too protective of me. He doesn't want me to be disappointed if the factory winds up closing or something."

Chewing her lip, Jill looked at the long, still-empty wall in front of them. "But aren't you concerned that he might have a point?"

"You mean, that the business might not be…what's that ten-dollar word he always uses? Like, '*Sustainable*,' or whatever?" She shrugged. "If something happens, I'll deal with it. I mean, nothing's guaranteed in this world, right?"

"Right. But…what about all these people?" She nodded toward the stacks of paper, each of which had a plastic-encased ID tag with a name and a photo next to it.

"What *about* them?"

"Well…" She paused to avoid having to raise her voice over what sounded like a jackhammer busting through concrete down below, then tapped the ID tag on the table in front of her. "What about Janice Jordan? Or…" She picked up the folder next to it. "Or Michael Donahue? They're really counting on their new jobs lasting, right?"

Kylie hesitated, a crease forming on her

smooth brow. "I guess so…"

"Don't you feel like someone should say something…" Her volume rose along with that of a couple of workmen yelling to each other downstairs. "…if they might not have the security they think they're getting here?"

"I don't know. I—"

Kylie's gaze snapped to something behind Jill, and she whirled around to see what it was.

The blood drained from her face at the sight of Mr. Steele standing just below them on the stairs glaring at them, as if he'd been on his way up and had stopped when he'd heard what Jill had said. The folder slipped from Jill's hands and hit the floor with a *thwack*.

Slowly, he continued to the top of the stairs, his steely gaze affixed to her. "Miss Martin."

Her body went numb. This was the first time he'd actually indicated that he knew—or cared—who she was.

"Yes, sir?"

"Would you come with me, please?"

As he strode purposefully toward his office, Jill quickly picked up the folder then turned to look at Kylie, whose wide-eyed look offered little comfort. Obeying Mr. Steele's command, Jill felt like her feet were made of lead.

By the time she entered his office, he was standing behind his desk, tapping at a keyboard and dividing his attention between two computer screens. He glanced up, his demeanor less tense than it had been just a few moments before.

"Oh, shut that door, will you? Thank goodness that construction won't be going on for much longer. I can't hear myself think."

She did as he asked, then took a few cautious steps into the room.

He glanced up again, then waved her forward. "It's come to my attention that you have a concern."

Her stomach fell so far she felt like she'd have to go downstairs to retrieve it. Obviously, he had heard at least some of what she had just said to Kylie. She fumbled for a reasonable explanation, but before she could speak, he continued.

"It's nothing." He waved a hand like the issue was some kind of pesky insect he wanted to kill. "Don't give it another thought."

"Oh. Okay." Her mind raced. How could he say her concern was nothing without asking her what it actually was?

"Tests for toxicity are standard practice in our industry." He kept looking down at his screen, adding to the casual lack of concern in his words. "That's one way we find breaches that need to be corrected."

Tests for toxicity? Was this about that report? But…how could he know she'd seen it? She hadn't told anyone, not even Kylie.

"Did you uh…" He frowned, distracted by something on the screen. "Did you read it?"

"Read it?"

"Yes." He looked up at her. "The toxicity report. Did you read it?"

"Oh...n..." Her jaw worked but her voice seemed to catch in her throat. What was going on here? "...no. I mean...not really."

One corner of his mouth lifted slightly. Or had she just imagined it?

"That's good." He gave a decisive nod. "Those things contain a lot of words that look scary to the unpracticed eye. There's no point in someone who's not been trained in the science of it all attempting to comprehend. The same would be true of many things you might come across around here. It's best for you not to try to decipher something you're not equipped to interpret."

She felt herself droop at the sting of his obvious affront. "I understand."

"Good." His attention returned to the screen and he began rapidly typing once more. "You, uh...shredded it along with the rest of the papers, then?"

Shredded? She hadn't. But it had been recycled with everything else. "It...it's..." she stammered, "...*gone.*"

"Good." He glanced up briefly, appearing satisfied with her vague answer. "That was all."

Feeling dismissed in more ways than one, she turned and reached for the doorknob.

"And I'm emailing you a list of basic questions about geothermal energy."

She turned back, puzzled.

He went on. "I'd like you to research the questions that don't have answers yet, and I'll use it as a Q and A for the employee orientation. Better to pass it out in written form than for me to have to answer the same things over and over again."

"Okay." Her hand hovering midair, she lingered awkwardly, questioning once again if he had any idea what her actual job was.

"Write the answers out in a way that the average novice can understand. You know." He flicked her a glance. "In a way that would make sense to someone like *you*."

She nodded, wondering if he was done insulting her for the day. When he didn't add any more, she reached for the door again.

"Oh, and Miss Martin."

The screech of a distant drill would have made it easy to pretend she hadn't heard him, but she faced him again anyway. "Yes?"

"Don't go onto the production floor." He flipped a casual hand in that direction. "The workers are moving fast to finish and they don't need any distractions. Besides, things can get dangerous. I'd hate to see you…" His eyes finally landed in solid contact with hers. "…*get hurt*."

What should have felt like concern for her well-being struck her as a warning of a more sinister nature. Struggling to get a good breath, she nodded and fumbled with the doorknob.

As she moved down the catwalk and back toward the conference area, her face started to burn. What had just happened in there?

Kylie met her halfway. "Is he mad? Because of what we were talking about?"

Feeling a little faint, Jill shook her head and veered toward her desk instead. "I don't really think he heard anything."

Kylie closed her eyes and let out a breath. "Well, what did he say?"

"Oh…uh…he's giving me a thing to work on. It's a Q and A to add to your folders."

Kylie frowned. "Why did he give it to you? The folders are *my* job."

She shook her head. "I…don't know. But maybe you should hold off on putting them together till I get it ready."

"I'm sick of working on that anyway." Kylie batted a hand in the direction of the table. "Hey, it's almost noon." She started toward her own desk. "Wanna go eat lunch down in the old picnic area?"

"That sounds really nice." But as Jill moved to retrieve her brown-bag lunch from her drawer, a thought struck her. "Actually, I have a better idea." She plucked her keys out of her purse. "We're taking a long lunch."

"Okay by me." Slipping an arm into her coat sleeve, Kylie smiled like a high schooler about to ditch math class. "Where are we going?"

Jill finally relaxed as a plan to put her mind at ease took form. "How about if we go have lunch with Jackson?"

Jill Came Tumbling After

Chapter 27

On the way to the Madison Falls Utility Commission office, Jill filled Kylie in on everything that had contributed to her feelings of unease. The toxicity report, then Mr. Steele's odd reaction when he saw her looking at the cracked wall. Jackson's outlook on the situation, and the entire bizarre conversation with Mr. Steele that morning.

"It's like a Nancy Drew mystery or something," Kylie exclaimed as Jill took the turn that would lead them east of Madison Falls, into farm country and toward the main highway. "That makes you Nancy and me Georgia Fayne. You can just call me George."

"I had no idea you were so into literature." Jill couldn't help but smile at her sidekick's youthful enthusiasm.

"I've read every single book in that series." Clearly, Kylie took genuine pride in that academic achievement. "Oh, turn left up ahead. Right before that barn."

Jill eased down the dusty road that she must have passed a zillion times and never noticed. No wonder she had no idea this place even existed.

"That's it," Kylie announced, as she pointed to an inconspicuous freestanding building up ahead. "Work, sweet work for my sweetie."

Jill parked in the small lot that was empty except for an older-model Corolla that she assumed belonged to Jackson.

As they got out of the car and started toward the building—Jill clutching her brown paper sack and Kylie swinging her pink PowerPuff Girls lunch bag—Jill blinked away a pesky tear. She remembered back in high school when she used to show up at the lumberyard to surprise Caleb with a picnic lunch. He always chided her for embarrassing him in front of the guys, but she knew he secretly loved it. Watching Kylie bounding enthusiastically toward the plain front door with an *Open* sign hanging in its window, Jill said a prayer that life would have kinder things in store for her young friend *George*.

A tinny-sounding bell announced their arrival, and Jackson glanced up from behind a tall counter. He broke into a lovestruck grin, then blushed slightly when his focus broadened to include Jill.

"Hi, honey!" Kylie swung her bag onto the counter, then leaned on her forearms to give him an innocent kiss.

"I feel honored." He nodded a greeting at Jill. "Nobody ever comes by to visit me. Not even my mom." He lifted a section of the countertop, then pushed a hinged gate and gestured for them to join him. "But this is a long way for you ladies to come for lunch."

"Actually…" Kylie took on a conspiratorial tone as they followed him to a desk with a computer and a small mountain of overstuffed files on it. "Jill and I are playing detective."

Jackson chuckled. "Detective?" He took a stack of binders off an old straight-back chair and moved it next to another one already situated by the side of the desk.

"Yes." Feeling a little silly now, Jill fingered the fold at the top of her lunch bag. "I'm sorry to bother you. But when we were talking the other day, you said something about Kylie's job maybe not lasting long. I was hoping you could tell us why you think that."

"I'm sorry." He gestured for them to sit, then opened a small fridge behind his desk and took out an ancient-looking black-metal lunch box. "I didn't mean to alarm you." Looking contrite, he sat in the cracked-vinyl desk chair that was probably twice as old as he was. "I believe in getting the facts, and sometimes I forget that other people get emotional. Kylie reminds me of that all the time."

"Yin to his yang." Perching on the chair closest to Jackson, Kylie waggled a finger between them.

"No, it's okay." Jill took the other seat. "But you said their plan is unsustainable. What did you mean by that?"

Sighing, Jackson removed a wax-paper-wrapped sandwich from his lunch box. "I don't want to stir anything up."

"Please." Jill took out her own sandwich, even though her appetite had dwindled. "A lot of people are counting on their new jobs at the factory. If there's a problem, I think we all need to know."

Jackson looked to Kylie for confirmation, then cleared his throat. "We approved the permits they applied for to allow them to drill into the mountain." He cast a quick look over at the door, as if to assure himself that no one else had snuck in unnoticed. "But when they hired Kylie, I dug a little deeper. Just to be sure."

"To be sure…of *what*, exactly?"

"I really didn't know." He took a bite of his tuna sandwich. "I didn't know anything about geothermal energy. It sounds like such a good thing, but something didn't quite sit right."

"What do you mean?"

"It was just a feeling I got. Not from Dean, but from that other guy." He looked at Kylie. "What's his name?"

"Mr. Steele." Kylie answered through a bite of bagel.

"Right. He didn't want to wait for the permits to be approved and he kept asking if there were ways around that. He said they wanted to do the drilling before the word got out that they were doing it. Like he was afraid of community resistance or something. I just kept thinking, if this thing is as great as you keep saying it is, why would anyone object?"

Jill nodded thoughtfully. "So, you looked into the company?"

"The company is new, so I came up dry there, so to speak."

Kylie tittered, prompting a half smile from Jackson.

"But then I researched the industry." He shrugged his eyebrows. "First time it's actually paid off for me to work for the UC. I have access to records that other people might not know how to get. Or how to read if they did find them."

Jill's stomach clenched. "Would you mind sharing what you found?"

Nodding, he wiped his hands on a paper napkin and adjusted the screen so they could all see it. "I'm sure you both understand how geothermal energy works." He began typing.

"Yes. They drill way down into the earth and bring up steam that they use to generate electricity."

"Basically. And it's a renewable energy source."

"Renewable. So, why would you say it's unsustainable?"

"Wel, the energy source itself is highly sustainable if the process is done right." He scrolled down a page filled with exposition. "But it has its complications. See, the steam that comes up from the earth's core isn't just water." He stopped scrolling and pointed to a list of chemicals on the screen.

Jill recognized the scary substances she'd seen on the report. "And what happens to all of that?"

"The toxic matter needs to be separated out from the clean steam. This produces a kind of sludge that then has to be disposed of."

Her stomach turned, and she put her sandwich back in her bag.

Jackson continued. "So I started to dig around in the water records from geothermal plants around the world."

He brought up a different screen, this one just a spreadsheet filled with numbers and words that might as well have been Greek as far as Jill was concerned. By the squinty-eyed way Kylie studied it, it was clear that she felt the same.

Jackson pointed to the screen. "These other power stations all have permits for proper disposal of the waste, and records of compliance. Nyland, on the other hand, hasn't applied for the permits to dispose of any hazardous waste."

"They got behind on some things," Kylie interceded. "Maybe they just haven't gotten around to that yet."

"It's not exactly a minor detail. Before they can apply for the permits, they have to order an environmental impact study, which they haven't done. That takes time to complete. And they've already done their drilling. They've scheduled test runs to make sure everything works. Those tests are going to generate toxic waste that will need to be properly disposed of. As far as I can tell, they haven't made a plan for it. At least, not a legal one."

"But…" Jill chewed her lip. "I read something in those papers they had us shred about groundwater contamination. Surely they're aware of the potential problems. Why wouldn't they want to properly dispose of toxic waste?"

"I wondered the same thing." He typed for a minute, then pulled up another screen. "This is the cost analysis for a small plant in Norway, about the same size as the one we have here. If you look at how much money they spend on toxic waste disposal every year…" He picked up his phone and started tapping. "…and convert that to American dollars…" He held up his phone.

Kylie almost choked. "That's a lot of zeros."

"That's over a quarter of a million dollars." Jill had to look twice to make sure she was seeing the number correctly. "Are you saying that if Nyland doesn't properly dispose of the waste, he stands to clear that much extra in a year?"

"Hey, I'm just pointing out the facts." Jackson shook his head. "But from where I sit, it looks like he would have a nice financial incentive not to play by the rules."

"But, Nyland Enterprises is all about environmental safety." Jill wanted so badly for this all to make sense. "They have to have a plan. And if they don't, people would find out, right? Isn't this a matter of public record?"

"Only if anyone bothered to ask. And in all the time I've worked here, no one has come in off the street to ask about a company's permits."

"But won't the EPA ask to see the permits?"

"Right." Kylie had put her bagel down and started fidgeting in her chair. "The EPA is inspecting us at the end of this week. If there's a problem, won't they call us out on it?"

"You would think so." Jackson's chair complained loudly as he sat back. "I mean, that's their job. But what if they don't? The company isn't up and running yet, they wouldn't necessarily see a problem. That kind of thing would show up later."

"Show up…" A bad feeling churned in Jill's chest. "…how?"

"If the chemicals got into the groundwater, that would affect anything living in the area. Plants, trees, wild life." He paused, his voice getting quieter. "People."

Jill drew in a sharp breath. "But…how could they let it go that far?"

"You hear all kinds of stories." Jackson's helpless look did little to inspire confidence. "About communities getting slowly poisoned. People getting sick and no one knowing why. By the time they start to connect the dots, it's too late, and the big industry has so much power and money behind it that no one can fight them."

Her stomach burning, Jill looked from Jackson to Kylie. "What do you guys think we should do?"

Kylie's lower lip quivered, like she might start to cry.

"I don't know." Jackson lifted a one-shoulder shrug. "It's like you said. A lot of people are counting on those jobs."

They sat in silence as the implications of his words sank in.

Then Jill jolted. "What time is it? We need to get back." She shoved her mostly untouched lunch back into her bag and stood. "Thanks for your help, Jackson."

Jackson rose to his feet and shoved his hands in his pockets, looking like he wished he'd had better news.

The three of them stepped out into the crisp autumn air that seemed to have gotten chillier while they'd been inside. Jackson accompanied Kylie to the passenger side and opened the door for her.

"Thanks, honey." She gave him a quick kiss on the cheek and slipped into the car.

Jill was about to open her door but paused as Jackson started back toward the building.

"Jackson?"

He stopped, then stepped toward her.

"Does it bother you that Kylie is working for a company that might be trying to cut corners?"

"A job's a job, I guess. But if we're really uncovering something here...I don't know." Looking off into the distance, his young face turned grim. "If they do improperly dispose of toxic waste, they could keep that up for who knows how long. By that time, the damage could be enormous."

Nodding weakly, she got into the driver's seat and shut the door.

"So." Kylie slumped low in her seat, her normally upbeat attitude having considerably diminished. "What do we do now?"

Jill sighed as she started the engine, then turned to check the long stretch of road for the unlikelihood of traffic. "I wish I knew."

Jill Came Tumbling After

Chapter 28

Jill spent the rest of the afternoon in a haze of confusion. No matter how much she told herself that the EPA would make sure that Nyland had a plan for handling its waste disposal, she couldn't shake Jackson's words. *The damage could be enormous.* What if this company really was trying to get away with something?

She sat at her desk, staring at her computer screen.

"You okay?"

Jill jumped, not realizing that Kylie was standing beside her. "I'm fine. I'm just trying to get the hang of this internet thing. I haven't really used it apart from sending email."

"I can help you." Kylie pulled up a chair and plunked down next to her. "What are you trying to do?"

"Just finding the rest of these answers for Mr. Steele's Q and A list."

"That is super easy. All you have to do is copy the question and paste it in the bar right here. Then click on the magnifying glass, and presto. Instant answers. You can click on whatever headline you want and it'll take you to that site."

"Thanks, Kylie." She tapped on the first tab, where she'd brought up the email. "I know you must think I've been living in a cave or something."

"Naw. Not a cave. Just a small town." Frowning, Kylie studied the questions on the screen. "Well, that's not right."

"What?"

She pointed to the bottom of the screen. "That last question. 'What are the potential dangers of geothermal energy?'"

Jill stared at the screen, her eyes narrowing on Mr. Steele's answer. *None.*

Kylie huffed out annoyance. "If what Jackson showed us is true"—she leaned down, biting out the words in a near-whisper—"there *are* possible dangers. Don't you think the new employees should be told the truth?"

Jill nodded. "Absolutely."

"Then change his answer. Sheesh. I mean, he gave you this assignment. You have to do it right."

"But, what if he—"

"So *what* if he doesn't like it? He can't argue with the facts."

"The facts, huh?" Jill chuckled. "You are *so* Jackson's girl."

She copied the question and pasted it into the search bar at the top of the screen, the way Kylie had shown her. When she clicked the magnifying glass, a daunting selection of headings appeared. Her breath caught in her throat.

"Oh my goodness." She scrolled down. "Kylie. There's so much information here. I wish I had time to read it all. If I had a computer at home—"

"I bet you could find some books. Go to the library website."

"Wait, they have a website? Our little library?"

"Welcome to the twenty-first century." Kylie tittered. "*Everyone* has a website."

An hour later, Jill had put five books on hold—two of them on alternative energy, two on environmental waste, and one on industrial whistleblowing. She'd had no idea that their little library branch had access to books from libraries all over the state. To her astonishment, Elaine—the head librarian—

actually thought they'd arrive tomorrow. Upgrading to this new century certainly had its perks.

Just as she finished composing the last answer to the Q and A list and hit the Print button, the phone on her desk rang and she practically jumped out of her skin. Why was she still so on edge?

She picked up the receiver. "Nyland Enterprises. This is Jill."

"I haven't been able to get to the grocery store. I'll be taking the children to the diner for supper."

"Mom?"

Silence. Then, "Who did you *think* it was?"

Jill let out a sigh. "Great. I'll meet you there after work. Oh, but where will you leave the puppy?"

"He'll be crated in my kitchen. You can swing by after you pick up the children." Pause. "He's a good dog. Riley's very fond of him."

Jill frowned. Her mom had never expressed the smallest sentiment for an animal, which was why Jill had never asked for so much as a goldfish when she was growing up. Strange to witness any hint of her mother's soft side.

"Did Sam finish fixing your sink?"

"He came on Saturday. It took him quite a while, but it's fine now."

"Okay, Mom. I'll see you after five." She ended the call and went to close the tab with all her research on it. But she stopped when something disturbing caught her eye.

Heart and lung issues in the older population are prominent. Various ailments in children, including asthma and cancer…

She closed the screen. This was too much for her to dwell on. Besides, it wasn't like she didn't have more pressing things to think about.

Like, for example, how she was going to save her house.

Chapter 29

When Jill entered the Country Kitchen, the smell of fried chicken and pie made her stomach growl, reminding her that she never had gotten around to eating the rest of her bagged lunch.

She spotted her mom and the kids in a booth by the window and headed toward them. The dim hope that her mom might offer to buy her dinner too evaporated the second Mom saw her and instantly slid out of the booth.

"There's your mama, Riley." Mom wasted no time pulling on her coat. "I was starting to think I wouldn't make it home in time for the *Wheel*."

Coming from anyone else, that comment would have brought a chuckle. But Jill knew how serious her mom was about her nightly game show lineup.

"Well, I'm here now, Mom. Thanks. We'll be by in a bit to pick up the dog." As she bent to kiss Emma's head and ruffle Riley's hair, she eyed the half-eaten chicken strips and fries still on Riley's plate. How pathetic would it be for her to have Glo box them up so she could eat them herself when she got home and save a little on the grocery budget?

As she straightened, she caught her mom eying her critically. "What?"

"You really should consider wearing lipstick, Jillian." Her own lips pursed in severe disapproval. "People will talk."

Jill huffed out a breath. "What are they going to talk *about?* My shocking lack of glamour?"

Mom shook her head and lowered her voice. "They'll speculate about the reasons why you can't keep a man."

Apparently uninterested in hearing Jill's response to that, Mom turned and beat a hasty retreat as Glo came around the counter carrying a coffee pot.

"Have a nice evening, Marion." Glo called after Mom, then gave Jill a wink. "Why don't you sit a spell and have some pie and coffee. On the house."

"Oh, that's awfully sweet, but—"

"No buts." Using the coffee pot, she gestured for Jill to sit. "You could stand a dose of sweet to counteract some of that sour." She tipped her head in the direction of the door still reverberating from Mom's exit.

Jill smiled. Nothing ever got past Glo. "Got any apple?" Inhaling the intoxicating aroma of coffee, she eased into the booth.

Glo turned over the cup and started to pour. "Any word about the..." She flicked a glance at Riley. "...w-e-l-f-a-r-e?"

"Not yet. I should hear from them this week. Did you know that having a job is a requirement in order to qualify?"

"Is it? Well then, thank the good Lord that new company decided to put down stakes here. It's everything we've been praying for ever since the mine shut down." She picked up Riley's abandoned plate. "I'll just box this up for you, sugar."

As Glo headed for the kitchen, a couple with a little boy entered the diner and headed for the empty booth next to Jill's. The woman smiled at her in recognition.

"Oh, hi." She touched the man's arm and gestured toward Jill. "Arnie, this is Jill from that Mommy and Me group that Trevor and I were in. You remember."

"My goodness. Vickie." Jill felt her face heat in humiliation at not even recognizing the woman she had practically begged to babysit for her just a week before. "Riley, say hi to Trevor."

Trevor had already climbed into the neighboring booth, and the two boys were playing some sort of air raid game over the back of the seat.

Vickie smiled warmly. "Sorry if we're a little exuberant. We're celebrating. My husband's been out of work and he just got hired at that new factory."

"I'm working there too." Jill smiled at Arnie. "Are you part of the crew that's starting next week?"

As Arnie filled her in on the details of his new position, Glo reappeared carrying a tray, along with a couple of menus, which she set on the table for Vickie and Arnie.

"I'll be with you folks in just a minute." She sidestepped over to Jill and transferred a to-go box and a plate of pie from the tray to the table. "I assumed you'd want it à la mode."

Jill inhaled the rich cinnamony aroma and her mouth started to water. "You assumed right." Picking up her fork, she eyed the box that was way too big for the tiny amount of food Riley had left. "Glo. What did you do?" She cracked it open and saw that Glo had supplemented the leftovers with an additional order of chicken and fries, and had even added a small container of coleslaw.

Glo gave her another wink. "Buck cooked up way too many fries tonight and they were just going to go to waste."

Blinking against threatening tears, she looked up at Glo and muttered, "Thank you." As she closed the box, she cast a quick glance around the diner, which hadn't been hit with the dinner rush just yet. "Glo, do you have a sec?"

"Why sure, sweetie." She relaxed her stance. "What's on your mind?"

"I've been meaning to ask you. Why *did* the mine shut down?"

"It was a real mystery. It just closed one day. People were sent home in the middle of their shift." Glo looked up toward the ceiling, like she was trying to remember. "There was some question about bookkeeping. Something about funds going missing. I don't think anyone ever knew for sure. And then the owners just up and left."

"No kidding? That explains why they abandoned personal belongings. The place feels like it was frozen in time."

"Well, isn't that just fascinating?" Glo brightened. "Maybe you'll come across that missing money."

"Wouldn't *that* be nice." As Jill dug into her pie, a movement outside caught her attention. Sam had backed his truck up to the sidewalk in front of the hardware store, and he and Caleb were loading some bags into it. Even in the waning light of day, she could tell that Caleb looked weary—like the effort it took to hoist those bags was almost too much for him.

"He's a good man, sweetie."

Jill blinked, shifting her attention from the scene outside back to Glo, who looked from the window to Jill.

Leaning in, Glo patted her on the shoulder. "He's just lost sight of what really matters is all."

"I know." Jill nodded. "I wish I could fix that for him."

"You've done all you can, and then some." Glo rested a hand on Jill's and gave it a reassuring squeeze. "All you can do now is keep taking it to the man upstairs."

As Glo went to take Vickie and Arnie's order, Jill pondered. Glo was right. She had to talk to God about this. About all of it.

She closed her eyes. *Lord, what should I do? About Caleb and our house. And now about this problem at work.*

Her eyes slowly opened, and she looked around, seeing several familiar faces, some of whom she knew were on the list of new-hires.

Lord, everyone is counting on this factory to turn around our economy. If I say something, will all these people lose their jobs before they've even gotten a chance to start?

Vickie and Arnie clanked their water glasses together. They looked so happy, like a weight had been lifted for them. Vickie's eyes caught Jill's and she lifted her glass toward her. Jill smiled wanly, then raised the half-full glass that her mom had probably sipped from while she'd waited for Jill.

She sighed. *But if I ignore the problem, will toxic waste contaminate our drinking water?* Her eyelids dropped again. *Please, God. If there's a problem, send someone else to take care of it. It's all just too much for me.*

Suddenly, a thought hit her and her eyes snapped open. *That report.* There was something about it that she was overlooking. Something important.

Mr. Steele had acted nonchalant about it, but he had obviously been concerned. Why would he have bothered to ask her if she'd read it and confirmed that it had been shredded if he didn't have something to hide?

Emma playfully slapped her palms down on the highchair tray, and her binky went flying. Both boys stopped their game and looked at her, then Riley scooted over to retrieve the binky from the seat where it had landed. He blew on it, like he'd seen Jill do a hundred times, then placed it gently in his sister's mouth.

A sob worked its way up Jill's throat. These precious children's future was worth more than anything. If even one of them, or one of *their* future children, was in danger because Jill had been too scared and shortsighted to do the right thing…

That was it. That was her answer. The future of this community was in danger, and it was up to her and Kylie and Jackson to put a stop to it. Yes, she needed this job as much as any of the new hires. But maybe God had something bigger in mind.

Shifting a bite of pie around on her plate, she pondered her next move. If only she had kept that half piece of paper, Jackson might have been able to see something on it that would help. It wasn't much, but, apart from their suspicions, it was all they had to go on. And she'd stuffed it into the bag with the shreds.

Then another thought struck her. Mom had said it had taken a while for Sam to fix her sink. Maybe he hadn't made it to the recycling plant on Saturday. And if memory served, the plant was closed on Sundays but stayed open late on Mondays. Knowing Sam, he wouldn't want to take time out of his workday to drive out there, but he might plan to do a run before heading home for the night.

She sat up straighter. Outside, Caleb disappeared into the hardware store while Sam started for the driver's side of his truck. Her heart thrummed at the realization that those bags they'd just loaded might be the store's recycling, and that hers might be in there too. If she didn't hurry, she stood to lose the only piece of evidence she had, for the second time. Some detective she was.

Before she knew what she was doing, she was on her feet, pulling Emma from the high chair. "Vickie. Would you mind keeping an eye on Riley for a few minutes? I just need to run outside and ask someone a question."

Vickie's puzzled look quickly dissolved into an understanding smile. "Oh, sure. No problem."

Hiking Emma on her hip, Jill hustled out the door just as Sam backed his truck away from the curb.

She darted into the street, waving her free arm. "Sam!"

His truck jerked to a stop, then he rolled back into his parking space. As he got out of the truck, Jill hurried the rest of the way across the street.

He eyed her curiously as he shut the truck door. "Everything okay?"

She paused to catch her breath. "Did you take those bags to the recycling center?"

He hesitated, looking at her like he was once again assessing her sanity. "I took them on Saturday, right after I finished at your mom's. Got there just before they closed. Why?"

Exhaling, she gave a slow blink. A hard lump of disappointment formed in her chest as she awkwardly hovered between telling him everything and returning to the diner where she'd left her son in the care of virtual strangers. What was wrong with her?

"I just…. Never mind. It's nothing."

"Okay..." He squinted at her, then shook it off. "Well, if that was all, I need to get this delivery made and get home. Grace has some free time after her rehearsal tonight and I don't want to miss her call. We haven't been able to talk much because of the time difference. And her rehearsal schedule is insane." His jaw worked and he let out a sigh. "I'm telling you, Jill, this is harder than I thought it would be."

She nodded. Why was she almost happy to hear that they were having a conflict? Like this was her opening to begin driving a wedge between them if she wanted to. She knew that would be wrong but part of her wanted to do it anyway.

If she could just say that perfect thing to make him see that maybe he should have looked at her as more than a friend way back before she chose Caleb. That the things that complicated his relationship with Grace would never enter into a relationship with her. That maybe it wasn't too late for all of them to make a fresh start.

But instead, all she could think to say was, "It's going to be okay, Sam."

He studied her, eyes narrowing. Then he drew in a long breath and looked away. When his gaze returned to her, he smiled lightly and opened up his arms to enclose both her and Emma in what felt like a very *brotherly* hug.

"I needed to hear that right now." He stepped back, his hands lingering on her shoulders. "You always know the right thing to say."

She tried to give him a self-assured smile that said "Yeah, don't I though?" Instead, she let out a nervous titter that sounded like a cat getting its tail stepped on. She *never* knew the right thing to say, and this pretty much confirmed it.

She was about to add something lame about love triumphing over all when the door to the hardware store burst open and Caleb appeared like a bull out of the chute.

"Get your hands off my wife!" he bellowed as he hurled himself toward Sam.

Jill screamed and leaped back, protectively enclosing Emma more tightly in her arms. The force of Caleb's charge propelled both him and Sam out into the middle of the street.

In a flurry of confusion, Sam's dad ran from the store and several other people appeared from up and down the block. The only thing that saved this from becoming a complete community spectacle was that most of the businesses on Main Street were closed for the night and the majority of the town was home having dinner.

A bunch of guys pulled Caleb off of Sam. He wiped blood from his lip as he shook them off and backed away.

He fired a glare in her direction, then looked around at the small crowd of expectant faces. He huffed out another breath, then turned and charged toward the hardware store. Then, apparently rethinking his aim, he swerved and set his course for the Spur.

As the crowd grumbled amongst themselves and began to disperse, Jill went to Sam, who still stood in the street catching his breath. "Are you okay?"

"He's given me worse." He rubbed his jaw. "Look, I'm really sorry, but I need to make this delivery." Giving her one last remorseful look, he got into his truck and started the engine.

Jill moved to the sidewalk and watched as he pulled away from the curb and disappeared around the corner. After casting one more rueful glance back at the Spur, she headed toward the diner, feeling more confused—and alone—than ever.

Jill Came Tumbling After

Chapter 30

When Jill arrived at work the following morning, the painters were already busy covering everything on the conference side of the second floor with tarps. The noise from downstairs, where the construction crew appeared to be working twenty-four seven these days, seemed to have grown louder as the deadline for the project's completion neared. Jill had begun to wonder if the place would feel tomb-like by comparison once the actual production began.

Glancing at the closed office doors, she assumed that her bosses were already busy doing whatever it was that kept them holed up in there most days. Her face went hot at the thought of disturbing Dean, especially now that they were so under the gun, but she'd come to the realization that the next best step was to just ask him what the plan was for disposal of toxic waste at this factory. She would know by his answer if she had anything to worry about.

Pushing aside an irritating wave of self-doubt, she approached his door and raised a jittery hand. But before she could knock, the sound of voices inside gave her pause.

"I gave you specific instructions."

Jill flinched at what sounded like Mr. Steele reprimanding someone, presumably Dean. Holding her breath, she angled her ear closer to the door.

"Yes, I fully realize that." Dean sounded justifiably upset. *The poor guy.*

"It was my understanding that we had filled those positions with…"

The sharp whine of a saw from the production floor cut into Mr. Steele's words, and she leaned in even closer.

"…with no knowledge of the industry. To take this kind of initiative…"

Jill felt her breath catch in her throat. What was he talking about? And was he being condescending or complimentary? It was impossible to tell.

As she strained to hear more, a whirring sound startled her. She reeled back, almost to the catwalk railing, before realizing that the sound had come from some distance away. She looked over at the old elevator just as Kylie appeared through the bars, rising slowly and beaming like she'd just experienced the latest attraction at Disneyland.

Catching sight of Jill, she bounced on her toes. "This thing still works!"

Giving up on both her mission to speak with Dean and her futile hope of doing more eavesdropping, she walked over to congratulate Kylie on her successful test run of the freshly awakened lift.

The platform came even with the floor and wobbled to a stop, then Kylie clanked open the cage-like doors and got out. "Now that was fun."

"I'm glad you're here. I've been thinking." Jill cast a quick glance at the still-closed office doors before continuing. "If *we* have questions about the waste disposal, other people might too, right?"

"Makes sense."

"So I'm going to ask Dean. It's a perfectly valid question."

The sound of a door opening turned their heads. As if on cue, Dean exited his office and headed their way.

Kylie angled toward her and spoke softly. "Looks like now's your chance."

"Good morning." Dean smiled tightly as he approached. "I have news."

Kylie and Jill exchanged a glance. Judging from the creases on his face, it didn't look like this was *good* news.

"Mr. Nyland will be arriving the day after tomorrow."

Despite the lilt at the end of his sentence, or maybe *because* of it, Jill suspected that Dean's stress levels had been amped up by this announcement. And something told her that the same would soon be true for her.

He lifted an index finger at Kylie. "I'm going to need you to make some changes to the training folders." He cleared his throat, then loosened his collar like he'd just realized that his tie was too tight. "If you'll get those ready, I'll be back with further instructions."

"Super." Kylie's jaw firmed in obvious frustration. She'd spent a good part of yesterday finishing those folders so she could move on to the next thing on her list.

"Come with me." Making an abrupt about face, Dean waved for Jill to follow.

The knot that had been in her stomach for the better part of the past week tightened as she trailed him onto the catwalk.

He skimmed a look over his shoulder in the general direction of the painters, who were now busy putting up their scaffolding. "When is the painting scheduled to be finished?"

"They hope to have this floor done in a week."

She expected him to lead her into his own office but when he kept walking, she stole a peek through the open door. No one was inside. The awareness that Mr. Steele had returned to his own lair made her suddenly feel like a lamb being led to slaughter. But when Dean passed that door as well, she breathed a little easier.

A glance at his watch seemed to quicken Dean's steps, and Jill hurried to keep up. She looked ahead in confusion. The only other possible destination was the door at the end of the catwalk. Mr. Nyland's office. In all her time here, she'd never seen anyone enter or exit that room.

Removing a substantial keyring from his pocket that looked like a prop from a prison movie, Dean stopped at Mr. Nyland's door and began sorting through the keys. "I know you have a lot on your plate." He selected a key and rattled it in the lock. "But I'm hoping you can do some work in here." He pushed the door open, and Jill tilted a look past him, having no idea what to expect.

He stepped into the room and she paused in the doorway. A strange sensation that she didn't quite know how to interpret slid over her as she took in the room that felt both out of place and exactly right, somehow. Utilitarian, like the rest of the building, but grand in a way, with its high ceiling and tall windows gracing two of its walls.

Apart from an antique desk and chair that were the focal point of the space, whatever had remained of this room's former tenant had been removed. The smells of disinfectant and fresh paint still lingered.

Dean seemed to read her thoughts. "I had it cleaned and painted before doing anything else in the building, of course."

She nodded, as though providing a tidy space for their absentee boss was a logical first step, even ahead of evicting the building's rodent population.

"I thought this would suffice," Dean said as he took a couple more steps into the room. "But now that I'm seeing what you're doing in the other rooms, I just want to be sure that this office is up to that level."

Jill turned her head so he wouldn't see her blush at that compliment.

"So…" He moved to the center of the room and spread his hands while doing a full three sixty. "What do you think?"

She regarded the barebones décor. Other than the desk and a sleek-looking computer sitting on it, it was basically empty. The drapes had been cleaned, but that long bank of observation windows next to the door looked even drearier from this side.

"I think I'd start by replacing those." She indicated the decades-old blinds that, in spite of what had probably been a decent effort by the cleaning crew, were all bent up and permanently coated in grime. She pivoted to the open area next to the front windows. "I picture a nice leather sofa and a couple of chairs over here. That would make the place cozier and give it an executive look."

Dean nodded in approval.

"I like the color of the walls, but they could use some artwork. I found a great black-and-white aerial shot of the building from when it was first built. That would look amazing behind the desk. And I know a photographer who sells framed shots of the falls and some other local sights. If you don't mind spending a little money—"

"No. I mean..." Dean's expression seemed more hopeful, like a load had been lifted. "That all sounds perfect. Do you think you can get it done in two days?" She must have winced, because he instantly looked apologetic. "I'm sorry I didn't realize the importance of this sooner."

"It's fine. I can call some furniture stores in Missoula and see what they have on hand. If we don't mind paying for the rush delivery—"

"Do what you need to do. We want Mr. Nyland to be pleased with what we've done here."

"I'll get right on it." She cleared her throat, calculating how to smoothly segue into her question about the waste disposal.

But before she could speak, Dean glanced at his watch again. A look of uneasiness washed over his face and she reconsidered her timing.

He shuffled his feet, a nervous move that was decidedly uncharacteristic for him. "There's something else that I need to discuss with you."

The tone of his voice, coupled with the way he suddenly wouldn't look her in the eye, felt disconcerting. What was going on?

"I just had a conversation with Mr. Steele. He's…concerned that you might be taking a bit too much initiative."

Too much initiative? So that conversation she'd overheard was about *her?*

"I…I'm sorry," she stammered. "I don't know what—"

"I explained to him that the Q and A should have been Kylie's responsibility. He never should have asked you to do that project."

"You mean, he's mad that I changed one of his answers? The one about the potential dangers?"

Dean nodded. "It's a public relations thing. Really, it's not your fault. They're being very pragmatic about how they present the details of this process to the public. No need to cause unnecessary alarm."

Unnecessary? "But, if there are actual dangers—"

"As I understand it"—Dean held up a hand—"the information you gave, while well-researched, doesn't apply to the process we'll be using here. Mr. Nyland has done extensive testing and has developed a new method of handling the potential hazards."

"You mean, the byproducts of the steam?"

"Yes. With this new method, the toxic substances are pumped back into the earth with the remaining steam. The environment is completely safe."

A cold feeling washed over her. Was he being truthful, or was there more to the plan than he was telling her? And, if push came to shove, would his loyalty be with the company or the community?

Giving a shrug, she hoped she appeared placated. "I guess I should have asked sooner."

"It's water under the bridge now. Or, through the turbines." He cracked a fleeting smile at his attempt at humor. "At any rate, I'll let you get to this."

He nodded again then made his exit, leaving her still reeling from embarrassment that Mr. Steele had been angry enough to speak to Dean about her. And exactly what else had he said? Something about her having no knowledge of the industry? That was true, all right. She'd demonstrated that in her lame excuse for an interview. But hadn't she proven herself in the job she'd been hired to do?

Rubbing her temples, she turned and looked at the room she had to make perfect for the big boss's imminent arrival. At least for now, she needed to keep her focus on her job.

There would be time later for addressing her deeper concerns.

Jill Came Tumbling After

Chapter 31

Jill had worked non-stop for hours on Mr. Nyland's office, and had left early to meet with Jerry, her local photographer friend, to pick out some prints to have framed. Then she'd picked up the kids early and hurried to the library before it closed.

Holding Emma in the sling, she secured her work bag, now weighted down with the five library books, over her shoulder. Riley skipped along the sidewalk beside her, contentedly clutching a picture book about dogs to his chest.

They reached the car and Jill opened the door to the backseat, where the crated puppy wriggled and yipped.

"Puppy!" Riley tossed his book onto his car seat and climbed in after it.

Jill sighed. At least it was easier to get him to cooperate with his canine cohort acting as an incentive. She dreaded the major meltdown he was sure to have when he realized they weren't going to be able to keep him.

Another worry for another day, she told herself as she shut his door and made her way around to the driver's side.

As she opened the backseat door for Emma, the startling sound of someone letting out a string of profanities drew her gaze to the front door of the bank. There, a hunched man wearing overalls and a grimace kicked a carved stone pilaster, then cursed even louder.

Lenny Simpson. Scowling Man.

That didn't look good. Maybe he'd just

had a meeting like the one she'd had with Mr. Stanley last week. Could be that he was behind on his mortgage too—only he probably had a farm and a family to support with the income it brought. And he'd been looking for a job to supplement that.

A wave of sympathy washed away some of the trepidation she'd felt about him. Maybe he was just another person trying to survive in a situation that had gotten away from him, and he didn't know how to handle his emotions about that.

Muttering to himself, he started down the stairs, and his eyes met hers. She froze. Why had Kylie made that comment about the chainsaw, anyway? It made it really hard to cultivate a feeling of good will toward him.

Shuddering, she hurried to get Emma's buckles secured, then straightened and looked up again. Scowling Man was gone.

She felt a hand on her arm and twisted around in a near scream.

"Sam." The tension in her body eased. "You scared me."

"Sorry." He held his hands up in mock surrender. "I'm glad I ran into you. We need to talk."

"I know." She glanced at the kids, not wanting them to be privy to any exchange about Caleb. Riley had opened his book and was pretending to read it to Emma and the puppy.

"So, tell me." She shut Emma's door and leaned against it. "What kind of shape is Caleb in today? How mad should I be?"

"I don't know."

"What do you mean? Didn't he go in to work with you today?"

"I haven't seen him since he walked into the Spur last night. He never came back to my place. I don't know where he is."

"Oh…" Confused, she ran through her mental checklist of all the places he might be, none of them good. "So…do you want me to go with you? I can ask Colleen if she can watch the kids—"

"Jill. I can't."

"What do you mean, you *can't?*" She stared at him. This wasn't the first time that Caleb had pulled a disappearing act, but this *was* the first time that Sam hadn't gone after him.

"Grace and I have been talking." Looking away, he rubbed the back of his neck. "She thinks I need to stop rescuing him, and she's right. I can't keep enabling him."

"Enabling? That's what Grace thinks?"

"And she's right." He nodded slowly. "I can see that now."

Jill went numb. "So, you're just abandoning me too then?" It was a completely unreasonable response, and she knew it. But she couldn't seem to help herself.

"It's not like that."

"Then what is it like? What am I supposed to do?"

"Please don't—"

"Forget it." She opened her car door.

"You're no better than him."

That wasn't true, of course. But, with what felt like a dramatic flair, she flung herself into the car, then gave the door a satisfying slam. Why was she acting this way? It was about as immature a response as she could have mustered, yet she was doing it anyway.

Adrenaline pumped through her as she stuck the key in the ignition and turned it. But instead of grumbling to life like it normally did, the engine made a grinding sound then went silent. She tried again. *Grind. Click.*

"No..." She muttered in defeat.

Her door opened.

"Want me to try?"

Could she possibly be more of a loser? She couldn't even manage a dramatic exit after pitching her lame diva fit.

Feeling like she had no other choice, she slid out of the car and stood there helplessly watching as Sam tried futilely to coax the engine to life.

He got out, looking at her with

sympathetic concern. "Let's put the kids in my truck. I'll take you all home, then give Bryce a call and see if he can fit you in tomorrow."

She briefly considered refusing his offer. But it was getting dark and she couldn't exactly haul her bags, the kids, and the dog home in one trip.

Wordlessly, she nodded.

"Need anything from your trunk?" He crossed around to the back as he spoke. "You might not have access to the car for a few days, so we really should take everything with us."

"Maybe." She retrieved her work bag and the diaper bag from the passenger seat, then shut the door. "I'll take a look."

As she stepped around to join him, a question roiled to the surface. "Sam. Be honest with me. Does Grace think you enable *me* too?"

He looked at the ground, then at her. "She loves that I look out for you like a sister." He looked down again, long enough for her to know there was more to his answer. "And that

I fill in where Caleb falls short. She's right. With your dad gone too. Not that he…"

He wisely left the sentence unfinished, undoubtedly knowing that she would complete it in her head. Her dad hadn't been much of a father.

He went on. "Someone has to fill that gap. Don't worry about it, Jill. You and the kids are like family."

Family. So he could help her with her car but not with tracking down her wayward husband. Where was that boundary supposed to fall? Sighing, she unlocked the trunk.

"I can take you to work tomorrow, if you want."

His offer was genuine, but sounded a bit too solicitous under the circumstances.

"It's okay." She lifted the lid. "You know my mom has that car she hardly ever drives."

He gave her a skeptical look. "You don't mind asking your mom for one more favor?"

She did mind, but at the moment it seemed more appealing than accepting another one from Sam, her professed enabler.

"She'll hate it, but she'll say yes."

While Sam went to get Riley, Jill scanned the contents of the trunk. All she saw were her tire jack, a little purple beach bucket from last summer's fishing trip to the Kicking Horse Reservoir, and an empty water bottle. Nothing she couldn't live without.

But as she raised her arm to shut the lid, something caught her eye. Frowning, she reached back into the shadows and clutched something soft and malleable. She pulled it toward her and gasped. A small white trash bag closed with a twisty tie.

One of the recycling bags?

Of course. She had told Sam that the bags that needed to go to the recycling center were black. He would naturally have assumed that this wasn't one of them.

A giddy feeling started in her stomach and worked its way up to her chest. That night when she'd found the report, her focus had been divided between what she was doing and her conversation with Colleen. She had a vague memory of shoving the report into a kitchen trash bag. Was that right?

She peered in, then poked around at the shreds. There it was…the corner of the report.

"What's in'a the bag, Mama?" Riley pointed from his perch on Sam's hip as the two of them appeared next to her.

"Just some…papers for work, sweetie." Smiling, she removed the half-page and stuffed it into her work bag then shut the trunk, feeling a renewed sense of hope.

At least something good had come out of her car not starting. She might not have had reason to look back here for weeks otherwise.

Chapter 32

After listening to what felt like at least a dozen versions of Riley's interpretation of his puppy picture book, Jill had finally escaped downstairs and settled on the sofa with a cup of hot tea. She retrieved her own library books from her bag and laid them out on the coffee table, then took out the report which was, not surprisingly, a little more crinkled than the last time she'd read it.

Positioned so the arm of the sofa supported

her back, she spread her crocheted afghan over her outstretched legs and studied the paper. She'd hoped for something to jump out as significant that she hadn't noticed before, but there was nothing. She took a sip of tea, and gazed out the front window at her dark, quiet neighborhood where nothing dramatic ever happened. Oh, how she longed for the days when life felt so uneventful it verged on tedium.

She set down her cup. If she wanted to understand what she was up against, it was time to get to work. Choosing the book closest to her—with the daunting title *Power, Profit, and Poison*—she said a quick prayer for some kind of enlightenment.

An hour—and two cups of chamomile—later, she found herself immersed in the chapter on government regulatory agencies.

Not only are the employees of government agencies overworked, but they are often under-trained. The result is an abundance of overwhelmed regulatory agents who are forced to rely heavily on the data provided by the very industry they've been assigned to regulate.

Well, *that* didn't seem right. Without looking up from the page, she took a sip of tepid tea and read on.

Adding to the conflict of interest inherent to such an underfunded system, many of these agents have backgrounds in the industries they are hired to regulate and, more often than not, will be returning to those very industries at some point in their career. The motivation for them to "overlook" potential problems can be enormous.

Disheartened, Jill stared at the page, the words blurring as her eyes started to tear up. She'd been hopeful that the EPA would be her saving grace, but now that hope waned.

She read on about several cases of small communities like hers becoming pockets of a peculiar array of symptoms. The victims were primarily children and senior citizens, but everyone was vulnerable.

And as if the loss of a loved one wasn't bad enough, the families were left to fight for justice against heartless industries that refused to claim responsibility or change their practices. In all of the cases described in this book, the working-class Davids were no match for the powerful and wealthy Goliaths, who could destroy them with legal costs before any kind of case against them made it to court. It was all incredibly depressing to read about.

Determined to ingest as much of this information as she could stomach, she kept reading.

Sadly, the effort to evaluate the effect of the multiple exposures of the hundreds of chemicals in our daily environment has been practically nonexistent. For the companies that profit from these poisons, there is just too much at stake.

Jill closed the book and rubbed her eyes, having reached her capacity for the night. This was all too much to take in.

Resting her forearms on the back of the sofa, she looked out the window and noticed a few snowflakes in the light from the streetlamp. She stood, stretched and yawned, then stepped out onto the front porch. Shivering, she pulled her sweater closer and sat on the top step next to the pumpkin she'd carved to look like a yowling cat.

There was something about the snow that made it seem even quieter out here. For a moment, she could almost convince herself that nothing bad could happen to them. That their home wouldn't be taken and the little issue at the factory would turn out to be just a misunderstanding.

But a tear rolled down her cheek, and then another. Who would take her in if she lost her house? Her mom would probably offer for the sake of the kids, but there was no way she'd put herself in that position, much less her kids.

Colleen would offer but, considering that she lived in a one-bedroom apartment, that would be a short-term solution at best. Of course, Sam wouldn't allow them to wind up homeless, but he and his dad had no room for them, especially if Caleb rematerialized.

She shuddered. Where *was* Caleb on this snowy night?

Not wanting to travel down that road of painful speculation, she redirected her thoughts back to her *own* need for shelter.

Grace was so kind, she would probably ask them to stay with her. But she shared a two-bedroom house with her mother. Of course, she'd be in New York for a while doing her opera, but still…. The last thing Jill wanted was to be a burden to anyone.

She wiped her wet cheeks with her sleeve. It was bad enough that she'd have to make ends meet on her salary—which had turned out to be what felt like a generous two thousand a month—but what if her amateur sleuthing cost her the only job she'd been able to find? She might be forced to move out of town just to get work.

The thought of uprooting her kids ignited

a slight panic. It wouldn't matter yet for Emma, but how could she take Riley away from the only life he'd ever known?

She pulled in a jittery breath. Who was she kidding? He was three. He would adapt just fine as long as he had his mommy and his toy car collection. It was Jill herself who didn't want to be uprooted. She loved Madison Falls. It was the only place she had ever lived or had ever wanted to live. She had to figure out a way to keep her life here.

And life *for everyone here…*

The unsettling feeling that the last thought had come from somewhere outside of her own head sent a shiver through her. The thought that she hadn't stumbled on this issue at the factory by accident but had in fact been given an assignment started to take root. Could that be true?

She gazed at the snow, which was coming down heavier now. In spite of everything, the soft blanket of white on the ground felt like a reassurance from God that they were covered.

Realizing that she'd probably stayed up way past her intended bedtime, Jill bent to turn off the battery-operated candles inside each of the jack-o-lanterns.

As she stood, a flash caught her eye and she noticed for the first time that there was a dark-colored sedan parked almost directly across the street. She wouldn't have noticed it at all, but the light from what had probably been a phone had momentarily illuminated the silhouette of a person sitting in the driver's seat.

A chill passed through her. This was a small town, and it was pretty unusual to see cars in her neighborhood that she didn't recognize. And for someone to just be sitting there, at this time of the night…

Her body began trembling. Whoever it was had been sitting there this whole time.

She hurried inside and locked the door, then went into the living room and pulled her curtains closed. A feeling of vulnerability threatened to overwhelm her, along with a fresh rush of missing her husband. Caleb wasn't good for a lot, but his presence in the house would have provided a sense of security.

The need to check on her kids propelled her up the stairs. After a quick reassuring look at each of them, she went into her own room and, leaving the light off, peeked through the curtain.

The snow was still falling, but in the place where the car had been, all that remained was a dark rectangle surrounded by white.

Jill Came Tumbling After

Chapter 33

"**H**old still, sweetie." Jill sat on the floor just inside the front door and said a little prayer that the snow boots she'd bought for Riley at the variety store's spring clearance sale would actually fit now that he needed them.

"Hurry, Mama. The snow's gonna melt." Riley held up his stockinged foot and leaned on her shoulder.

"I don't think there's an immediate danger of that." Holding her breath, she pushed his wiggling foot into the boot with ease. If anything, they were a little too big. *Thank You, Lord.* At least *something* had gone in her favor.

After getting the second boot on, she stood. "Now put your coat on. We need to get going."

In spite of her spending the night waking to the slightest sound—thanks to her getting worked up over what had probably been someone parked to answer a phone call or something equally innocuous—she'd gotten the kids up early. It would take a few extra minutes to walk to her mom's, not to mention the time she needed to allow for begging Mom to let her borrow her car to get to work. Sam had offered to pick them up, but she had refused. Maybe it was time for *both* of them to set some new boundaries. Besides, it was only a few blocks to her mom's, and the walk would do her good.

Of course, she hadn't realized that the first snowfall would coincide with her first day of being a pedestrian, but at least it had been easier to rally Riley with the promise of time in the snow.

Once she had her own coat on, she secured Emma in the sling and reached for the puppy-occupied crate. She hoisted it, noting with dismay that he was getting heavier by the day and would require a larger crate if she didn't rehome him soon.

The second she opened the door, Riley bounded out, and Emma let out a squeal, more likely from the burst of cold air than from delight at the winter wonderland that was now their front yard.

"Wait for us, Rile." Jill shut the door and turned to lock it, then stopped cold. Someone had left a large basket filled with fruit, canned goods, and her favorite ginger cookies right there on her porch. She bent to examine it for any clues as to who might have left it, but all she saw was a tag that said, *Enjoy!* punctuated with a little heart.

Jill bit her lower lip, fighting tears. She

sure did love this town.

Fifteen minutes later, she and Riley stomped the snow off their boots on her mom's porch as Mom opened the front door.

"Can I stay'a out, Dwandma?"

"You come inside and eat a bowl of oatmeal, young man. Then we'll see about going back out in this mess." Mom folded her arms and stepped aside for Riley to enter. "And leave those boots by the door. There's enough snow in my driveway. I don't want to have to shovel it out of the house too."

"Good morning, Mom." Jill struggled against a sardonic tone as she set the crate inside and slipped Emma from the sling. "I have a tiny problem."

"What is it now?" Mom repositioned herself in the center of the doorway as she took Emma, clearly not planning to invite Jill in.

"It's my car. It won't start."

Her mom sighed.

"So, I was wondering if I could borrow yours. It does better in the snow than my Honda, anyway."

"Jillian—"

"I know what you're going to say. But it will only be for a few days. You never drive when it's snowy anyway."

"That may be true. But I have the children here. What if something were to happen?"

"Then you'll call a neighbor. Or 9-1-1. Please, Mom. I need to get to work."

"You should call Caleb. He's always been good with cars."

Jill just nodded, resisting the urge to respond further.

"And when you call him, be sure you're nice. Men need to feel appreciated. Tell him you're sorry about everything, then maybe, just maybe he'll forgive you. Men need to feel respected, Jillian."

Respected. Jill practically growled. "Since when does respect not have to be earned?"

"He's your husband, Jillian. You need to

respect the role."

"Respect the role? Mom, *he's* not respecting that role. Why should *I?*"

Mom's face soured. "You're impossible. For the sake of the children, try to suppress that poor attitude of yours when you speak to Caleb."

"Mom. I'm not *going* to be speaking to Caleb anytime soon." Jill sighed. She might as well be the one to tell her mom before the town grapevine squeezed out this juicy bit of news. "He got into a fight with Sam. It was pretty public. Right in the middle of town. You'll be hearing about it, I'm sure."

"A fight? What about?"

Jill rolled her eyes. There was really no way to cushion this. "Sam and I were...I mean, I was giving Sam some reassurance about his situation with Grace. The next thing I knew, Caleb launched himself at Sam like they were twelve years old again."

"Oh, Jillian." Mom shook her head and pursed her mouth in disgust.

"What do you mean, 'Oh, Jillian'? Like it's my fault he can't control his temper?"

"His temper shouldn't have to be tested like this. If you hadn't kicked him out—"

"I kicked him out because he drinks our grocery money and won't even try to get a job. Why do you talk like you think this is all my fault?"

"Because it *is* your fault. All of it."

Jill felt like she'd been stabbed in the back, right to her face. She stood there, having no response that wouldn't just make things worse. "I'm going to be late for work." Shaking, she half-turned then stopped. *Shoot.* She turned back. "I need your car key."

Puffing like a bull, Mom reached just inside the door and produced a key ring. "It's ridiculous of you to think that you can support a family on your own, you know. You have no skills. Women all over the country stay with their husbands because they themselves are incapable of supporting a household on their own."

"And lots of other women get jobs and make ends meet just fine." Hoping that would suffice as a parting shot, she turned and started for the steps.

"Yes. Women who have gone to college and worked hard. You have done neither."

Jill spun around. "I haven't *worked* hard? I've done nothing *but* work hard. While your favorite son-in-law stays out drinking till all hours and sleeps the day away. Then picks a fight with his best friend and runs off and disappears when things get hard. Why do you act like he's some kind of hero and I'm the one who's failed? *I'm* your child, not him. I'm the one you're supposed to support."

Her mom's eyes widened in horror. Too late, Jill realized what she had said.

"What do you mean, he ran off?" Her mother pierced her with a glare. "What have you done?"

"I haven't..." She stopped and caught her breath. There was really no point in trying to explain something that her mom refused to understand. "After the fight, he retreated to the Spur and didn't go home to Sam's or to the hardware store yesterday. He's gone, and we don't know where he went."

Mom tightened her grip on Emma, her expression turning sad. Was she finally seeing the truth of Caleb's behavior?

"Really, Jillian."

Guess not.

"If you allow this to continue, there will be a custody battle and he might win. You know that, don't you?"

"That's ridiculous. Why would he win? He's never there for the kids, and he's never been a provider." She cringed as she said it. He had been a provider in the beginning. What had happened to change that?

Jill shook her head. "I have to go." She stomped across the porch and down the steps.

"Two parents who can't provide for their children," Mom called out after her, like she didn't even care if the neighbors heard. "The court would have to grant custody to someone in the family who can ensure a roof over their heads."

Jill stopped at the bottom of the steps. She took in a long draft of cold autumn air and counted to ten. Her mother's threat was absurd, and she couldn't let herself be baited. Refusing to look back, Jill kept walking.

But her heart thrummed as she marched down the walkway toward the garage. What if there was something to what her mom was saying? If she lost her job, could she lose her kids too?

Chapter 34

Jill had Kylie accompany her to the one place in the factory where she knew neither Dean nor Mr. Steele would walk in unexpectedly—the ladies' room.

The two of them perched on the old-fashioned radiator that Jill had scrubbed clean, along with the rest of this room, on her very first day there, studying the recovered half-shredded document.

"It's just like you said," Kylie confirmed.

"A bunch of science-y nerd-speak and the scary part about the chemicals in the groundwater in Japan. It's totally sketchy, but I don't think it proves anything. Except that some other company had a problem disposing of their waste."

Jill sighed. "But why would Mr. Steele be so adamant about making sure this got destroyed?"

"No clue." Kylie hopped down from the radiator. "He was whipped into a frenzy about all those papers he wanted us to shred."

Jill slid to her feet as well. "Which makes me wonder what else was in those boxes."

Together, they left the ladies' room and stepped carefully across the large tarp that the painters had spread across the floor.

Once back at her desk, Jill made a quick check of her email. There was one from the furniture store in Missoula, confirming the delivery of a leather couch and two chairs for later that day. And one from Jerry letting her know that he'd finished the framing and she could pick up the photos any time. There was also a reply from a local furniture maker whose work she'd admired for years, saying that yes, he did have a coffee table in stock that he thought would suit her purposes. One look at the photo he'd attached and she quickly wrote back to ask if he'd be able to deliver it.

Things were coming together.

Just as she was about to sign out of her email, a new one popped up at the top of the screen. She sat there, staring at it for a long moment before working up the nerve to open it.

Angela Hoyt, according to the email, was pleased to inform her that she had indeed qualified for the Temporary Assistance funds. *Congratulations.*

Jill let out a jittery breath as she closed her eyes against impending tears. She'd qualified for welfare. That wouldn't solve everything, but it at least counted for something.

A quick scan of the rest of Angela's message assured her that she should receive her first check next week. So maybe she could afford to tuck something away in a Save the House fund.

Just as the celebration in her head was about to turn into full-blown fireworks, the phone on her desk interrupted the party.

She picked up the receiver. "Nyland Enterprises. This is Jill."

"Hi, Jill." The male voice on the other end sounded tense. "This is Bryce. From Bryce's Auto."

"Oh hi, Bryce." She hadn't expected to hear from him so soon. Sam must have called him right when he'd opened that morning. "Have you figured out what's going on with my car?"

For several seconds, all she could hear was the indistinct sound of clanking tools and staticky radio tunes that provided the constant soundtrack for Bryce's shop. When he spoke again, it was in jumbled partial sentences. "I'm…not sure that I…. Sam said it was parked in front of the bank, but…. I didn't see it anywhere."

"What are you talking about? It's got to be right where I left it."

"I'm sorry, Jill. I'll go look again. Maybe Sam got it running? I can give him a quick call."

"Yeah. That must be it." Although the fact that Sam could pretty much fix anything *but* cars made that prospect seem unlikely.

She hung up the phone, frowning at it like it was somehow partially responsible for this new complication in her life. How could her car possibly be gone? It wasn't like it was worth stealing even on its best day, much less right now.

She let her face rest in her hands, pressing her fingertips against her eyes to ward off an approaching headache. What would she do if she didn't have a car? She obviously couldn't afford to replace it. But if it had been stolen, would her insurance cover it? Did she even still *have* insurance?

It wasn't quite time for her morning coffee break and already she felt like going home and crawling back into bed.

Doing her best to set that worry aside, she stood and headed for Mr. Nyland's office. She'd had some of the guys haul up a treasure she'd found in one of the rooms downstairs—a carved oak barrister's bookcase with leaded-glass doors. The glass, thankfully, was in pristine shape, but the wood needed to be refinished. She had enough varnish left over from the counter in the lobby, and enough time—she hoped—to get the first coat done before lunch.

Just as she was about to pass Dean's office, the door flung open and he burst out, looking down at the tablet he held and nearly barreling into her. They both rebounded back, startled.

"I'm so sorry—"

"—please excuse me."

They each let out an uncomfortable chortle at the awkwardness of the encounter before recovering an air of professionalism.

Dean secured the elastic belt around his tablet and clutched it in front of himself. "How's the room coming along?"

"Great. There's not too much to see yet, but you can take a look if you'd like."

He checked his watch. "I have a few minutes now." He pivoted and took off at no-time-to-waste pace.

Jill chewed her lip as she scurried to catch up. This could be a good opportunity to question him in private and determine whether or not she could trust him.

"I'm looking forward to meeting Mr. Nyland." She did her best to sound conversational as they approached the door.

"Hm?" Dean seemed distracted, like his mind was still on whatever he had catapulted out of his office to go do. "Oh, yes. I'm looking forward to working with him as well."

"So, you haven't actually gotten to work with him yet?"

"To be perfectly honest, I've only met him once. The day I did my interview. That…" He paused. "…seems strange, doesn't it?"

"Not really. Well…" She angled him a look. "…maybe a little."

"Since then, it's been a whirlwind and Mr. Steele has been the one to communicate with him directly." The edge to his tone softened as she pushed open the door and he followed her in. "Well, this is shaping up nicely. I'm very pleased." He crossed to the bookcase which stood on a tarp in the center of the room. "This looks like an antique. Did you find it here?"

"It was downstairs covered in dust." A rush of satisfaction trailed after his positive appraisal of her design decision. But he could bolt from the room at any second, and she needed to stay on task. "It sounds like you sold Mr. Nyland pretty quickly on your vision for the company."

"He's quite an innovator. He appreciates forward thinking."

"I'm not surprised. I mean, considering that he developed a method for eliminating the toxic byproducts of geothermal production. Do you know how he came up with it?"

"Trial and error, I'm sure." Seeming only partially involved in the conversation, he crossed the room to study the spectacular aerial shot that looked like it had been framed with that space behind the desk in mind. "This company has come a long way."

"A long way in a short time?"

"Not such a short time, really. It's taken Mr. Nyland years to get his business to where it is."

"Years? But..." Pretending to be more involved with her refinishing project than the conversation, she looked around for a place to plug in the big work light she'd borrowed from the painters. "I thought that Nyland Enterprises was new."

"Oh, the name is new." Still looking around, he crossed to the front of the desk. "It used to be called Clean Green Associates."

Well, that was a twist. Why hadn't anyone mentioned *that* little nugget before?

"Clean Green Associates. That's a good name. Why did he change it?"

"I'm sure it had something to do with the issues he had with the factory he owned in Japan."

Her jaw practically *thunked* against the floor. Mr. Nyland had owned a factory in Japan? That didn't necessarily mean that it was the one that had been responsible for poisoning a community's water supply, but that *would* explain why Mr. Steele had been so insistent that they destroy the paper trail.

"I-issues?" she stammered.

He shrugged like he assumed this wasn't new information for her. "Mostly labor-related."

Not wanting him to see the confusion coloring her face, she quickly dove behind the desk under the guise of needing the power strip that the computer was plugged into. She shoved it out into the open area, then crawled out to plug in the light.

She popped to her feet, hoping he'd attribute whatever tension might be in her voice to the effort she'd just exerted. "What happened to that factory?"

"They closed it." Dean went on, evidently unaware of the mental sinkhole she'd fallen into. "It's apparently very hard to work with the unions over there."

Jill crossed the room to get her brushes, having no idea what she should ask next. Why hadn't she read more Nancy Drew books as a kid? "So they just closed the factory there and opened a new one here?"

"Mr. Nyland saw the importance of bringing jobs to this country. Relocating was a win-win."

Not such a "win" for the people whose water got poisoned.

She nodded dumbly. Was Dean handing

her the company line or was this what he believed to be true?

"Of course"—Dean held up a hand—"it's probably best not to mention this to anyone. There are people who are against any kind of alternative energy, and if word got around that there were problems with the Japan location, it could potentially cause unnecessary unrest. You understand."

"Sure." She didn't. Not yet, anyway. In fact, this new bit of information had her more confused than ever.

"But, I'm sure Mr. Steele explained that to you."

"Mr. Steele?"

"Yes. When he spoke with you about the report you read. He did talk to you about that, didn't he?"

"Yes. I mean, sort of. He basically told me that I should ignore anything I read around here because I haven't been trained to understand it."

The little lines around Dean's mouth

tightened. "Mr. Steele is a very intelligent man, and he tends to believe that the rest of us don't quite…measure up." He winced apologetically. "Please don't take that personally."

"Okay." Jill couldn't help a small smile at his show of support. She really wanted to trust Dean. "Don't *you* take that personally either."

He chuckled, like a barrier had just come down. Then he jolted and took a step toward the door. "I really should—"

"Wait. Before you go, can I ask you one more question?"

He nodded.

"I don't understand…" She measured her words. "…how Mr. Steele even knew that I had seen that report."

His eyebrows lifted, like the question had surprised him. "I told him."

"*You* did? But how did *you* know?"

"Colleen told me about it."

Colleen? But…how did she…

Oh, right. Jill had told her about the report, when she'd wanted to steer their conversation away from Sam. But, that had been on Saturday, the day *after* their little flirtation in the cereal aisle. That still didn't make any sense.

Dean must have read the confusion on her face because he attempted to fill in the gaps. "She told me about it when we were at dinner the other night. She said you were concerned, so I said I'd look into it."

His words felt like they'd been delivered on a cold platter of betrayal. Dinner? *Really?*

"You and Colleen had dinner?" She hated the quiver in her voice, but she couldn't seem to prevent it. "When?"

"On Saturday. I'm sorry." His face went pale. "I assumed you knew."

Jill fought to get a good breath, uncertain which part of this bothered her more—that Colleen had told him about the report or that she'd gone on a date with him and hadn't bothered to inform her.

She turned away, not wanting him to see that her cheeks were probably turning all shades of red. Why hadn't she told Colleen to keep the information about the report to herself until she knew more about what was going on? Of course, how could she have known that her best friend would be engaging in a secret tête-à-tête with one of her bosses? The whole situation ignited a flame in the center of her chest that would take more than an antacid to quell.

"I'm so sorry." Dean sounded both confused and remorseful. "I seem to have spoken out of turn."

"No." She faced him again. "It's fine. I mean, I'm really glad you two hit it off. She's terrific."

A hint of a grin crept over his face that said he agreed.

As he excused himself to take care of his next order of business, Jill wiped a hand across her forehead and took out her paint brushes.

Everything about this situation just kept getting stranger.

Chapter 35

While the brisk walk home from her mom's felt invigorating, it definitely increased Jill's anxiety. The days were getting shorter and the snow would soon be getting deeper. She needed to get her car back.

At least her load was easier to manage, since she'd hauled Riley's red wagon out of the garage. The puppy and her bags now rode along behind them and, as long as Riley remained enchanted by the crunch of the snow under his slightly too-big boots, this system would work.

As they approached their house, a shadow moved across their front porch. She stopped, alarmed, straining to see what it was.

"Auntie Cole!"

Colleen. Releasing Riley's hand so he could gallop across the yard in greeting, she drew in a relieved breath. Then she remembered she was mad at her, and her shoulders tensed.

"Hey, buddy!" Colleen met Riley at the base of the stairs, then bent down to give him a quick hug. She looked at Jill, who made her way up the walk. "You really should keep your porch light on, you know. It's dark out here."

"I'm conserving electricity." Noting that the day's snowfall had already made their tracks from this morning undetectable, Jill tried not to think about how long she'd be able to get away with not shoveling.

"Of course." Without offering, Colleen

picked up the crate and made a kissy sound through the bars as she started up the steps.

"What are you doing here?" Jill walked a fine line between gratitude and gruffness.

"I brought dinner." Colleen nodded toward a couple of shopping bags next to the front door. "And I thought you might like some help with your Halloween costumes."

Halloween. With everything else that had been on her mind, she'd practically forgotten. She'd pulled something together for Riley, but had done nothing about outfitting herself and Emma. "That was really thoughtful. Thanks." Her words came out sounding forced as she unlocked the front door, noting with relief that there were no notes either on it or shoved under it.

"Hey, why were you guys on foot, anyway?" Colleen followed her in, setting the crate on the floor then stepping back out to retrieve her shopping bags.

Jill winced as she grabbed the crate and hauled it, along with both of the kids, to the kitchen. "You're not going to believe this, but I think my car got stolen."

"What? No, it didn't."

Jill tossed a look at Colleen, who had trailed her to the kitchen with one of the shopping bags. "What do you mean, 'no it didn't'? I haven't even told you—"

"It's in the garage." Removing a to-go container from the bag, Colleen looked at her like she might be crazy. "I peeked through the window to see if you were home."

"What?" Jill put Emma in the playpen, then hurried back out the front door. As she trudged toward the garage, she surveyed the driveway. Sure enough, a pair of tire tracks had been filled in with the afternoon's snowfall. She flung open the garage door and, to her astonishment, saw the car parked there.

"What on earth…?"

She opened the driver's door and stared. There on the seat was a colorful bouquet of flowers. When she picked it up, she found the key and a chocolate bar. *Special Dark.* She closed her eyes and let out a breath. *Sam*.

She got into the driver's seat, leaving the door open, then put the key in the ignition and turned. The engine hummed to life, sounding smoother than it had in years.

So Sam had fixed the car for her. Why hadn't he just told her? She sighed. Maybe he had left her a phone message but in all the busyness of last night and the rushing around this morning, she hadn't remembered to check. She'd have to call him later to thank him.

Since the last thing she needed was to admit to Colleen that Sam had come to her rescue again, she left the flowers and candy. She could come back out for them later. Stepping back into the house, she heard Colleen and the kids happily chattering and smelled dinner being warmed up.

Colleen appeared through the doorway with a stack of plates. She looked up at Jill, curiosity filling her gaze. "So, what's going on with your car?" She began setting out the plates.

Jill approached the kitchen with a casual shrug. "The short answer might just be that I'm losing it."

Colleen raised her eyebrows. "You're acting weird. Is everything okay?"

Jill looked down at the playpen, where Emma poked her nose through the mesh until the puppy licked it, which sent both kids into a fit of giggles. She then shifted to another hole in the mesh and repeated the process. This could keep the three of them entertained long enough for Jill to say what she needed to say to Colleen.

"Come on." She motioned for Colleen to follow her.

Colleen looked skeptical as she trailed her into the living room.

"So." Jill turned, folding her arms. "How was your little *date?*" She made the word sound more accusatory than she probably should have.

Colleen let out a breath and stared at her

shoes. "He told you."

Jill kept her volume down. "At least *somebody* did."

"I was *going* to tell you."

"When? As a P.S. on my invitation to your wedding? Cole, he's my boss. Do you have any idea how embarrassing it was to hear about this from *him?*"

"I'm sorry. It's just that given my history of picking guys who turn out to be duds, I wanted to be sure before I said anything."

"But I'm your best friend. You've always included me in the 'being sure' part. Besides, I actually know this guy. Why wouldn't you want my opinion?"

"*Because* you know this guy. You know him as your boss, and I didn't think you'd be able to be impartial."

She was right. But the truth was, Jill still didn't know if Dean could be trusted, as either a boyfriend for Colleen or as a boss. There was so much more to this than Colleen realized.

Of course, she didn't realize it because Jill hadn't told her. But the reason she hadn't told her was that she'd wanted to be sure first. And now…. Her jaw worked as she remembered her other reason for being mad. "You told Dean about the toxicology report. Why would you do that?"

"I thought I was helping you. He knows everything that goes on in that factory. It's his job. And you didn't tell me not to say anything."

"If I had known you were going to be rendezvousing with my boss, I would have mentioned it. I thought it was part of the friend code. We should be able to trust each other."

"Oh, like you're trusting *me* right now?"

That stung. Jill stood there, at a loss for a response. Colleen was right. Here she'd been furious at Colleen for not trusting her, but Jill had been just as guilty. She let out a breath. "I trust you."

Colleen looked away, fingering the edge of her sweater. "So. Was he able to put your mind at ease?"

Jill lifted a one-shoulder shrug. "Not really. But I have other things to worry about." She tried to lighten the mood. "Like how to turn us into an awesome pirate family without spending any plunder."

"Now *there* I can help." Colleen reached into the bag she'd tossed onto the coffee table and took out a white blouse with puffy sleeves. "Does this not scream 'pirate mom'?"

Jill nodded, feeling terrible that they were at odds. She needed Colleen's support right now, and she really didn't want to stay mad. "Thanks."

"You're welcome. And, wait for it…" She pulled out a little long-sleeve onesie with a skull and crossbones on the front. "Isn't this the cutest?"

Jill sputtered out a laugh. "In a very disturbing sort of way, yes."

"And look at this." She took out a fringy

shawl and wrapped it around her waist. "I was going to be a fortune teller, but I think it would look better on you. And I brought a ton of costume jewelry for you to wear as your pirate treasure." She lifted the bag and shook it, making a clanking sound. When she went to set it down again, her brow furrowed. "What's this?"

Jill followed her gaze to the half-shredded report she'd tossed down the night before.

Colleen looked confused. "I thought you said you didn't have this anymore."

"I thought I didn't. But then it turned up."

Colleen lowered herself onto the sofa, studying the paper. "This doesn't look good. You think it's about your company?"

"I do now. Dean told me they used to have a factory in Japan. Only it was called something else then. Clean Green, I think."

Colleen sorted through the library books. "And what are you…? You're learning how to be a whistleblower? Jill, what's going on?"

"That's what I'm trying to figure out."

The sound of the doorbell startled Jill. She looked at Colleen, then peered through the curtains out the front window. A man she didn't know stood on her porch holding some sort of folder in his hand.

"What now?" Shaking, she went to the door with Colleen following close behind. She cracked it open a few inches.

"Mrs. Martin?"

"Yes?" Her heart skittered into her throat and she considered slamming the door and calling the sheriff.

He stuck out his hand. "My name is Joseph Carter. I'd like to speak with you about your house."

Oh no. Was he here to take her keys? Set up the auction date?

Ignoring his outstretched hand, she opened the door a few more inches so he'd be able to see the full impact of her begging. "I…really…I mean, I'm trying. If I could just have a little more time."

"Mrs. Martin, I understand what you're

going through."

"Mama!"

Riley's urgent cry drew her around.

"I'll go." Colleen cast a concerned look over her shoulder as she started for the kitchen.

Jill faced the door again. "Please, Mr…?"

"Carter." He reached into his black leather folder and removed a sheet of paper, which he presented to her like he was granting her a diploma.

Her head felt like a top spinning out of control. Wasn't there some kind of law that you had to physically accept the paper in order for it to count as being legally served? Or was that just something she'd seen on TV? She held up both palms in what she hoped read as an official refusal.

"I understand this is a difficult time." His manner remained annoyingly calm as he peered into the room, then slid the paper onto the table just inside the door. "I'll just leave this here for you to look over when you have time."

Was that a fair tactic? She glanced down at the paper like it was a bomb he'd placed in her house. She wanted to read him the riot act for pretending to be so nice, like he was there to do her some kind of favor or something instead of—

"Jill!"

The urgency in Colleen's voice yanked Jill's attention away from her outrage. She held up a hand to Mr. Carter as she whirled around, her mind filling with every possible disaster scenario in the three seconds it took her to get to the kitchen.

There she found Riley and Colleen on the floor with the puppy, who was panting heavily and looking like he wanted to stand but couldn't. She hurried to him and put her hand on his side. His tiny heart beat like a bongo.

Colleen pushed to her feet and ran from the room, then returned a few long seconds later with her phone to her ear.

"What's wrong with him?" Jill tried to

sound calm for Riley's sake, but he already had tears streaming down his tiny cheeks.

"It looks like he might have eaten something he shouldn't have."

Jill's head snapped at the male voice coming from the kitchen doorway. Mr. Carter stood there, looking uncertain.

"Do..." She swallowed hard. "...do you know about dogs?"

Taking that as an invitation to come closer, he kept a concerned eye on the puppy. "I have three myself. One of them has a penchant for getting into the trash. Any chance he might have gotten hold of something toxic?"

Was there? Jill couldn't think straight. "We're pretty careful."

"No one answers at the vet's office." Colleen paced as she tapped at her phone. "I'm calling Dr. North at home."

"Mamaaa!" Wailing, Riley pulled himself onto her lap.

As she wrapped her arms around him, she noticed something next to the playpen, just past where Riley had been sitting. A chewed wad of brown and red paper.

Realizing what it was, she snapped a look at the hooks next to the back door where her apron—the one with the chocolate bar in the pocket—was supposed to be. But it lay in a heap on the floor.

She opened her mouth to yell at her son for letting the puppy get the candy, but this wasn't his fault. She shouldn't have left it there. This was on her.

Colleen had evidently gotten hold of the vet, and had been explaining the situation. She held the phone from her mouth and spoke to Jill. "Do you have any idea what it—"

"Chocolate." Jill grabbed the wrapper. "Tell her it was chocolate."

Mr. Carter placed a hand on the puppy's side. "Mrs. Martin, I—"

"I'm sorry." She really couldn't deal with this guy from the bank, or foreclosure office, or whatever institution had sent him. "Please, can I just have a few more days?"

"Dr. North says she'll meet us at her office." Colleen crowded in between them and bent to scoop up the puppy.

Mr. Carter reached for the crate. "If you'd like some help, I could—"

"If you wouldn't mind." Still holding Riley, Jill pushed to her feet. "I need to get the baby…"

As Mr. Carter and Colleen helped her transport the whimpering puppy and two crying children out of the house, Jill lifted a panicked prayer. *Please, God. I can handle losing the house if I have to, but please don't let us lose this puppy!*

Two things had prevented Jill from just rolling over and ignoring her alarm clock that morning. First, she only had a few hours before Mr. Nyland's arrival to put the finishing touches on his office. And second, it was Halloween.

At least the air of anticipation at the factory provided a substitute for some of the sleep she'd lost because of the puppy. He had responded well to treatment, but Dr. North had wanted to keep him at the clinic overnight on an IV to restore his fluids.

By early afternoon, she was starting to drag. As she stood back to survey the office, the heavenly smell of coffee turned her attention to the door.

Kylie entered holding a couple of steaming cups. "You looked like you could use this."

"You're my coffee angel." She reached out to accept the offering, even though she'd had more than her usual intake of caffeine that day already.

"It looks great in here." Sipping from her own cup, Kylie commenced a self-guided tour around the room. "Hey, any word from the vet?"

"The puppy's doing great. My friend Colleen is picking him up for me and keeping him at her place until after the event tonight."

"That's good." Kylie gave her a sympathetic look. "You know, today's our first payday. That ought to cheer you up."

It didn't. In fact, Jill found that thought especially depressing now that saving the puppy had meant waving goodbye to her Save the House fund.

Not that it mattered. Mr. Carter had been kind enough not to press the issue in the face of her canine emergency, but he had left the notice of foreclosure on her table, where it remained untouched like a ticking time bomb.

"Looks like you finished the office without a moment to spare." Kylie had ended her tour at one of the front windows, overlooking the parking lot. Jill joined her in time to see Mr. Steele's blue Mercedes pull up to the front steps of the building. Three of the doors opened, and three men got out. Dean, Mr. Steele, and a dignified-looking man whose charcoal-gray wool coat was just a few shades darker than his graying hair.

Jill's stomach tightened at her first nervous

glimpse of Harvey Nyland.

Jill Came Tumbling After

Chapter 36

In the whirlwind of the next few hours, Jill and Kylie trailed the three men around the factory, taking notes whenever Mr. Nyland commented on anything that might fall within their realm of responsibility. Jill had expected him to be all-business but instead found him surprisingly personable—kind of a cross between Mr. Rogers and Santa Claus. In fact, the more time she spent in his presence, the more she felt her anxiety melt away.

After the informal tour, they watched from the conference area as he stood with his hands on the railing of the second-floor observation area giving a speech to the construction crew down below like a general addressing the troops.

"I'm very pleased and impressed with the work you all have done."

Jill glanced over at Kylie, who had been unusually quiet all afternoon.

"As you well know"—Mr. Nyland continued, his voice carrying like an opera singer through the large space—"the regulators from the EPA will be here tomorrow to give us our final approval. Having seen for myself what a top-notch job you all have done to prepare, I am convinced that they will have no concerns." He paused, seeming to enjoy the agreeable murmur from the crowd. "Thank you for your contribution to what I hope will be a major boon to the community and an asset to the entire world."

Everyone, including Dean and Mr. Steele, broke into applause.

Kylie twisted her mouth and gave three slow claps before folding her arms. What was up with her?

"But, it's Halloween. Go home." He gave a friendly wave of dismissal. "Enjoy this spooky holiday with your families."

More applause, then the buzz of cheerful conversation as the workers celebrated their unexpected early release for the day.

The three men headed toward the catwalk while Jill and Kylie started for their desks. As Jill passed the railing, she looked down and realized with a hint of sadness that most of the crew had finished their work here and wouldn't be returning after the weekend. She and Kylie had gotten to know a few of them on their trips over to the trailer for coffee and stale pastries, and she'd miss the feeling of comradery.

A peripheral movement pulled her from her melancholy and she realized that Dean was over on the catwalk, well behind the other two men, gesturing for her to join them. A nervous tremble moved through her. Even though Mr. Nyland had been very positive about her work so far, the thought of witnessing his initial response to his office made her want to hide under her desk. She looked to Kylie for reassurance but she was already across the room, engrossed in something on her phone screen.

Gulping in a breath, she said a prayer that this would go well.

By the time she slipped into the room, Mr. Nyland had made himself at home behind the large desk and stood when he saw her.

"Miss Martin." He smiled in approval. "This is the most well-turned-out office I have ever had. I thank you."

Jill felt her face flush as both Dean and Mr. Steele looked her way, the former beaming with encouragement while the latter remained stone-faced.

"Please." Mr. Nyland indicated that she should take a load off in one of the two plush chairs she'd positioned opposite his desk.

She looked to Dean, who gave a subtle nod of confirmation as he pulled up a straight-back chair for himself, clearly leaving the other comfy one for Mr. Steele. Once they were all seated, Mr. Nyland folded his hands together on the desk in front of him and spoke.

"Miss Martin. May I call you Jill?"

"Please." She fidgeted, making a mental note to find some small pillows to put in these chairs for people with shorter legs to lean back on.

"I understand you have a concern regarding our former location in Japan."

She jerked her head up, both alarmed and humiliated that she was being "spoken to" about this by the owner of the company.

An inconvenient lump appeared in her throat. "Uh…well…yes."

"Allow me to put your mind at ease." He nodded patiently. "The truth, which I don't believe was included anywhere in the report you saw, was that we experienced a small leak in one of our holding tanks that resulted in a minimal amount of seepage into the groundwater. As soon as the breach was brought to our attention, we found the source and fixed it."

"Oh." Relief washed over her. "That's good to know."

"Sadly, the incident was misrepresented in the Japanese press. It's a natural consequence of trying to do what's right for the environment. The people who want to promote the big-profit money-grubbers will do anything in their power to take down the little guy who's trying to do the right thing."

Her head bobbed in understanding, assuming that he'd cast himself in the role of "little guy" in that concise scenario.

"Perhaps"—Dean sat forward—"you could explain the process being used here."

"Ah, yes." Mr. Nyland's demeanor reminded Jill of her favorite high school science teacher who, even after explaining a concept for the umpteenth time, would patiently go over it again if asked. "I wanted to prevent the possibility of another minor mishap such as the one in Nagosaka." On the phrase "minor mishap," he flicked his hand as if it had been just that easy to put to rest.

A conviction that had been fluttering around in Jill's head all afternoon finally settled in her gut. She could trust this man. She felt it deep down.

He pivoted his chair and gestured to the window behind him. "See that building? We call that the separator station. That's where the waste gets separated from the usable steam that's been brought up from the production well."

Jill scooted forward in her seat, seeing for the first time that there was a small building between the factory and the large cooling tower.

"In our old system, this brine got transferred into barrels to be transported to a hazardous waste site. It was at that point in the process where the breach occurred. So we have eliminated the need for transporting the waste off-site by pumping it back into the earth via an injection well located underneath the separator station. It's a patent-pending process and, I believe, one that all geothermal plants will adopt in the future."

Pumped back into the earth. That made perfect sense. Jill felt slightly awed to be in the presence of a man who could come up with something so ingenious.

Dean had stood and was looking out the window, as if the details of the procedure were just now coming together for him as well. The thought that he hadn't been out there to get a closer look at the mechanics of the operation for himself crossed her mind, but she brushed it aside. Like everyone on the crew, he'd been working day and night just to keep up.

"I hope that satisfies your concerns."

Jill nodded, totally reassured that the toxic sludge was inevitable, and they had a plan for properly disposing of it.

"Oh, and I almost forgot." Mr. Nyland reached into the inner pocket of his suit jacket and brought out a folded paper, which he then slid across the desk. "Dean tells me you're a single mother."

She snapped a look at Dean, who gave her a subtle look of apology like someone who'd been caught spreading gossip. Obviously, Colleen had been even more loose-lipped than Jill had realized.

"I believe in valuing our employees." Mr. Nyland gave the paper an extra nudge. "I've taken the liberty of setting up a trust in the names of each of your children to be used for college."

College? Jill stared at him for a long moment as his words sank in. She hesitated, then took the paper and unfolded it. It was full of financial jargon, none of which made any sense. She glanced up. "I don't—"

"I'll contribute to both funds every year as long as you remain in the employ of Nyland Enterprises."

A second, more careful perusal of the paper supported his explanation. Her mouth went dry as her thoughts raced. *College*. A secure future for Riley and Emma. This man really *was* Santa Claus.

She cleared her throat. "I don't know what to say."

"Dean was right about you." He shook an index finger. "You're a sharp employee, and you've done your homework. I find that admirable."

She looked over at Dean, who seemed pleased but not surprised, like he'd known this was in the works.

"Also, I understand you're having an issue with your house."

"Oh…"

"We talked about it"—Mr. Nyland pushed his chair back from the desk—"and I feel we're justified in changing your job classification to a higher bracket. One that would pay twice what you're earning now."

Twice? She did a quick mental calculation. Was he serious? This meant that, if she could get hold of the right person at the foreclosure company, it might not be too late to defuse that ticking time bomb.

Restraining her impulse to leap across the desk and hug him, she instead just blurted out, "Now I *really* don't know what to say."

"No need to say anything." He pushed back from his desk and stood, signifying an end to the meeting. "I appreciate your contribution to a prosperous future for Madison Falls."

As the men congregated in the center of the room, discussing tomorrow's inspection and their plans for treating the inspectors to a round of golf on Sunday, Jill forced her weight onto her shaky legs. It had been silly of her to get so worked up without knowing all the facts. This factory was a great thing, and not just for Madison Falls. And Mr. Nyland was so kind. Thanks to his generosity, her kids were going to be able to go to college. And live in a decent house. To think that she had almost jeopardized all of that with her naïve suspicions.

Mr. Nyland and Mr. Steele headed out of the office, while Dean lagged behind to close the door after Jill.

"I hope you don't mind that I shared what Colleen told me. It seems to have benefited you."

"It's fine. I mean, thank you." Tears started to well, and she blinked them away. She did not need to cry in front of her boss. "I just can't believe it."

"He's a very generous man."

They began traversing the catwalk, far enough behind the other two for Jill to get the impression that Dean wanted to speak to her without them overhearing.

The softness of his voice confirmed it. "I was hoping you could pass a message on to

Colleen for me. I left her a voicemail, but…well, I know she's busy."

Jill drew in a breath, recalling where she and Colleen had left their conversation the previous night. But they'd have plenty of time to talk tonight while they took the kids around town gathering candy. She couldn't wait to tell her how wrong she had been—about the factory, and about Dean.

"Sure." She tried not to let on that she had any trepidations. "What's the message?"

"I told her I'd see her at tonight's festivities. But now, Mr. Nyland is taking the men from the EPA to dinner at the Fountain and he wants me to be there."

"That's a good place. Nicest restaurant in town."

"I know. It's where I took Colleen." An endearing blush swept across his cheeks. "Anyway, would you tell her I'll try to get away as soon as I can?"

"Oh. Of course."

He flashed a hesitant smile, and for a moment Jill saw him not so much as her boss but as a man with all the insecurities that anyone had in the hopeful first days of a new romance. As he caught up to the other men, she sighed. Colleen deserved a really great guy. Hopefully, Dean would prove himself worthy.

Laughing and joking like they weren't concerned in the slightest about tomorrow's inspection, the men disappeared down the stairs. The second they were out of earshot, Kylie bombarded Jill with questions.

"What went on in there? Did you get to ask him any questions?"

Feeling a little foolish for having gotten Kylie all riled up for no reason, Jill crossed to her desk and grabbed her things. "He explained everything. Kylie, this is so good. I'm not worried at all anymore."

As the two of them headed downstairs, Jill filled Kylie in on what she now knew to be the truth.

"I'm so relieved." Jill stopped at the base of the stairs to button her coat. "We don't have to worry about blowing the whistle on this factory. And people aren't going to lose their jobs."

Kylie lingered on the bottom step with one hand on the railing and the other on her hip, saying nothing and frowning.

Jill adjusted the strap of her bag on her shoulder and took a couple more steps, noticing how disturbingly silent this building was now that everyone had gone home for the weekend. It dawned on her that she'd never been there without the noise of the construction crew, and the thought of the building being vacant except for her and Kylie gave her a sense of foreboding that she was more than anxious to shake free of.

"Oh, and I almost forgot to tell you the best part." She spoke over her shoulder to encourage Kylie to keep moving. "I got a raise."

Kylie, who had taken a couple of measured steps, skidded to another stop. "You did?"

"Yeah." Jill looked back at her but kept moving. "It's because Mr. Nyland found out about my situation. Being a single mom and all."

"Huh." Working her jaw, Kylie started walking again, her steps uncharacteristically slow and contemplative.

"And he started a college fund for each of my kids. He said he'll contribute to it every year as long as I'm still working for the company. Do you know what this means?"

When Kylie didn't answer, impatience quickly turned to irritation. Jill turned, feeling a chill from the weird vibe Kylie was giving off. Then she realized how incredibly insensitive she'd been to just blurt out her good news without thinking about how it would sound to her equally hardworking co-worker.

"Oh, Kylie." She took a couple of steps back to where Kylie stood with shadows casting lines that added to the strain on her face. "I'm so sorry. He only did this because Dean put in a good word for me. I'm sure he'd do the same for you if—"

"Don't you see what he's doing?" Her voice held an edge that sliced through the air like a hatchet.

"What do you mean? He's helping me."

"He's buying your loyalty. And apparently, it's working."

"He's not…buying my loyalty." Not wanting to give credence to that possibility, she turned her back on Kylie and made a beeline for the exit. "That's crazy."

"Is it?" Kylie hurried to catch up. "I think it's pretty smart. You asked all these questions and now suddenly he's making it really hard for you to blow the whistle."

"That's not what's happening." Jill grabbed the big brass handle on one of the doors and gave it a dramatic yank, then stepped out into the rapidly dimming afternoon light. She paused, wanting to distance herself from what Kylie was suggesting but not wanting to be rude and leave her there alone to make sure the doors were locked.

As Kylie fussed with her keys, Jill half turned and gave what she hoped would be a convincing close to the discussion. "The EPA people will be here tomorrow. If there's a problem, they'll see it."

"But what if they don't? Don't you remember what Jackson said? After they give the factory their approval, it might be too late."

"But what more can we do?"

Kylie looked around, her young face filled with frustration as she pulled her coat more tightly around her shoulders. "I just liked thinking we were in this together."

Jill opened her mouth, but all that came out was a puff of mist.

Shaking her head, Kylie started down the steps. Jill followed, feeling like a real jerk.

Taking care not to slip on the snow that had turned to a coating of ice, they walked to their cars in silence. Jill shivered. The tall pine trees surrounding the factory did little to prevent the mountain gusts from piercing her too-thin coat like so many frozen needles.

"I'll watch for you tonight." Unlocking her car, Jill called out over the top of it to Kylie, who was parked on the other side. "What's your costume?"

Kylie turned, wiping her cheek like she might have been crying. "I'm a princess." She gave her a sad smile, got into her car, and pulled away.

Jill started her engine, grateful that the heater still worked. Reminding herself that she still had to thank Sam for fixing the car, she shifted into reverse and made a cursory check of the rearview mirror. But something stopped her short.

A person stood among the trees, over near the razor-wire fence that surrounded the cooling tower. At least…she thought it was a person. A shiver grazed her skin as she twisted around in her seat to get a clearer look. Yes, someone moved, barely visible against the shadowy branches.

He disappeared around the corner of the building, a distinctive dragged-foot limp making him impossible not to identify.

Chapter 37

Jill spent the entire drive home debating about what she should do. Report her sighting of suspicious activity around the factory to the sheriff? Say something to Dean? Chalk it up to her overactive sleep-deprived imagination?

By the time she'd picked up the kids, fed them, and gotten all three of them into their costumes, she'd pretty much decided to let it go. She just wasn't up for any more pot-stirring.

Before darkness fell, the merry band of pirates set out to pillage and plunder around the neighborhood before heading to Main Street for the main event. Each business had at least one employee stationed out on the sidewalk, most of them in costume, handing out treats to the kids. Practically the whole town, and several people from the outlying areas, turned out for the night of family fun.

The street, which had been blocked off to traffic at either end, was already filling with costumed kids, adults, and even dogs. Scanning the crowd for Colleen, who was supposed to meet them at the stack of hay bales that the feedstore always set up as a photo area, Jill balanced Emma in the sling. Riley, who was in a state of perpetual motion, thanks to the combination of candy-consumed and candy-anticipated, looked like a runner waiting for the starter pistol.

Jill smiled at her friend Lucy Branigan, who perched on one of the bales, leaning on her husband, Bob, and waiting for Jerry to snap their photo. Lucy, who had a talent for all kinds of design, looked gangster-chic in a form-fitting black-and-white dress with a black beret, and Bob had traded his safety vest and hard hat for a pinstripe suit and black fedora. He held up a toy machine gun, while she toted a bag with a large dollar sign on it.

Their nine-year-old son, Casey, looked like all his sports heroes rolled into one. He wore a baseball cap, a football jersey and basketball shorts, and proudly held up a hockey stick. When it came to sports, the kid was definitely obsessed.

Jill scanned the immediate vicinity for their teenage daughter, Taylor, but wasn't surprised not to see her. She was a bit on the rebellious side, but she and Jill had bonded over strict-mother stories—Jill had won—and Taylor was one of Riley's favorite babysitters.

As soon as Jerry snapped the shot, the Branigans stepped down so the next group could move into position.

Approaching Jill, Lucy gave her costume

an admiring once-over. "Don't you look fancy."

"You too. Just don't go near the bank."

"Good point."

"Where's Taylor tonight? Off with her friends?"

"She got a second job. Hostess at the Fountain."

"And she's still at the bistro?" Jill raised an eyebrow. "I didn't know she was so ambitious."

"She wants to be able to live on her own after graduation. It's time for her to learn that in the working world, you don't always get to hang out with your friends on Halloween."

"Harsh life lesson." Jill turned to Bob. "The factory is so quiet without your crew. I miss you guys already."

"A few of us will be around, at least for another week." He smoothed the brim of his fedora. "We have to finish cleaning up after ourselves."

Lucy slung the money bag over her

shoulder. "We're heading over to the bakery to get Jack-o-lantern cake pops. Want to come with us?"

"Thanks, but we were supposed to meet Colleen. You haven't seen her, have you?"

Bob and Lucy shook their heads, then hurried to catch up with Casey, who was pretending to skate down the sidewalk in pursuit of an imaginary hockey puck.

Jill sighed. Riley was way too revved up to wait any longer for the *shop-or-treating*, so she gave him the go-ahead nod. Knowing Colleen, she had probably worked late and was still in her apartment trying to decide if she should be a Jedi warrior or Superwoman.

Unless, of course, she had decided things weren't going to work out with Dean and she intended to stay home feeling sorry for herself. It wouldn't be the first time a broken heart had resulted in a last-minute change of plans.

Working their way down the block, they made it to the diner, where Glo sat outside in a red vinyl chair at a card table heaped with platters of saran-wrapped miniature donuts.

"Hi, sugar." She plunked a donut into Riley's pumpkin. "Happy Halloween."

"Thank you." Riley's eyes grew even wider than the donut.

"And for the bigger kids." Glo held up a small orange flashlight with a purple plastic cord looped through one end. "We like to encourage a safe-and-sane Halloween." When she flicked the switch, a shadowy ghost appeared in the center of the beam.

"Glo." Jill scoffed. "You know I don't believe in ghosts."

"Neither do I." She held up another one. "Would you rather have a spider?"

"Ew. I'll stick with the ghost." Jill accepted the gift and slipped the cord around her neck, then tucked the light neatly inside her tapestry vest to prevent Emma from chewing on it. At least it would keep Riley occupied on the walk home. "Have you seen

Colleen? She was supposed to meet us at the photo area."

"I haven't seen her come home yet." Glo tipped her chin toward the door across the street, on the corner right next to the hardware store. "But I've been pretty busy."

Jill sighed. Glo had a knack for keeping track of people's comings and goings, no matter how busy the diner got. It was like a sixth sense with her.

She was about to encourage Riley to move on to the next stop when a sharp recrimination zinged into her ear like an arrow hitting its mark.

"Why are none of you wearing coats?"

Jill turned to see her mom, expert hurler of accusations, advancing toward them. "Mom, it's Halloween. Look around. Nobody's wearing their coat."

"But surely you—"

"Happy Halloween, Marion." Glo greeted her warmly, then turned back to Jill. "If I see

Colleen, honey, I'll tell her you're looking for her."

"Thanks, Glo."

As Glo turned her attention to a pair of enthusiastic young superheroes, Mom stepped gingerly back into the flow of the foot traffic alongside Jill. "I thought I might run into you here."

"Mom, you knew this was where we'd be. I told you. I thought you said you were staying home in case anyone came to the door."

"They all came at once, as usual, then nothing. I thought I might as well get a little shopping done." She held up a small bag from the drug store.

"Shopping? Why, did you run out of aspirin?"

"You know I like to be prepared."

"I know, Mom." She smiled to herself. Why couldn't Mom just admit that she'd wanted to come with them? "So. Would you like to walk with us?"

"I'm here. I might as well." She paused as Riley found the line for the table in front of the flower shop. "We used to have such fun on Halloween."

Jill shot her a confused look, wondering who she meant by "we." She was about to ask when Mom continued.

"Do you remember that year I made you the ladybug costume?"

Jill thought for a few seconds, then a dim memory surfaced. "Oh, yeah. I must have been about four."

"You insisted on being a ladybug and of course the dime store had everything but. I wasn't about to drive to the city just to look for a ladybug costume, of all things, so I—"

"So you made me one. You hated sewing, but you made me that costume. I totally forgot about that."

"Figures." Mom gave her a sideways look, flashing just a hint of an uptick at the corner of her mouth.

Was she actually being jovial?

Jill sputtered out a laugh. "I loved that costume." She paused, surprised to find herself genuinely enjoying a conversation with her mother. "You were a good mom. You know that, right?"

Mom blinked a couple of times. "And you were a *terrible* daughter." She kept her gaze forward, her smile threatening to spread. "Completely ungrateful."

Jill let out a chuckle. "Thanks a lot."

"But you're a good mother too. These children are very blessed." Mom swallowed, like saying something nice made her throat ache. "You can do this on your own, you know. I never could, but you're stronger than me."

Jill looked at her, not quite sure if she'd heard right. It sounded like Mom was admitting that at some point she'd considered breaking free from Dad but had been too afraid. Having no idea how to respond to that cracked-open can of worms, Jill just let out a quiet, "Thanks."

They had moved on to the line in front of the theatre, which had been turned into a fun house for the night.

Mom put both of her hands on Riley's tiny shoulders. "Why don't I take the kids through this while you go over and check on Colleen."

"Really? You don't mind."

"I offered, didn't I?"

Not wanting to press her luck with Mom's holiday spirit of cooperation, Jill handed over Emma and instructed Riley to stay close to Grandma. Then she cut a diagonal across the crowded street.

The sight of Sam handing out candy with his dad in front of their store reminded her that she hadn't thanked him yet for fixing her car. It had been a busy day, but that was no excuse.

Seeing her, he said something to his dad, then edged his way out from behind the card table piled so high with sweets that it looked like they'd robbed a chocolate bank.

"Ahoy thar." He smiled. "Where are your shipmates?"

"Mom is taking them through the fun house." Realizing how cold it was out here now that she didn't have the benefit of Emma's warmth, she folded her arms. "Has Cole come out yet? She was supposed to meet us."

"No, I don't even think she's gotten home from work."

"Seriously? That girl needs to loosen up and have some fun."

"Yeah, try telling her that." He looked distracted. "Hey, I'm sorry about your car. My guess is it'll turn up after tonight."

She frowned. "Turn up?"

"Probably just a dumb Halloween prank. You know, bored teenagers."

"But...it—"

A group of miniature ninjas cut between them, throwing her off-balance. By the time she'd steadied herself, Sam had changed the subject.

"Hey, I have something I need to tell you." He glanced at his watch. "I'm taking off for a few days."

"What? Where are you going?"

He looked around, like he didn't want his plans to become the subject of town gossip, then reached into the inside pocket of his coat and pulled out a small box. Sheltering it from prying eyes, he popped it open, revealing a sparkling diamond.

"Oh...Sam..." All remnants of fatigue instantly left her. "It's your mom's engagement ring."

He held up a hand to shush her, then snapped the box shut and returned it to his pocket. "It seems like a good time, don't you think?"

"Sure. But...how did you convince your dad?"

"He's the one who gave it to me. So, maybe you're right. Maybe he's finally getting ready to move on."

"That's wonderful, Sam." Her lower lip quivered at the unexpected combination of emotions. "All of it."

"Yeah. I still hate cities though."

She took in a breath as the full weight of what he was saying hit her. "Her opening night. Oh, Sam. That's so romantic."

"I hope I still think so when I'm stuck in Manhattan traffic trying to get to the opera house."

"You'll be fine."

"Yeah." He smiled, then patted her shoulder. "You'll be fine too."

"When do you leave?"

"I'm taking the red-eye out of Missoula. I promised Dad I'd help here as long as I could, but I should hit the road in about half an hour." He jarred to attention. "When you find my sister, tell her I'll call her tomorrow."

"Will do. Wait, does she know?"

"Oh, yeah. She's already got her bride magazine collection out for Grace to go through."

Jill shifted awkwardly. This was real. He was leaving and when he came back, he'd be an engaged man. She was genuinely happy for him, so why did this news make her feel like crying?

As Sam returned to his place next to his dad, Jill ambled toward Colleen's door. Her chest felt like it was going to cave in with a perplexing sense of loss. She'd lost Caleb, and now she was losing Sam too.

What was she thinking? If she had ever stood a chance with him, she'd missed it a long time ago. And the truth was, she didn't want to start up with someone new. As impossible as it seemed, she wanted to have her old life back, the way things were before Caleb went so far off-course. She still loved him, and her true desire was for the marriage to be restored.

Just as she reached Colleen's door and pressed the doorbell, the sound of "Ghostbusters" yanked her head around to where the town band was set up in the park at the end of the block. People were dancing in the street, and the sight both lifted her spirits and weighed down her heart.

Then a woman in a poofy blue Cinderella gown swirled out into an open area, her dress shimmering in the moonlight. Jill smiled. It was Kylie. And then Prince Charming—aka Jackson—moved into position in front of her. He took her in his arms and they started dancing, a bit awkwardly at first, but there was a joy to their movements.

Jill felt a little of her mood lift. Every woman deserved a prince like Jackson. Or Sam. Or maybe even Dean.

Sadly, *she* had married a guy who had looked like a prince but then acted like a frog and drank like a fish.

When Colleen didn't come to her door— no surprise, really—Jill decided to walk over to her office and save her from her workaholic self. This was Halloween, after all. And if Jill was going to walk around town wearing an outfit that was a bit outrageous and not nearly warm enough for this time of year, her best friend should do the same.

A few minutes later, she was a block off Main, away from the crowd. The spooky chords of "Thriller" and the sound of happy banter grew indistinct at her back. Off to her left, she could see that the reception area at the front of Colleen's office building was dark, but the light shone in the window in the back where Colleen had her desk.

Caught ya, Working Girl.

Jill walked through the front door. "Cole! You stood us up."

Stepping into the back office, she saw a familiar sight. Colleen sat at her desk, her focus glued to the screen of her computer.

"Come on, Cole—"

"This is bad, Jill." Colleen barely acknowledged her entrance, but the urgent quality in her voice sent a shiver down Jill's spine. "We have to stop them."

Chapter 38

After hearing a quick summary of the phone calls and emails that had granted Colleen official clearance to access Clean Green's file, Jill stood behind her staring in disbelief. There in front of them on the screen was the complete toxicity report. Why hadn't it occurred to her that working in a law office gave Colleen access to legal documents?

"This is so much worse than you thought." Colleen's voice shook as she scrolled down the screen.

"No…Cole." This was all mixed up, and now Jill had to undo the damage she'd previously done by foolishly crying wolf. She grabbed a chair and plunked down next to her. "I met with Mr. Nyland today. He explained everything. There was a leak at their site in Japan. They found out about it when they got this report."

"A leak? That's what he told you? Look at this." Colleen pointed to the screen and read. "*In excess of two thousand barrels of toxic chemicals buried on property owned by Clean Green Associates*. That was no 'leak.'"

"But…he said they didn't know."

"Oh, they knew all right. Look at this article I found when I looked up Clean Green's history." She brought up a different screen and read. "*Clean Green Associates pulled up stakes in Nagosaka with no warning.*"

"No warning?" Jill's voice sounded weak. "What about the workers?"

"Good question." Colleen read on, her jaw tightening even more. *"Reportedly, the shutdown occurred because of poor labor relations. But according to Haru Tanaka, a union representative in Nagosaka, Clean Green left because the Ministry of the Environment had uncovered a stash of unlawfully stowed industrial waste in the area behind their plant. When this was discovered, CGA abandoned its plant without notice."*

"That can't be true." Jill's stomach churned. "He said the situation was misrepresented in the press. They didn't know their plant was polluting the groundwater."

"Of course they knew. Look." Colleen tapped the screen with a perfectly polished red nail. *"Clean Green was the subject of several lawsuits, at least one involving a death.* Lawsuits, Jill. They knew. And they continued to cover it up."

A death?

"But…" The room started to spin, and Jill honed her focus on the vase filled with yellow Gerberas and rust-colored chrysanthemums, wondering vaguely if Dean had given them to Colleen. "…if they were sued, wouldn't that stop them from doing business?"

"It doesn't mean anything. They settled out of court and left the country. Started up here under a different name."

"Yes. And a different method of handling the toxins. They pump it all back into the ground."

"*Different?* Jill, that's what they claimed to be doing in Japan." She tapped at her keyboard, then brought up another screen.

"What's this?" Acid worked its way up Jill's throat.

"This is the business plan they had on file in Nagosaka. It claims that they would be exempt from the need for a permit to dispose of toxic byproducts because they wouldn't have any."

Jill read, not wanting to believe it. "*All waste products will be pumped back into the ground at the factory site via an injection well.*" A lump of rage and humiliation formed in her throat. "I can't believe it. Mr. Nyland told me himself that this was a new process that he invented because of what happened in Japan. Are you sure that business plan is from before they had the problem?"

"This plan predates that toxicity report by over a decade."

A decade? Jill felt all the air leave her lungs. Just a few hours ago, she'd been so sure that she'd been wrong. But she'd been right all along. Horribly right.

"But…why? Just for money?"

"Money is a powerful motivator. I'm sorry, Jill. Even working in a small-town law firm, I see heartbreaking things like this. People do the wrong thing and get away with it, and don't care that other people will have to pay the price."

"We need to show this to Dean."

Colleen's jaw hardened. "He's one of them, Jill."

"No. Colleen, you heard him talking about his long-term vision for this company. And he didn't work for them when they were in Japan."

"But what if that's just his story?" Colleen's face started to contort like she was about to cry. "Why can't I pick a decent guy just once?"

Jill's heart broke for Colleen. And for herself.

The notion that they could just plain ignore all of this taunted her. She could keep her great job with the raise and the college fund. Colleen could pretend that Dean was who he appeared to be. A real prince.

Then she thought about Riley and Emma and all the little superheroes and princesses innocently running around outside at this very moment. How could she move forward in her job, knowing what she now knew? That if she didn't do something to stop Nyland

Enterprises from poisoning the groundwater, people would get sick.

Kids Riley's age would die young. Then their kids—maybe even her own grandkids—would be born with mysterious birth defects. How could she live with that, knowing she could have stopped it but chose not to?

Colleen was so right. Money was a powerful motivator. Money and the stability it provided. But as much as she wanted that stability, the desire to protect her community had to be even more powerful. They had to be better than the Mr. Nylands of the world. Something bad was happening here, and they were being called to stop it.

Sitting up straighter, she gestured toward the screen. "Can you print all of this for me?"

"Sure, but what are you going to do?"

"I need to make sure the regulators from the EPA see it tonight. Before they tour the factory."

"How are you going to get it to them tonight?"

"I know where they are right now."

Colleen rolled her chair back. "I'll go with you."

"No. I really think it's best if you don't get involved. It's bad enough that the whole town's going to hate *me*."

Colleen opened her mouth, probably to argue, but closed it again and nodded.

"You go find my mom." Jill put a reassuring hand on Colleen's arm. "She has the kids in the fun house. I'll meet you there." She swallowed hard. "This won't take long."

Chapter 39

Jill walked the short block to the Fountain Restaurant, clutching a manila envelope on which she'd written in bold black letters *Confidential Information for the EPA*, and trying to either work up her courage or talk herself out of what she was about to do.

Remembering what she'd read in the book about whistleblowing, she'd devised a plot to get this to them anonymously. She hadn't wanted to say anything to Colleen, but that book was filled with stories about how dangerous things like this could get when big money was involved. Whistleblowers having their lives ruined, or worse. She shuddered at the thought.

She approached the restaurant, one of the tall, freestanding old brick buildings that gave Madison Falls its character. Her heart pounded in syncopation with the town band's distant rendition of "Little Blue Man" as she crept into the dark woodsy area at the side of the building. Watching from a safe distance, she had a perfect view through the lofty windows into the softly lit dining room.

Discreetly positioning herself behind a thick tree trunk, she scanned the room. There at a table in the back corner, she could see Dean, Mr. Nyland, Mr. Steele, and three other men in suits. Two of them looked to be in their twenties, and one at least fifty. It seemed safe to assume that he was the one with the most clout in the group.

Shifting slightly, she had a nice view into the front entryway. As she had hoped, Taylor stood at the podium in her new job as official gatekeeper.

Jill gave one more confirming look at the men, who were currently occupied with their meals. That was good. The more distracted they were, the better for her. She was about to act on her plan when Mr. Steele reached into his pocket and took out his phone, which he glared at as if it had just insulted him.

He excused himself, then left the table and headed toward the front of the restaurant. Jill held her breath. Thank goodness she hadn't moved from her spot any sooner or she would have walked right into him. Cautiously, she crept around the stand of trees and closer to the street. She saw through the side window closest to the front that he was in the entryway near Taylor, still scowling at his phone. Then he burst out the front door and, to her surprise, got into his car and drove away. She stood there, listening as the sound of his engine grew dim.

Where on earth was he going?

She drew back into the shadows, remaining completely still, and having no idea if she should act quickly in case he was coming back soon, or just wait and see what happened.

But too many precious seconds had slipped by already. Since getting caught in the act was the worst outcome she could think of, she just stood there frozen in an inert stupor.

After about five minutes, judging by the number of Halloween hits she heard the band play, the car returned. Still looking agitated, Mr. Steele got out and went back inside.

Jill let out a long breath. She scooted to her original position, where she saw Mr. Steele return to the table, cheerfully explaining away whatever he had run off to do.

Their server appeared, apparently to take their dessert orders, and creating the perfect diversion. Jill moved quickly around to the front of the building and looked through the leaded-glass window in the tall front door. When she caught Taylor's eye, she motioned for her to step outside.

"Look at you. I love your costume," Taylor said approvingly as she let the door shut behind her, rubbing her arms against the cold air. "What's going on?"

"I have to ask you to do something." Jill motioned her off to the side, as an added precaution. "There's a table in the far back corner with six men in suits sitting at it."

Taylor nodded. Jill knew she'd know which table she meant, because nobody wore a suit in this town unless they were going to a wedding or a prom.

"I need you to give this to the man in the navy-blue suit." Jill handed her the envelope. "And if anybody asks who it's from, you don't know. Okay?"

"Sure. Why the mystery?"

"I promise I'll tell you when I can, but for now, just give it to him."

Taylor gave her a *whatever* shrug and went inside.

Jill hurried back to her hiding place and watched through the windows, praying that she hadn't just put her young friend at risk. But enlisting a bored, indifferent teen to make this delivery worked better than she could have hoped. Taylor handed the envelope to the man in blue and was out of there before anyone had a chance to ask any questions.

Scowling, the man slipped the papers from the envelope and started reading. His scowl deepened as he said something, then passed the first paper to the man beside him and went on to the next page.

Jill waited, not knowing what to expect. Would they calmly discuss it? Or would the conversation become defensive and heated?

No...the men started laughing, like they thought it was a joke. Then they raised their glasses and recommenced with their celebratory conversation.

Jill felt her jaw drop. They might as well have given each other good ol' boy pats on the back.

This was awful. She had given the EPA a smoking gun and they had laughed it off. Was this like one of the situations she'd read about? Did Mr. Nyland have them in his back pocket?

The only one who wasn't laughing or joining in the merrymaking was Dean. He was studying the papers with a look of grave concern. If she had to guess, she would say that Dean was taken completely off guard by this information, and that he was as stunned by it as she had been.

Not knowing what else to do, she stepped grimly back to the sidewalk and away from the restaurant. What now? Take it to the press? Find someone higher up in the EPA? There had to be something.

Glumly, she turned the corner a block from Main. But when she glanced over at Colleen's office building, she slowed. That was strange. The light in the back was still on. Colleen had been about to lock up and turn out the lights when Jill had left her at least half an hour ago. Why would she still be there?

Knowing her, she'd probably gone down another research rabbit trail. She really did need Jill to rescue her. Besides, it was almost time for the costume contest, and they should salvage what fun they could out of this night.

She crossed the street and marched through the front door toward the light spilling from Colleen's office. "You know, Cole. You really shouldn't leave your front door unlocked when you—"

Stopping abruptly in the doorway, she nearly choked on her words. There was no sign of Colleen, but her chair lay on its back. The vase had been knocked over, and water dripped from the desk into a pool on the floor.

Horror filled her, and her mind went numb. If her involvement with the factory had caused her best friend to be endangered…

That thought trailed off as another, even more frightening one took hold. She had to find her mom and the kids.

Urgency whirled her around but she froze at the sight of a shadowy figure just inside the front door. Her heart lurched and she let out a shriek that caused the figure—a man—to draw back. His face was now illuminated by the light from the streetlamp and she recognized him. It was that red-haired college kid…Glenn? The one who'd been hired to hand out the brochures on her interview day. Fear fell away, replaced by a fierce protective instinct.

"Where's my friend?" She barreled toward him with the force of a bulldozer. "Colleen. Where is she?"

"I don't know." He backed up like a scared rabbit, his hands flying up in self-defense. "I was just supposed to follow you."

"Someone told you to follow me? Who?" Standing so close, it became clear that she was almost as tall as him.

"He told me not to tell—"

"Who?" She raised her arms, like she

wanted to grab him by the front of his jacket.

He whimpered, then swallowed so hard she could see his Adam's apple move even in this dim light. "That guy from the factory. Mr. Steele." He rapid-fired out his answer like something had him even more scared than she was.

"How long have you been following me?"

"I don't know. A little while."

"Hours or days?"

"Days."

He'd been following her for *days?* The image of that car parked in front of her house creeped her out all over again. "Why?"

"He has me tell him whenever you do anything that might mean you could be trying to interfere."

Interfere? Whatever this was about, she didn't have time now to figure it out. "Look, you better tell me what you know about my friend. The one who works here. Because if anything happens to her, I swear I'm going to tell the sheriff you were directly responsible."

"I don't know anything." The kid's lip quivered like he might cry. "All I know is I followed you in here and stood outside that door while you two were talking. Then after, I did like I was supposed to and messaged what you said to Mr. Steele."

Jill felt sick. That must have been the text he'd received at the table.

"And then what?"

"I followed you again. That's all I did."

The thought that he'd been watching her while she was outside the restaurant made her shudder, but she shook it off. The kid himself was harmless—just dumb and gullible and probably desperate for cash.

Sidestepping toward the door, she jabbed a warning finger at him. "Stay away from me."

Jill stumbled outside, having no idea what to do. But with no time to waste, her gut told her she had to confront the men she knew were responsible.

Jill Came Tumbling After

Chapter 40

A few minutes later, Jill burst through the door of the Fountain, whizzed past Taylor, and slammed into a waiter, sending his tray of drinks crashing to the floor. She stopped in the center of the room, staring at the vacant back table.

"When did these people leave?" She cried out to the room in general, getting nothing in return but stunned silence.

She darted back to the entry and caught

Taylor by the arm. "Did you see them leave?

"Yeah, like, five minutes ago. But what—?"

She ran outside, her thoughts desperately racing. Sam was gone, leaving her without her safety net. The sheriff…of course, that was it. She needed to find him.

Knowing that he would probably be out patrolling the event, she tore her way back to Main Street.

Cutting across a sea of people as they worked their way toward the park for the costume contest, she scanned the crowd in the hope of seeing the sheriff or one of his deputies. The sight of Colleen's pitch-black apartment windows tore at her heart, but a movement at her front door yanked her to a stop. It was Dean, urgently pressing the bell.

The hope that he could help surged through her as she tried to disentangle herself from a cluster of giggly Disney princesses. She'd just reclaimed her momentum when she felt herself being yanked to one side by someone who had a firm grip on her arm. Before she could let out a protest, a hot-breathed voice snarled in her ear.

"If you don't want your friend to die, you won't draw any attention to yourself. Do you understand?"

Stark terror ripped through her. She snapped a look at Mr. Steele, who maintained his hold on her arm as he steered her away from the crowd.

"Where is she?" She felt like she was shouting, but in reality, she sounded more like a frightened mouse.

"Shut up!" he barked through gritted teeth. "I'm taking you to her."

She went willingly, in the hope that he was telling the truth. When he stepped into the alley behind the flower shop and she saw his car parked haphazardly next to a dumpster, her terror grew. Before she could protest, he opened the backseat and shoved her in. She watched as he crossed behind the car at a rapid pace.

As he got into the driver's seat and started the engine, she pulled at the door handle, but it wouldn't budge. Then she slammed painfully back against the seat as he stepped on the gas.

"Where are we going?" Her voice had some power behind it now, not that it did her any good.

"You're done asking questions." He spit out the words like they tasted bad in his mouth.

Jill sat forward, positioning herself as close as she could get without vaulting over the seat. "If you've done anything to my friend Colleen, I swear—"

"You were supposed to be stupid." Mr. Steele smacked a palm against the steering wheel. "I told Owens to hire anyone he wanted to get the place up and running. 'Just make sure they aren't industry people,' I said. 'We need people who will do what we tell them and not ask any questions.'"

Jill stared at him, horrified. When she had overheard him say that she had no knowledge of the industry, he hadn't meant it as a simple observation. He had meant that hiring her and Kylie because they were ignorant had been intentional. They weren't supposed to be smart enough to question anything.

The stinging realization that Dean had given her the job because he thought she was dim struck her to the core. But she couldn't blame *him*. He'd only been following orders.

She snapped back to her more pressing concern. If she was going to find out where Colleen was, she would have to get Mr. Steele to talk to her. "You had someone follow me. Why?"

Mr. Steele glanced out the side window at the dark residential neighborhood they were passing through. "Do you know what my job is, Miss Martin?"

The question caught her off guard, then made her a little angry. Why was he wasting time?

Before she could venture an answer, he went on. "My job is to protect Mr. Nyland.

And do you know how I do that?"

If he hadn't been driving, Jill would have been tempted to slap the back of his head. *Enough with the rhetorical questions, you pompous jerk!* She held her tongue and waited for him to get to the point.

"I have made sure that Mr. Nyland's reputation as being concerned for the environment and the local community has preceded him. Have I not done an excellent job of that?"

"Stellar."

"And you, Miss Martin, will not undo all the work I've done to lay the groundwork for this company to succeed."

"Succeed? By poisoning our water? You can't do this. What about the people who live here? Do you realize how many lives are at stake?"

"That's not my concern." He lifted a shoulder. "It doesn't matter if we add more pollution to the environment because it comes from so many uncontrollable sources as it is.

No one can really prove cause. We're all in it for ourselves. It's just that some of us are luckier and smarter than the rest of you."

As he turned onto the old highway that would lead them away from town, she swallowed back a lump of cold fear and fumbled for her safety belt. From where she sat in the center of the backseat, she could see his eyes in the rearview mirror. There had to be something human in him that she could appeal to.

"Don't you have kids? People you care about? What if it were your family…"

His eyes widened for a brief moment, like she'd touched a nerve. Then just as quickly, they turned ice cold. "I know enough to keep the people I care about a safe distance from places like Madison Falls, Montana."

The coldblooded sentiment hit her gut like a cannonball. What could lead a person to be so heartless? But there was no time to dwell on that thought. "This isn't going to work, you know. People here are smart. They'll figure it out."

"By the time anyone notices a problem, we will have found other reasons to vacate the place. I won't be forced out before I'm ready again. I learned from the Japan fiasco."

The way he talked made her wonder who was really in charge. Was it his job to do all the behind-the-scenes dirty work while Mr. Nyland turned a blind eye?

He abruptly jerked the wheel, throwing her against the seat in a way that made her glad she'd buckled herself in. Then her heart leapt into her throat at the realization that he had pulled over to the side of the road. She looked around. They were on a part of the highway where there was nothing but the dark woodsy embankment leading down to the river to one side, and the steep incline of the mountain off to the other. And pretty much no one drove this way at night unless they had to.

Her nails dug into the seat on either side of her. What was he planning to do?

Keeping the engine running, he leaned over like he was retrieving something from the front passenger-side floor. Then he got out of the car and slammed his own door but opened hers. She undid her seatbelt and twisted to face him, choreographing in her head a maneuver that would propel her into the driver's seat before he could stop her.

He probably guessed what she was thinking because he snarled out something that almost sounded like a laugh. "You're a lot smarter than I gave you credit for. But still not as smart as you think." He was busy doing something, but his hands were just a little out of her view.

She edged closer to the front seat, both to try to see what he was up to and to prepare to make her move. "Why are you doing this?"

"Why do you think? There's money to be made. Lots of it." Whatever he was doing out there made a splashing sound. "And I'm not going to let a little thing like a meddlesome employee stand in my way."

Panicking, she lunged across the seat and grabbed the steering wheel, but before she could get her legs over he leaned in and clutched her by the hair, wrenching her head back. Something soft covered her face and she fought to get a breath, but the smell of disinfectant overpowered her. She tried to push free, but her body went numb and her strength faded.

Darkness overcame her. Her will to fight evaporated and she slowly gave in to a welcoming unconsciousness.

Chapter 41

Jill ached all over, sleep tugging at her and making it impossible to open her eyes. She felt cold…so cold. But when she reached for her blanket, her hand flailed, grabbing at air.

What had woken her? The baby? She strained to listen but there was no sound. Then she heard a *flapping* from somewhere overhead. She groaned. Maybe she had left the window open and a bird had flown in. That would explain the cold…

Again, she tried to wrench open her eyes. Why wouldn't her lids move?

A dull ache pulsed through her head, and she struggled to sit up but couldn't. Once again, she tried to pry her eyes open, then blinked. They *were* open. Then why couldn't she see?

Something…wasn't…right.

Slowly, she spread out her fingers, feeling a cold grittiness beneath them. A *chirping* sound from somewhere to her right grew louder, more distinct. Something skittered past her ear, then across her arm. She jerked, sitting up and protectively pulling herself into a ball as whatever it was dashed away.

Wide awake now, her head thrummed with confusion. Where was she?

A sense of danger clung to her like the last remnants of a nightmare. Why couldn't she remember how she got here? She pushed to her feet, unsteady in shoes that felt unfamiliar. Wait…she had gone to sleep in her shoes?

No…she was still in her pirate costume. But, why…?

Slowly, her recall started to click in. The Halloween festival. People dancing. Her search for Colleen.

Then raw panic grabbed her by the throat. Where were Riley and Emma? Right…she'd left them with her mom. But where were they now?

Holding her hands in front of her, she took a cautious step on the soft, uneven ground, then another. The unsettling sensation of not being able to see her hand right in front of her face made her dizzy, and she stumbled, her fingers brushing against something. One more careful step and she felt the damp, gritty surface of a wall. No. Not solid enough to be a wall—more like the crumbling side of a steep hill.

But she wasn't outside. The air felt too stifling. Not to mention the complete absence of light like she had never experienced before.

Clarity pushed through the ache in her head and brought with it a horrifying comprehension. It couldn't be…but there was no other obvious explanation.

She was in the *mineshaft*.

But, how? How had she gotten there? No, that didn't matter. She just had to find her way out.

Don't panic, Jill.

Forcing in deep breaths, she continued to move along the wall. That had to lead to a corridor, or the exit. The thought of that massive door terrified and confused her. Someone had to have broken through that lock and chain to put her there, but who? And *why?*

Stumbling, she tried to catch herself, then hit the ground hard. She reached to push herself back up, clutching at something that she thought was solid but crumbled in her hand. An eerie feeling swept over her, leaving in its wake the sensation that she wasn't alone.

That thought sent a tremble through her as she forced herself upright. Her body felt like she'd been run over by a fleet of buses, but she had to keep moving.

Continuing on, she stepped over whatever it was that had disintegrated at her touch. Then a sound like a soft moan stopped her cold. Had she imagined it? She thought it had come from somewhere near her feet, but with the darkness playing tricks on her equilibrium, it was hard to know for sure.

She stood completely still, listening. When the sound didn't come again, she slowly dipped down, reaching for anything that could be used as a weapon if need be. Her hand hit something solid and she fumbled to get a grip on it, then paused. It felt like a handle of some kind. She reached down with the other hand and felt a smooth flat surface attached to it. A briefcase, or maybe a small suitcase. So strange. And not very helpful as a means of self-defense.

She was about to abandon the idea of needing to defend herself when the moaning sound happened again, this time louder and somehow...*familiar*.

Suddenly, a huge tsunami of nightmarish memories threatened to drown her. Something had happened to Colleen, and when Jill had gone to look for her, something had happened to her too. Mr. Steele. A car...then that awful smell.

Oh, good Lord. Chloroform.

Then he had dumped her in the mine? Of course, that made sense. Or as much sense as any of this did. He would have access to the key to the mine.

Another moan cut into her thoughts and she knew with horrifying certainty what had happened. Mr. Steele had said he was taking her to Colleen. And he had meant it.

"C...Cole...?" Her voice rasped like she'd swallowed sandpaper. She lowered herself to her hands and knees, feeling for something that she wasn't so sure she wanted to find. Her fist bumped against something warm. An arm. She grasped onto it, working her way up a silky sleeve to a shoulder, then a face. It was her.

"Colleen!"

She was breathing but not conscious. Jill looked around, frantically trying to see, but not able to make out anything more than the vaguest of shapes. She sprang to her feet, then felt for the wall again, determined to find the way out. But after what felt like an eternity of painful staggering and stumbling, she reached a horrifying conclusion. Not only were they trapped in the mineshaft, but they were in some sort of pit with no discernable way out.

Her attempts at getting a foothold on the sides only intensified her panic. After one more failed try, she ricocheted back, panting, sweat dripping from her forehead.

"God!" She wanted to cry, but instead she cried out. "What do You want from me? Please. You have to help me. I can't do this on my own. Show me the way out."

Falling to her knees in uncontrollable sobs, she buried her face in her hands. This was hopeless. She reached around in the dark, found Colleen's hand, and held it to her chest.

Then she pulled in a breath, straining to listen. Had she heard something? It sounded like—

"Jill!"

It was! The blessed, dim sound of someone screaming out her name.

She jumped to her feet. "I'm here!" As she raised her hands to cup them to her mouth, her thumb hooked something around her neck. She tugged at it and let out a gasp. A flashlight? Why hadn't she remembered that Glo had given her a flashlight?

Laughing in crazed, exhausted relief, she yanked it out of her vest and clicked it on, rejoicing in the beautiful glow it gave out. She lifted it upward, making the hazy image of a ghost dance across the ceiling above her. She sputtered out another laugh at the thought of telling Kylie there really was a ghost in this mine.

Now she could see the depth of the pit they were in—probably a good twelve feet on one side, culminating in what looked like a few boards nailed together to serve as a makeshift fence. The other sides continued up to the cavernous ceiling.

"Jill!" The voice had gotten closer.

"I'm here!" Her throat ached, but she called out with all her strength. "Down here! Be careful. It's some kind of hole."

A beam of light appeared. Then a face looking down at her. The face of a prince.

Tears came again. "Caleb."

"I'm here, honey. Are you okay?"

"I think so." Tentatively, she turned her light on Colleen, bracing herself for the worst. But apart from a few scratches on her face, she didn't look as bad as Jill had imagined. "But we have to get help for Cole."

He shone his light around the pit, lingering at the far end. Jill's stomach did a flip as she realized that the thing she'd inadvertently shaken hands with earlier was a skeleton. She shuddered. So, she and Colleen hadn't been the first ones to wind up down here.

Trying not to think too hard about that, she focused on the task at hand. "What do we do?"

"Hold on." He moved away from the edge and his light faded, like he was looking around for something he could use to pull her up with. Colleen stirred, her face contorting like she was in pain.

"It's going to be okay, Cole." Jill knelt next to her and took her hand. "God sent Caleb to us."

A sharp *snap* from above returned her attention upward. Caleb was ripping the fence away from the edge.

"Stand back, Jilly."

She stood and scampered to the other side of Colleen as he lowered the framework into the pit, then rested it against the side like a ladder.

"You're a genius. Do you think it'll hold me?"

"It's held up all these years. I think it can take your feather weight." He shifted the beam over to Colleen again. "We shouldn't try to move her. Let's get you out, then we'll go get help."

Jill couldn't argue. "We just have to hurry."

As Caleb held on from the top, Jill took hold of the splintery side rails. She raised a foot and tested her weight on the bottom rung. Semi-confident that it would hold, she pulled herself up.

"Oh, God." A bead of sweat rolled down her forehead and landed in her eye with a painful sting. "Please help me do this."

"Don't look down, Jilly." Caleb's voice was calm and soothing. "Remember that time we climbed the rock wall at Lolo Pass?"

"That…was…insane." She took a fortifying breath and lifted her foot to the next rung. "I thought I was going…to die."

"But you didn't. You did great."

"I was on a rope."

"True. But you didn't fall."

"If I had known I was going to do this today, I would have…" She paused, reaching for the next rung. "…worn better shoes."

Caleb laughed, a joyful sound that she hadn't heard enough of in the past few years.

"You've updated your fashion style since I left." He was obviously trying his best to sound lighthearted, but the strain from supporting the rotting wood was evident in his voice. "I think I like the old you better."

"Thanks. Maybe next Halloween, I'll let you design the wardrobe."

"Oh, man. I missed Halloween."

Tipping her head back, she gauged where she should put her hand next. Then something flitted past Caleb's head, making a nauseating *flap, flap flap* sound.

Bats!

In a horrible instant, she felt her foot slip and she let out a shriek, but Caleb caught her wrists. She looked up to see that he had dived over the edge almost to his waist. She regained her footing, and with his help made it the rest of the way up.

At the top, she folded into a heap on the cold ground, wanting to kiss it. Then as Caleb pulled her into his arms and held her, she turned into a sobbing mess.

"It's okay, Jilly." He ran a hand over her head, uttering a few soothing reassurances, then set her from him. "Come on." He stood, then helped her to her feet. "We have to go."

With his arm securely around her, she let him guide her. Taking one painful step at a time, she kept her focus on what she could see in the beam of Caleb's flashlight. They turned a corner, and he lifted his light higher, barely illuminating the huge double doors at the far end of the passageway.

Every muscle ached, but she kept her eyes on the exit. When the corridor opened into the large room that she remembered from all those years ago, a thought struck her.

"Wait…how did you get in through that door? It was locked."

"Easy. There's more than one way in."

Tightening his grip on her, he turned to the right and maneuvered them down another narrow passageway. For a long while, they trudged forward in silence broken only by the occasional critter skittering across the floor in front of them. She tried not to think about poor Colleen back there all alone, and prayed for her sake that she wouldn't wake up before help arrived.

"Caleb." She looked ahead at what seemed like nothing but an endless dark tunnel. "How do you know where we're going?"

"You remember, back in high school. The guys and I used to break into the mine. I know I told you."

"Yeah, you told me. But I never believed you."

He stopped abruptly and turned to the left, shining his light up a steep set of stairs that would have been easy to miss. At the top, she could see trees silhouetted against a moonlit sky. An open door!

"I guess you believe me now, huh?"

Sputtering out a laugh, she was about to move forward up the stairs when something swooped down, flapping so close to her face that she felt the cold tip of a wing against her forehead. She stumbled back, letting out a shriek that echoed through the passageway.

Caleb followed the shape with his light as it winged away, catching a hint of something sticking out of the wall about six feet beyond the exit hallway. As quickly as it was visible, it was engulfed in darkness again as he turned the light back on the exit and stepped toward it.

"Wait." She flung out her arm to stop him. "What was that?"

"What?"

"Shine your light back that way." Giving him a shove, she pointed into the darkness.

Clearly impatient, he swooped the light over again, to where a hot-pink pipe about two feet in diameter jutted out of the wall near the ceiling and cut across the corridor, then abruptly ended. It looked alarmingly clean and new in this place where everything was rusty and decaying.

She took a step closer, straining to get a better look. "Do you remember ever seeing that before?"

"No."

"Are you sure?"

"Uh...it's hot pink. I think I'd remember. Besides..." He stepped in closer too. "It's obviously pretty new."

She looked back, realizing that they'd been walking parallel to the side of the factory building, and this door had to be somewhere near the separator station.

"Caleb...I think I know what this is."

He looked down at her with both brows raised.

"They told us they're pumping the toxic waste back into the ground, but they're not." The words tumbled out of her mouth and she knew she probably wasn't making any sense. "They've been planning to dump it into the mineshaft. They're just going to let it flood the mine until it seeps out into our groundwater." She stumbled back toward the stairs, her urgency to get help intensifying.

"What?" Caleb followed. "Why?"

"Because if they don't have to pay to dispose of it, they'll make a huge profit. At our expense."

She stepped into the stairway, then jolted to a stop at the sight of Mr. Steele standing at the top and blocking the exit.

"So, you figured it out, Miss Martin. Good for you."

Her blood started to boil. "There's nothing *good* about this." She grabbed Caleb's hand. "And the name is *Mrs*. Martin."

"I see." He advanced a step. "Well, the two of you obviously belong together, which is fortunate because you're going to be down here for a very long time." He held up a lock like the one she'd seen on the gate to the razor-wire fence. "I have you to thank for pointing out this breach in our security. It will be locked up nice and tight from now on."

He paused, seeming to relish his moment of ultimate control. Then a dark form moved into the doorway behind him. A glint of moonlight on metal flashed as the shadowy figure raised something then brought it down hard across the back of Mr. Steele's head, sending him plummeting downward.

Caleb grabbed Jill and swept her past the groaning heap on the ground, then up the stairs and out into the blessedly fresh air.

A siren wailed and she looked around, getting her bearings as red and blue lights flashed through the trees from the parking lot. They were in the woods near the separator station, just as she'd thought.

She looked over at their rescuer, who still held a shovel in his hands. Caleb spoke to him, then pulled him into a very manly bear hug. As the two parted, Jill let out a gasp.

The man moved toward the gathering vehicles, waving the shovel over his head to get their attention. Watching him, Jill stepped in beside Caleb, who flung a protective arm around her.

"Caleb." She leaned against his side, finally feeling safe. "How on earth do you know Lenny Simpson?"

"You know Lenny too?" His chin jerked downward and he looked at her, surprised. "I've been going to AA meetings with him at the church. He's the one who let me know you needed help."

Jill Came Tumbling After

Chapter 42

Curled up on the sofa with her feet tucked under her, Jill pulled the afghan closer around her shoulders and snuck an admiring look at Caleb. He sat in the chair next to her relaying his side of the events of the previous night to Kylie, who sat crisscross on the other end of the sofa, leaning forward in rapt attention.

"So I was just sitting there at the pastor's house—that's where I've been staying. With him and his wife. Anyway, they were down at the church handing out candy. The phone rang, and it was Lenny—"

"Lenny?" Kylie aimed a confused look at Jill. "Lenny Simpson?"

Jill placed a hand on Caleb's knee. "You have to tell her how you two know each other."

Caleb nodded. "See, I went to church last Sunday, just to help set up the worship band. On my way out, I smelled bacon. I was hungry, and I asked someone what was going on. They said it was the AA meeting and that anyone was welcome to come in and have some breakfast. So I went in for the food and wound up staying for the meeting. That's when I met Lenny."

Kylie looked to Jill, who gave her a nod to confirm his story.

"Anyway, this meeting was powerful. The guy running it talked about God and how we can't do anything in our own power. He reminded me of all the things I used to know about faith that I'd let slip away. And that I was making alcohol more important than anything. More important than God...” He reached over and took Jill’s hand. “And my family.”

Jill offered him an encouraging smile and squeezed his hand. This was the first glimpse of real hope for their marriage that she’d had in a very long time.

“Afterward,” Caleb continued, “Lenny and I stuck around talking and he opened up about his situation. He said he tried to get a job at the factory, so I told him you worked here. Next thing I knew, I was telling him all about us. He’s a real good listener.”

“Him?” Kylie crinkled her nose in disbelief.

“Yeah. So he told me he didn’t get a regular factory job but Mr. Steele had offered him some nighttime security work.”

“What?” Kylie scoffed. “Nobody told me they were hiring security.”

“Of course not,” Jill explained. “They didn’t want anybody to know that some of the guys they brought in to do the drilling were coming back at night to put that pipe into the mineshaft. It was Lenny's job to make sure no one came around while they were working. Mr. Steele must have thought he was too dense to figure out what was going on."

"And too desperate for money," Caleb added. "He's trying to keep from losing his farm, so he took the work. It's a good thing too, because—"

"Because he saw Mr. Steele drag Colleen out of the trunk of his car, then me out of the backseat." Jill still couldn't believe it, no matter how many times she'd relayed it. "Then he saw him carry both of us inside the building. Fortunately, Lenny recognized me and called Caleb."

"And then he called the sheriff," Caleb added.

"I never trusted that Mr. S." Kylie hissed out his name. "I can't believe he just dropped you and Colleen in a pit. It's a miracle you weren't both killed."

"That's the only word to describe it." Jill shifted, still feeling the all-over pain that blessedly hadn't been caused by anything getting broken. "I think we've hit our quota of miracles for the year."

"So." Kylie leaned forward like a kid anxious to hear the end of a story. "Colleen is going to be okay?"

"She'll be in the hospital for a few more days." Jill couldn't believe how protected they'd been. This all could have been so much worse. "Then yeah, the doc says she'll be fine."

A movement outside caught Jill's eye, and she looked over to see Glo's car pull up in front of the house. Glo got out, then lifted a box from the seat next to her and started up the walkway.

"I'll go give her a hand." Caleb stood and went to the entryway.

The second he was out the door, Kylie's eyes brightened and she turned to Jill. "So. What's going on with you two? Is he staying here?"

"I might keep him around." Jill watched through the window as he jogged out and met Glo, then took the box from her. "It's nice to have someone to shovel the walk."

Kylie swatted her leg. "I'm serious."

"He's been going to Alcoholics Anonymous meetings every day this past week. Got his old job back at the lumber mill, plus he's working at the hardware store. He said he realized he hit bottom, and the pastor has been helping him get back up."

Kylie made a humming sound. "AA is a big step. That's really encouraging." She reached out to give Jill's knee a friendly squeeze. "So, everything's going to be back to normal?"

"I don't know, Kylie. It seems like he's had a real heart change, but it's going to take some time to know for sure. I think it's worth giving it another chance. It's what I really wanted."

"I'm so happy for you. Oh, but does that

mean you're quitting your job?"

"I don't think I have a job *to* quit. How would they possibly be able to keep the place in business now?"

Biting her lower lip, Kylie nodded sadly. "Hard to run a business from prison."

The front door opened and Glo entered then hurried to the sofa to give Jill a hug. "Oh, sweetie. It's all just so awful. Are you okay?"

"I'm fine." She exchanged a look with Caleb as he carried the box toward the kitchen. "Better than I've been in a long time, in fact. What's in the box?"

"Just a few things." Glo settled in the chair Caleb had vacated. "I thought you shouldn't have to cook for a few days."

"You're the best. Glo, this is my friend, Kylie."

"Cinderella." Glo smiled. "We met last night. Along with that tall, handsome prince of hers."

"I wasn't the only one who had an interesting night last night." Jill bobbed her head at Kylie, who took her cue and held up her hand, showing off a modest but beautiful diamond.

Putting her hands to her cheeks, Glo gasped. "Well, look at that. Congratulations, sweetie."

As Glo and Kylie chatted about wedding plans, the phone rang and Caleb emerged from the kitchen to answer it. His face turned serious and he disappeared back into the kitchen.

Glo reached over and patted Jill's hand. "I heard what you found out about the factory."

"I guess it's probably all over town by now."

Glo's face tensed. "Do you think they'll be able to open after all this?"

"I really don't see how." A tinge of illogical guilt pinched Jill's nerves. It wasn't her fault, but she couldn't help but feel at least partly responsible for the economic impact this would have on the town. "I mean, who's going to trust them now?"

Glo let out a *tsk*. "And we all thought that Mr. Nyland was such a humanitarian."

"From what we heard, it was mainly Mr. Steele." Kylie said his name like it tasted sour. "Mr. Nyland wanted the money, but he let Mr. Steele do all the dirty work."

"What about that young handsome one?" Glo asked.

"Dean?" Jill sat up a little straighter. "I'm sure he'll be investigated, but I don't think he was in on it. He seemed as surprised as we were to find out about the illegal dumping."

Caleb came back into the room with the phone still at his side, his mouth slack. "That was the sheriff."

A knot tightened in Jill's stomach. "What now?"

"You are not going to believe what they found when they went to get Colleen last night."

"You mean aside from Jack Skellington?" A fresh shudder ran through her at the memory of the chalky handshake that would no doubt be with her for quite some time. "Because he and I met, remember?"

"Yeah, but it was what he had with him. A suitcase." He paused, like even he didn't believe what he was about to say. "Filled with cash."

"Oh…" Jill had totally forgotten about that mysterious suitcase.

"My goodness." Glo's eyebrows shot up. "Jill, you found the missing money from the sapphire mine."

Jill looked at Caleb. "Is that what it is?"

"The sheriff told me they're checking it out."

"If it is, you really are a hero," Glo said. "People have been speculating about that missing money for years."

"You're going to be in the news." Kylie sat forward. "That's almost as good as finding DB Cooper."

"But I didn't really find it. I mean, it was there but I didn't open it or anything."

"Still." Glo patted Jill's knee. "If you

hadn't done what you did, that money would have been lost forever once those men started flooding the mineshaft." She scrunched her face, then her expression lightened like the image had been too much to linger on. "Why don't I make you some tea?"

"Great." Jill gave Kylie a wink as Glo made her way toward the dining room. "And one of those ginger cookies."

Without even hesitating, Glo reached for the "care" basket that Jill had found on her porch a few days ago and had left sitting on her dining table. She stopped then turned to Jill with a *you-got-me* look on her face. "It's impossible to keep a secret in this town."

Jill chuckled. "Do you want your basket back? You might need it. I'm afraid lots of people in town are going to be unemployed again."

"You don't worry about that." Glo wagged a finger at her. "You're our town hero, even if it takes some folks a while to come around to appreciating it."

Kylie stood, casting a meaningful look from Caleb to Jill. "I'll go help Glo with the tea."

Caleb stepped in closer and kissed Jill on the forehead, then continued toward the entryway. "If you're okay here, I'm going to go to your mom's and get the kids. I want to spend some time with them today."

"That sounds great." She watched him put the phone back on the stand in the entryway. "My car key is hanging by the door."

"No…that's *my* car key." He tossed her a light smile. "How do you think I got the car back home?"

"Wait." A slow realization moved through her tired brain. "*You* fixed the car? How did you even know it wasn't running?"

Pulling on his coat, he stepped back into the living room. "I was sitting in the Spur, wrestling with my conscience. I saw you having trouble starting it, so after you and the kids left with Sam, I went over and had a look. I realized that you still needed me, and that was my chance to prove to you that I was man enough to deserve you."

Jill blinked, then swallowed back a sob. "Why didn't you say something?"

"I thought you'd know. Who else would leave you flowers and chocolate?"

A slow smile crept over her face. It was just the first step, but it was huge. Caleb was making an effort, and that was all she could ask of him.

He turned for the door, then stopped, his brow furrowing. He lifted something from the table by the door and held it up to examine it. "What's this?"

Jill threw her head back, then winced at the remnants of last night's headache. She hadn't even looked at that paper Mr. Carter had left. "It's the score to the music we have to face."

"What are you talking about?" He studied the paper.

"Our foreclosure notice."

"Uh...Jill..." Frowning and still looking it over, he walked back into the living room. "I don't think this is what you think it is." He looked up from the page, then held it out to her.

"What do you mean?"

"This guy wants to buy our house and rent it back to us so we don't have to move."

She stared, then snapped the paper from his hand. "What?"

"Yeah." He chuckled. "I guess maybe we didn't use up our quota of miracles last night after all."

Chapter 43

Jill stood at the top of the factory's front steps savoring the warm sun on her face. June had always been one of her favorite months, and it looked like they were in for a beautiful summer.

Sweeping her gaze over the parking lot, she could hardly believe the crowd that today's event had drawn. It had been a good move to organize shuttle buses to drive everyone in from town, because, as spacious as this lot was, there was no way it would have been big enough to accommodate all of the cars and the onlookers. And judging from the extra runs the buses had made, they'd attracted at least twice as many people as she'd anticipated.

Dean appeared beside her, loosening his collar in spite of the fact that he'd stopped wearing ties months ago.

Stifling a smirk, Jill decided not to give him a hard time for his endearing nervousness. "Are you ready?"

"I don't know." He gulped, then raised his gaze to take in the entirety of the scene in front of them. "I still can't believe this is really happening."

The place looked exactly as he'd always described it—first to Jill, Kylie, Colleen, and Bob, whom he'd appointed as his board of directors—then to the town council. The latter had voted unanimously to accept his proposal to use the found-mine-money for a community betterment project that would benefit the environment and bring in tourist dollars. A total win-win for Madison Falls.

"You did this, Dean." Jill patted his arm. "This is your big day." She motioned for Kylie to stop handing out brochures to the crowd and join them on their makeshift stage. "Now let's get this party started."

As Kylie happily bounded up the steps, Jill approached the microphone that stood at the edge of the landing. "Welcome to Ever Green Technologies." She waited as everyone cheered and repositioned themselves to face her. "I'm sure you all know as well as I do what we've been through to get to this day."

A murmur ran through the audience, and Jill looked down to catch Colleen's eye. If possible, they'd become even better friends after the ordeal they'd been through.

"But we are a community that believes in taking care of each other, and that good is always a more powerful force than evil." Another ovation broke out, this one even more raucous. Jill swallowed a cry-laugh and waved her hands to encourage silence so she could continue.

"And now please welcome the CEO of this amazing company, and a good friend, Dean Owens."

Clapping along with everyone else, she turned to take her place next to Kylie as Dean approached the mic.

As the volume of the onlookers ebbed, Dean began to speak. "When I first accepted a position with Nyland Enterprises—" He paused as a good-natured groan rose up from the crowd. "I had no idea what I was in for. None of us did." He shot a glance over his shoulder at Jill and Kylie. "But today I want to thank the city council and you, the people of this community, for understanding that the vision behind the original geothermal concept was bigger than the shortsighted tactics of its founders."

This wasn't the time to elaborate, and there was no need to. Everyone knew that William Steele and Harvey Nyland were in the

Deer Lodge prison awaiting their trials—Mr. Steele for attempted murder, and Mr. Nyland for conspiracy to commit fraud.

"This site will not only function as a closed-loop geothermal plant, providing ample clean, sustainable energy, but as an educational facility and tourist destination."

As Dean continued to describe the features of this mountainside campus, Jill scanned the crowd. She easily found Caleb, who held Emma on his hip and had Riley standing next to him on an apple crate. Next to Riley, the puppy—long since known as Wriggly—lay in a patch of shade.

She looked around, noting several familiar faces. Lenny Simpson stood with his wife, over near the organic snack stand. Jill couldn't help but note that he looked really happy these days, a result of both his sobriety and the fact that he was back to spending his days doing what he truly enjoyed—farming. Both he and his friend from the interview were now leasing some of their land to Ever Green for organic farming and getting paid to do the work. Thanks to Dean, they'd both been able to keep their farms.

"…also a wildlife rehabilitation and refuge center…" Dean went on, listing the attributes of this site. "A camp curriculum that includes lessons in environment-friendly practices like composting, planning of endemic trees in denuded areas…"

They truly had so much more to be thankful for than just the hundred or so jobs that Ever Green was providing. Every business in town had already seen an uptick in revenue, including Sam and Caleb, who had gone in together to buy the retail space next to the hardware store and had opened a fishing gear business. Starting this summer, Caleb would be leading fishing excursions for tourists, which Dean had also incorporated into the camp itinerary.

She smiled at the thought. Between Caleb's income from the fishing business and hers from working part time at the factory and the repurposed-home-furnishings business she'd started with Kylie, they were going to be able to make Mr. Carter an offer to buy back their house even sooner than they'd originally agreed to.

"And now, I'd like to introduce you to my executive team." Dean lifted his arm in presentation. "This is Kylie York. Very soon to be Kylie Gillespie. She's our head of PR and facility tours."

Kylie curtsied, and the crowd let out an appreciative cheer.

"And this is Jill Martin, our solutions strategist and my right hand." Jill lifted a wave, losing her battle with the tears she'd hoped would wait at least till she was off the stage. But it was okay. These people were all her friends.

As Dean went on to name the rest of the key staff members, Jill reached down to retrieve the shiny pair of shears she'd stashed in one of the cement planters.

"Let's not waste any more time." He took

the shears from Jill and approached the big double doors that had been draped with a thick green ribbon for today's ceremony.

As the audience went crazy, everyone on the steps gathered for Jerry to step forward and snap a commemorative shot. Jill already had plans to frame a big print of it to give to Dean for his "well-turned-out" corner office.

Dean cut the ribbon and the whooping increased. As he shook hands and accepted congratulations from everyone on the stage, the town band kicked off their rendition of Peter Gabriel's "Down to Earth."

"That was super fun," Kylie said as she and Jill sauntered down the steps. "Now I can totally focus on my wedding plans."

"Hey, speaking of wedding plans." Jill lifted her arms as Grace made her way through the crowd and gave her a hug. "Where's Sam?"

"He's sitting in with the band for a couple of songs." Grace beamed like a woman in love. Between her opera schedule and Sam's new business venture, they had decided to set their wedding date for December. "I'm going to check out the gift shop. I heard you two had some new pieces for sale."

"It was Kylie's idea. All the proceeds go to the camp scholarship fund."

As Grace gave her another hug and took off to go shopping, Kylie scanned the crowd.

"I have to go find Jackson. He promised he'd do the zipline with me."

Jill looked over her shoulder to where Colleen had joined Dean on the stage. She chuckled. Talk about beaming like a woman in love. And Dean wore a smile that seemed to come easily these days.

As Jill made her way to where she had seen Caleb and the kids earlier, the band started a new song, and she recognized a familiar voice. It was Sam, singing the lead on Paul McCartney's "Mother Nature's Son."

When she turned around again, she saw Caleb sauntering up to her with his thumbs hooked in the front pockets of his jeans, looking at her like he had some kind of secret he might or might not want to share.

She stopped, playfully folding her arms and enjoying how easygoing he seemed these days. It hadn't been easy, but Caleb had been giving it his all. Going to AA meetings, regularly attending church, working hard, focusing on showing Jill she could trust him. He wasn't perfect, but most days he showed her that his heart had truly changed.

She looked around. "Where are the kids?"

"Your mom took them to the petting farm."

"They love that place."

"Yeah." He leaned in to kiss her in the way he always used to. The kind of kiss that had started to make her feel loved and appreciated again. "I have something for you."

Putting a little space between them, he reached around to his back pocket. When he brought his hands to the front again, he was holding a small box. He popped it open, revealing a delicate gold band that had a small blue gem set in the center surrounded by tiny diamonds.

Jill let out a surprised yelp. "Is that my sapphire?"

"The one you kept all these years. I thought you might like to actually wear it."

"Oh, Caleb."

"It's an anniversary band. Six years. I always meant to give you a bigger ring. I think this is a good time."

Crying full out now, she took the ring from the box and popped it onto her finger, then threw her arms around him, still admiring the way the stone glimmered in the sun.

She always thought that when given the choice, people would generally follow the path of least resistance, but that wasn't always true. Sometimes, even in the face of life's biggest upheavals, people still surprised her.

She looked up at the crystal-blue Montana sky and said a silent *Thank You* to the One who made it all possible.

The End

Jill Came Tumbling After

Thank you for taking the time to read *Jill Came Tumbling After*. If you enjoyed it, please consider telling your friends or posting a short review. Word of mouth is an author's best friend and is much appreciated.

Jill Came Tumbling After

Please enjoy this sample chapter from

Lefty Lucy
Book 3
in the **Madison Falls** Series

Sample
Chapter 1

Lucy Branigan hunched over a stack of unpaid bills on her kitchen table, her forehead resting in her hand. Closing her eyes, she asked God to show her how to make the numbers add up.

For years, she had somehow managed to find innovative ways to stretch their household budget that went mostly unnoticed by her family. No one had ever gone hungry, and no debtor had ever gone unpaid.

But sadly, for the past several months, her husband's construction business had suffered with the downturn in the economy, and their income had taken a nosedive. Now, with Christmas just around the corner, her budget had transformed from challenge to unsolvable puzzle.

The sound of work boots clunking down the stairs drew her chin up and she forced a smile. With all her husband, Bob, had on his plate—keeping his crew employed and handling all the issues that came up at his worksites—Lucy had always made a point of making sure he didn't have to concern himself with the household finances.

But now...she wondered where the line between protecting him and excluding him lay, and if she'd know when she crossed it. They were a team, after all. For better or worse.

In the few moments it took him to make it down the stairs and through the front entryway, she decided that when he asked how the billpaying was going—which he always did—she would let him in on her concerns.

But when he entered the kitchen, he gave her a quick glance and headed straight for the coffeemaker without saying a word.

Her heart sank at what irrationally felt like a slight. She watched his back as he poured coffee into his thermos. Judging by the tautness across his shoulders, this wouldn't have been the best time to add to his stress. Good thing he hadn't asked.

Tightening the lid to his thermos, he twisted her a look. "Want me to pour you a cup?"

A measure of lightness filled her. He was acting like his usual caring self after all. No doubt he'd just been preoccupied when he'd entered the room.

"No, thanks." She gave him what she hoped would read as a carefree smile. "I'm meeting Grace and Jill at the diner."

"That's right," he said. "Wedding talk with the girls."

She rubbed her hands together playfully. "Just wait till you see what we have up our sleeves."

"An opera singer having a Christmas wedding." The little wrinkles around his eyes softened as he ambled over to her. "Something tells me Grace and Sam's wedding is going to be like nothing this town has ever seen." He leaned down and waited for her to tip her head back so their lips could meet.

She closed her eyes, enjoying the too-brief but still lovely kiss.

"That looks daunting."

Startled by that unexpected response to their good-morning smooch, she opened her eyes to see him looking at the bills she had spread in front of her.

"It's not as bad as it looks." Inwardly, she winced at what had seemed truthful until she heard herself saying it. "It's just going to take an extra dose of creativity to pull Christmas out of our hats this year." She felt better at his implied inclusion in that statement. *Our* hats, she'd said. Not just hers. They shared equal billing in this monetary magic act.

His jaw tightened and the little lines made a return appearance, making her instantly wish she'd left out the part about Christmas. It had been selfish of her to want to lighten her own load by shoveling some of it onto him.

She quickly changed the subject. "Oh, and don't forget, I'm helping Grace with auditions tonight."

"Right." He leaned closer and lowered his voice. "Have you talked any more with Casey about that?"

"I haven't mentioned it." She kept her voice down too, even though both of the kids were still upstairs and far out of earshot. "I've been waiting to see if he brings it up."

Bob pulled in a breath. "Sometimes I wish kids came with an instruction book."

"Or at least a troubleshooting guide."

Nodding, Bob straightened. "I better hit the road." He gave her shoulder an extra squeeze. "That snow we had overnight is going to slow everyone down."

She hated how cold her shoulder felt when he took his hand away, almost as much as she hated the idea of his being on the road in the wintertime. But the job for his core crew renovating a senior residence in Lolo was a blessing. It was also a commute, but at least they got to work mostly inside.

"Bye, honey." Lucy pushed her chair back, but he gestured for her to stay in her seat. "Love you."

"Love you too." He lifted a wave as he headed out of the kitchen.

She listened to the sound of the closet opening and closing, then to the rustle of his arms slipping into his coat. The front door opened and shut, and she let out a soft sigh. There was an empty feeling in the house whenever Bob wasn't in it. A hollowness that she'd feel until he returned.

She sat there staring mindlessly at the papers in front of her till she heard his truck start up, then pull out of the driveway. An uneasy feeling had settled in her gut that she couldn't quite shake. She hated that Bob wasn't his normal, jovial self. As his wife…his better half…shouldn't she be able to do something about it?

The *clunk clunk* that could only be her eighteen-year-old daughter, Taylor, bounding down the stairs jarred her out of her thoughts.

"I'm going!"

"Don't forget your lunch."

Hearing a dramatic groan, Lucy rolled her eyes. She'd heard stories of polite, grateful, loving teenagers, and wondered daily why she hadn't managed to raise one.

Taylor stomped into the kitchen and eyed her pink-with-daisies lunch bag—the one she had enthusiastically picked out herself just last year—then shot her mother a glare as she snapped it off the counter.

"This is so uncool." Her upper lip curled and she actually stomped her trendy little

North Face-booted foot. "Why can't I just buy my lunch?"

"You know how I feel about the nutritional value of school lunches. And we're on a budget. Please don't keep asking."

"I work. I can spend my own money on lunch."

"You are working so you can save for college and moving out."

The blare of a car horn turned Taylor's head. She hoisted her backpack onto her shoulder and darted out of the kitchen. "Bye, Mom."

"Bye. I love you."

Lucy leapt to her feet and trailed after her daughter, arriving in the entryway just as the front door slammed shut. She hurried into the living room and watched out the front window as Taylor hopped into a beat-up yellow VW Bug that Lucy didn't recognize. The car sputtered a little as it tore away from the curb, leaving Lucy straining in vain to get a look at the driver.

She frowned. Taylor had never been the most forthcoming kid when it came to her social life. But Lucy had worked hard to keep track of who her friends were and what they drove. She hated having to play detective, but when her daughter acted like she had something to hide, it left her with little choice.

"Hey, Mom."

Switching gears, Lucy turned at the sound of nine-year-old Casey thumping down the stairs.

As always, just seeing him brought a smile to her face, and both eased and added to her strain. Ever since they'd found out that he had Barth Syndrome—a rare condition he'd been born with—every moment with him held a special melancholy sweetness. Lucy never wanted to dwell on the thought that his condition could take him from them at an early age, but she couldn't keep that reality far from her mind.

Meeting him at the bottom of the stairs, she gave him a quick hug, which he willingly participated in.

"Don't forget your lunch." She crossed back to the kitchen to grab his Ninja Turtles bag while he got his coat, then met him at the front door. "There might or might not be something left over from Halloween in there. You'll have to wait to see."

His eyes lit up. "Thanks, Mom."

A flash of yellow school bus through the front window jarred them both into action. Casey grabbed his backpack and headed out the door, just as the bus pulled up in front of their house. Lucy stood on the front porch, her arms wrapped around herself to fend off the November chill. That fresh layer of snow might be slowing everyone down, but as she took in the serene beauty of their neighborhood, she couldn't help but think that might not be such a bad thing.

Casey took a seat next to a window and waved to her as the bus pulled away. He'd always been her sweet boy. God help her if he turned caustic in his teen years, like his sister had. After everything they'd been through to keep him healthy and safe, that kind of rebellion from him might just send her over the edge.

Seeing the mailman coming up the street, she lingered on the porch. Might as well grab her mail while she was outside.

"Morning, Mrs. Branigan."

"Morning, Scott." She made her way down the front steps to meet him on the walkway. "Good to see that the weather isn't keeping you from making your rounds on foot."

"Got the chains for the truck out last night. But I won't give in until it's deep enough to slow me down."

"Will we see you at the audition tonight? I know Grace is counting on your baritone to carry the ensemble."

"Wouldn't miss it." He presented her with a thick stack of mail. "Who wouldn't want to be a part of a musical version of *A Christmas Carol?*"

"Who, indeed."

She couldn't help but smile at his enthusiasm, wishing she could bottle it and inject some into her own son.

Thumbing through the envelopes in her hand, she made her way back inside and into the kitchen. She let out a disgusted groan as she tossed it all next to the paperwork she already had piled up. Like she needed more bills.

A glance at the clock made her stomach jump. She'd better get a move on if she wanted to be on time to meet the girls at the diner. Maybe some girl time was what she needed to recalibrate her perspective and lighten her mood.

End of Sample

I hope you enjoyed this sample chapter from *Lefty Lucy,* book 3 in the Madison Falls series. This book can be found at my website:

www.lesleyannmcdaniel.com

Or on my Amazon author page:

www.amazon.com/author/lesleyannmcdaniel

My Thank You Gift to You...

High and Dry

CRESCENT COVE Series Prequel
Available only to my newsletter subscribers.
Get your copy for FREE!

Do you love Inspirational Fiction? Join my
Newsletter family and receive all the latest
news about my books, plus contests,
giveaways, and insider info.

www.lesleyannmcdaniel.com

While earning a degree in acting at Willamette University in Salem, Oregon, Lesley fell in love with theatrical costuming, and pursued that as a career while nurturing her passion for writing on the side.

Between working as a homeschooling mom and professional theatre costumer, she has completed several novels. She would have done more by now if she didn't also occasionally stop to clean the house and fold laundry. Fortunately, she loves to cook, so no one in her family has starved yet.

In her spare time (ha!) she chips away at her goal of reading every book ever written.

Lesley loves to hear from readers. Please visit her website at: **www.lesleyannmcdaniel.com** ...or on Facebook at **www.facebook.com/LesleyAnnMcDaniel**